next page

# SECOND BOOK
## OF
# LOST SWORDS

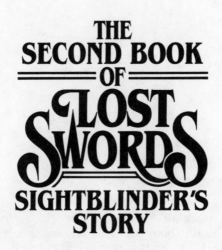

# THE SECOND BOOK OF LOST SWORDS
## SIGHTBLINDER'S STORY

# FRED SABERHAGEN

SABE
c. 1

TOR

THE SECOND BOOK OF LOST SWORDS:
SIGHTBLINDER'S STORY

Copyright © 1987 by Fred Saberhagen

First printing: November 1987

A TOR Book

Published by Tom Doherty Associates, Inc.
49 West 24 Street
New York, N.Y. 10010

ISBN: 0-312-93032-1

Library of Congress Catalog Card Number: 87-50477

Printed in the United States of America

0  9  8  7  6  5  4  3  2  1

# CHAPTER 1

THE sun was up at last, somewhere beyond the cliffs that stood above the far end of the lake. While the bright disk itself remained invisible, it projected a diffuse radiance through morning mist and lake-born fog, making a pearl-gray world of land and air and water. It was a world in which no shape or color was able to remain quite what it ought to be. Small waves of soft pearl nibbled at the slaty rocks of the uneven shoreline. On the steep slopes rising just inland, pine trees with twisted trunks and branches grew thickly, their gray-green needles gathering pearls and diamonds of moisture out of the leaden shadows that surrounded them. Land and lake alike seemed to be giving birth to the billows of almost colorless vapor that moved softly over earth and water. Fog and light together worked a brief natural enchantment.

A man was standing alone on the very edge of the lake, leaning out into the mist. With one of his huge hands he gripped the twisted trunk of a stunted tree, while the other hand held a black wooden staff in a position that allowed him to brace part of his weight on its support. He was very nearly motionless, but still the attitude of his whole body showed the intensity of the effort he was making, trying to see something out over the water. He had a large, round, ugly, stupid-looking face, his forehead creased now with the effort of trying

1

to see through the pearl-gray air. His mouth was muttering oaths, so softly as to leave them totally inaudible. Gray marked his dark hair and beard, and his age appeared to be closer to forty than to thirty.

Somewhere, only a matter of meters to the man's right as he looked out over the water, a lake bird called, sounding a single, mocking, raucous note. Despite its nearness, the impertinent bird was quite invisible in mist. The watcher paid it no attention.

He was thinking that a clear midnight, even with no moon, would have made for better seeing than this hazed near-nothingness imbued with sunlight. At least at midnight you would not expect to be able to see anything. As matters stood now, the man could only suppose that there were still islands out there in the middle of the chill lake, the islands he had seen there yesterday, no more than a couple of kilometers away. He supposed he could take it for granted too that there was still a castle on one of those islands, the castle he had seen there yesterday. And maybe he could even be sure that—

Nearby sounds, the scramble of feet in heavy gravel, the impact of a blow on flesh, jolted the watcher away from suppositions. The sources of these sounds were as invisible as the noisy bird, but he was sure they were no more than a stone's throw away, along the shoreline to his right. After a momentary pause there followed more energetic scrambling and another blow, and then a cry for help in a familiar voice.

The watcher had already launched himself in the direction of the sounds, moving with surprising speed for someone of his great bulk, well past his early youth. And as he ran along the jagged shoreline, avoiding boulders and trampling bushes, new sounds came from behind him, those of another pair of running feet. Those pursuing feet sounded lighter and more agile than his own, but so far they had been unable to overtake him. He paid them no attention.

The big man's wooden staff, a thick tool of black hardened wood somewhat longer than he was tall, was raised now in his right hand, balanced and ready to do the service of either spear or club.

And now, after only a couple of dozen strides, the younger feet behind him had begun to gain. But still the big man did not turn his head. The sounds of struggle ahead continued.

Both runners saw that, despite their quickness, they were too late.

Rounding a spur of the rugged shoreline, one after the other in rapid succession, they came in sight of the noisy struggle, in which three men had surrounded one. The three men, though wearing soldiers' uniforms in gray trimmed with red, were all unarmed. The man surrounded had showing at his belt the black hilt of a great Sword, but he was not trying to draw the weapon. And now, an instant later, even if he had wanted to draw it, it was too late, because his arms were pinioned. He was a tall and powerful man, and still conscious, but he had lost the fight.

The huge man roared a challenge and ran on, doing his best to reach the fighters. But he and the runner who followed him were still too far away to have any influence upon the outcome. The three who had the one surrounded were now lifting him up between them, as if they meant to make of him an offering to some strange gods of mist or lake.

And now indeed, coming down out of the low, tree-grazing clouds, a winged shape appeared. Those descending wings surpassed in span and thickness those of almost any bird, reptile, or flying dragon that either of the would-be rescuers had ever seen before. But still those wings appeared inadequate to support this creature's body, which was as big and solid as a riding-beast's. The head and forelimbs of the quadruped were those of a giant eagle, covered with white feathers shading into gray. But the body and the rear legs resembled those of a lion, clad in short, tawny fur and thick with muscle. The thing appeared too bulky for its wings, despite their size, to get off the ground. And yet it flew with graceful power.

Whatever the nightmare creature was, it had already fastened the taloned grip of its forelimbs on the heavy body of the man who was being held up for them. Up he went again, right out of the hands of his human captors, the undrawn Sword still at his belt.

And now at last the huge man running came within reach of the victorious three, and sent them scattering with a swing of his black staff. They did not run far. Instead they were quick to seize up weapons of their own, swords and knives that had been lying concealed among the low bushes and the rocks.

The big man and his companion, who had arrived right at his heels, met their three opponents. The length of black wood, held now like a quarterstaff, knocked a long knife from one man's hand, and then with a straight thrust doubled up the man who'd lost the blade.

"Ben!"

Thus warned, the big man spun around quite gracefully, in time to catch a hurled rock on his left arm, which by now he had adroitly shielded in his rolled-up cloak. He advanced on the thrower. Off to his right he could hear, and see from the corner of his eye, young Zoltan and the third opponent sparring, a clash of swordblades and then another clash, with gasping pauses in between.

Mist still flowed in from the lake and purled around the fighters, in billows sometimes so thick that one pair of them could not see the other. The man who had thrown the rock now sought to win against the staff by dancing in and out, waving his battle-hatchet. But he could make no headway against the tough wood of that long shaft, and the arm that held it. A few hard-breathing moments later, the staff came crashing against his skull, ending plans and trickery for good, driving out all thoughts and fears alike.

Ben quickly turned again. The third opponent, seeing the fight going against his side, risked all on a deceptive thrust. Young Zoltan, well-taught, sidestepped as was necessary, and the enemy impaled himself on Zoltan's blade. He staggered back, uttered a strange sound, and fell. The fight was over.

But yet, once more, feet scrambled in the gravel. The man Ben had knocked down at the beginning of the skirmish had now got his brain working and his legs under him again, and was rapidly vanishing inland amid the mist and dripping trees.

"After him!" Ben roared. "We need to find out—" He saved his breath for running. Young Zoltan was well ahead of him, already sprinting in pursuit.

Running uphill as best they could, the two allies separated slightly, chasing the sound of their quarry's receding footsteps inland. Trees grew thickly on these slopes, and their branches of soggy needles slapped, as if with a malignant will, at every rushing movement. Having been through a run and a fight already, Ben's lungs were laboring. Whenever he paused to listen, his own blood and his own breath were all that he could hear. The mist rolled round him, blinding him effectively. The chill sun seemed to make no headway in the sky.

Then there came Zoltan's voice, calling him from somewhere ahead. Ben ran again, stopped to listen once more, and once more resumed the chase, or tried to.

When he had labored onward forty meters or so he paused again and choked out breathless curses. The sounds of running feet were fainter now, and they were all behind him. The surviving enemy must have doubled back toward the lake.

Panting more heavily than ever, Ben caught up with young Zoltan at last, though only on the very shoreline. Side by side they stood, their sandaled feet in the small waves, watching as a small boat, its single occupant furiously working the oars, vanished into the mist, heading directly out from shore.

"What do we do now?" Zoltan gasped at last. "The Prince is gone. Whoever they are, they have the Prince —and Shieldbreaker with him. What do we do?"

Ben leaned against a tree. "Seek help," he got out at last, and paused for a wheezing breath. "And pray"—he drew another desperate breath—"we find it."

# CHAPTER 2

THE mirror was made of real glass, smooth and relatively unblemished, so clear that it almost certainly had a silver backing. Even the wood carving of the frame fastened so carefully to the wall was not entirely inept. All in all, it was a finer thing than you would expect to find out here in the hinterlands, in the only inn of a small town that was very little more than a fishing village. Certainly it was the best mirror that the lady who now occupied the little room had seen in a long time. And during the tedious days of waiting for the boat that was to carry her on down the Tungri, she had been taking full advantage of the opportunity offered by the glass for a new self-appraisal.

The face that the mirror showed her had never been ethereally beautiful—it had too much of a nose for that. But a dozen years ago—no, say only ten—it had possessed considerable attraction. Or at least a number of men had found the lady who wore this face desirable as recently as that. Even now it was still a good face, its owner thought, comely in its own earthy way. Or it would be a comely face, and even relatively youthful, if you thought of it as belonging to a woman of sixty.

The trouble with that qualification was that she was scarcely more than forty, even now.

The woman who had been waiting for days in the small, cheap, temporary room, she who had once been

7

Queen Yambu, dropped her grayish gown—it was almost a pilgrim's garment—from her shoulders, and stood before the mirror unclothed in the light of midday. She was still trying to give herself a more complete and objective appraisal.

Her silvery hair went well with the gray eyes, but stood in discordance with her full breasts and her upright bearing. Her body looked much younger than her face, and now the overall effect was nearer her true age.

Women—and men too—who had the skills of magic, or the resources to hire those skills, frequently turned to magic to fight back advancing age, or at least its visible effects. But Lady Yambu had no great aptitude of her own for working spells, and as for buying the appearance of youth, she had never seriously considered that course of action, and did not do so now.

Had she been truly dissatisfied with her appearance, a first step, simpler than magic and less risky, would have been to dye her hair back to its own youthful raven black. That might have made her look younger—would certainly have done so until the beholder looked upon her face.

Yes, the problem, if it was a problem, was in her face.

She had one of the Swords to thank for that.

"Hold Soulcutter in *your* hands throughout a battle," she had once said to a man she knew almost as well as she knew anyone, "and see what *you* look like at the end of it."

The good mirror on the rough wall was giving her a harsh truth, but truth was what she wanted, now more than ever, and she did not find it devastating. Really, the glass only confirmed what she had been telling herself of late: that youth no longer really mattered to her, just as for a long time now neither power nor the thrill of competition had been subjects of concern. More and more, with time's accelerating passage, the only thing that she found of any importance at all was truth.

Pulling on her gown again, the lady turned from the mirror and took the three steps necessary to approach the open window of her second-floor room, through which a chill breeze entered.

Like the mirror, the single window presented a vision that seemed worthy of a finer setting than this poor room in a rude settlement. The sun, now approaching noon, had long since burned away the morning's mystery of mists from the glassy surface of Lake Alkmaar. Much of the twisting, irregular length of that body of water was visible from the lady's window.

Fifteen or twenty kilometers from where she stood, beyond the distant eastern end of the lake, rose the high scarp of land walling off the eastern tip of the continent. Above and beyond those cliffs lay Yambu's former life, her former kingdom, the other lands she had once fought to conquer—and much else.

But the truth she wanted did not lie there. Not her truth, the truth that still mattered to her. Not any longer. Where it was she did not know exactly, but certain clues had pointed her downriver, far to the south and west.

Halfway between her window and the far end of the long, comparatively narrow lake, a couple of dozen small islands were clustered irregularly near the center of the kilometers of water. Even at this distance, in the clear sunshine, Yambu could descry the gray bulk of a castle upon the largest of those bits of land.

If she had ever suspected that any portion of the truth she sought might lie out there upon those islands, the events of the last few days and the stories spreading among the townsfolk and the travelers at the inn had effectively changed her mind. The good wizard Honan-Fu had been conquered, overthrown. That was not his castle any longer.

She raised her eyes yet once more to that even more remote scarp of land, blue with distance, that represented her past. Then she turned from the window. She was not going to retrace the steps of the journey she had begun. There was nothing for her back there now.

Approaching the most shadowy corner of her little room, the lady was greeted by a peculiar noise, a kind of heavy chirp. It came from her toy dragon, which was perching with great patience upon her washstand. This dragon was a peculiar, winged beast, no bigger than a barnyard fowl but of a quite different shape—the joint product of the breeder's and the magician's art.

Going to stand beside the creature, whispering into its gray curling ear with soft strange words, Lady Yambu fed it the living morsel of a mouse, which she took with firm fingers from a cage beside the stand. Delicacies were almost gone now, for the lady and her pet alike. She still had a substantial sum of money left, and a few jewels, but she meant to save her modest wealth against some future need; her journey downriver might be very long. Tonight, she thought, the dragon might have to be released from the window of this room to forage for itself. She hoped that the creature would come back to her from such a foray, and she thought it would; she trusted the one who had given her the pet almost as much as she had ever trusted anyone.

Restlessly Lady Yambu moved back to the window again. Down at the shabby docks, some of which were visible from this vantage point, there was still no sign of the long-awaited riverboat that was to carry her out of the lake and down the Tungri as far as the next cataract. The *Maid of Lakes and Rivers,* she had heard that the riverboat was called. The *Maid* was days overdue already, and she supposed more days were likely to pass before it arrived.

If it ever did. She had heard also that traffic on the lower river was at best far from safe.

This was her eleventh day of waiting in this inn. It was good that the earlier years of her life had schooled her thoroughly in patience and self-sufficiency, because—

Making a brisk decision, the lady suddenly scooped up a few small essential items that she did not want to leave unguarded in the room while she was out of it, and moved in two strides to the door. Locking the door behind her, she strode along the short and narrow upstairs hall of the inn, and down a narrow stair. This stair, like most of the rest of the building, was constructed in rustic style, of logs with much of the bark still on them.

As the lady descended, the common dining room, now empty, was to her left, and the small lobby, with three or four pilgrims and locals in it, was to her right.

She had almost reached the foot of the stairs when she saw, through the open front door of the inn, to her right, the figure of a man who moved along the middle of the unpaved street outside, advancing toward the waterfront with a steady, implacable-looking tread. No doubt it was the size of the man, which was remarkable, that first attracted her attention—his form was mountainous, not very tall but very bulky, and not so much fat as shapeless. Lady Yambu could see little of this man but his broad back, but still his appearance jogged her memory. It was not even a memory of someone she had seen before, but of someone she ought to know, ought to be able to recognize. . . .

Moving quickly through the lobby and out the front door, she stood on the log steps of the inn above the muddy and moderately busy street, gazing after him. A second man, much younger and much smaller, was walking with the one who had caught her attention, and already both of them were well past the inn, heading down the sloping street in the direction of the docks. The big man carried a staff, and the smaller wore a sword, which was common enough here as in most towns. Both were dressed in rough, plain clothing.

The lady, on the verge of running after the two, but not choosing to brave the mud and the loss of dignity involved, cast her eyes about. Then with a quick gesture she beckoned an alert-looking urchin who was loitering nearby, and gave him a trifling coin and a short verbal message. In a moment his small figure was speeding after the two men.

"Alas," the lady was saying to the huge man a quarter of an hour later, "I doubt that there is any messenger, winged or otherwise, to be found in this village who could reach Tasavalta sooner than you could yourself."

She was back in her room at the inn, sitting on one end of the small couch that also served as a bed, while the two men she had invited in from the street stood leaning against the outer wall, one on each side of the window. They had now been in the lady's company long enough to tell her their story about the kidnapping of Prince Mark at dawn, only a few hours ago. She had heard them with considerable interest; the Prince of Tasavalta had been a person of some importance in her old life.

The lady asked her informants now: "And he still had Shieldbreaker with him when he was taken?"

The smaller, younger man nodded. He was called Zoltan, and had been a total stranger to Yambu until today. He said: "But my uncle did not draw it. As you must know, lady, that would have been a mistake in a fight against unarmed attackers—doubtless they knew he was carrying a Sword, and which one of the Twelve it was. And they knew the only way to fight against it. Or they would not have attacked him without weapons of their own in hand, or at least at their belts."

"So Shieldbreaker has presumably gone to the master of those men now, whoever he may be. And he commands a griffin. That is not good. I have never even seen a griffin," said the lady, and sighed, reminding herself that the time was long past when she had to concern herself with such things as the balance of power. "And of course now you are in a desperate hurry to send word to Tasavalta, and get help from Princess Kristin and the others, or at least let them know what has happened. But I have no messenger to lend you."

In response, the huge man, Ben of Purkinje, looked pointedly at the lady's pet winged dragon, which was still perched on the washstand.

Yambu nodded. "Yes, that creature could serve as a messenger, of sorts. But I fear my pet could not be made to carry any word back to Tasavalta for you. Still I would like to do something to help Prince Mark, provided he is not, as you fear, already beyond help. Though we were enemies, I suppose he is now as close to being my friend as anyone who walks the face of the earth today." She paused. "And you, Ben of Purkinje, though I think we have never seen each other before today—you have been much in my mind for the past several months."

That surprised the big man, distracting him if only briefly from his deep concern over his Prince. "Me? Why me?"

"Because between us, you and me, there is a connection of a sort—I mean apart from our having been enemies across the battlefield. You knew my daughter."

"Ah," said Ben, distracted even more, against his will. "Yes. I knew Ariane."

"That is her name. I have no other daughter. And you were with her, eleven years ago or thereabouts, in the vaults of the Blue Temple."

The impression made by her words on Ben was deepening. Eventually he said in a dull voice: "She died there, in my arms." And Zoltan, so young he was, perhaps not even fully grown as yet, looked at the older man with sympathetic wonder.

Yambu said: "And you had been with Ariane for a long time before that."

Ben gazed back at her in silence. His face was grim, but beyond that hard to read.

She who had once been the Silver Queen went on: "As you know, I have been living for years in a White

Temple, withdrawn from the world. Almost, I have ceased to have either friends or enemies at all. Now I am only an old woman, making my way out into the world again to try to wring some answers from it. I am sure you can provide me with some of the answers that I want—a portion of the truth about my daughter. In return I will be willing to do whatever I can for you, and for your Prince. Perhaps there will be nothing I can do; but I am still not entirely without resources."

For a little time Ben prolonged his thoughtful silence. Then he said: "As I suppose you know, lady, Ariane suffered a head wound when we were fighting down there in the Blue Temple's vaults. For a time after she received the injury—for many minutes, perhaps an hour—she was able to speak and move about. Then suddenly she collapsed. I was standing beside her, and I caught her as she fell. A few minutes later she was dead."

"The two of you were lovers?"

The huge man turned away to look out of the window momentarily, and then turned back. His ugly face was full of pain. "We had known each other for a matter of a few days—no more. From the day that Mark and I and the others broke into a Red Temple and brought her out, until the day she died in that damned hole."

"I want to know," said Yambu, royally persistent, "whether Ariane was still a virgin when she died."

"How can that matter now?"

"And I want to know much more than that." The silver-haired woman was still capable of ignoring questions in the manner of a queen. "I would like you to tell me everything, any detail you can remember, about those days the two of you spent together. Whether the truth is harsh or tender, I would know it. Lately the fate of my only child has come to be of tremendous importance to me."

"I have no objection," Ben replied, "to telling you the whole story. Someday when I have time. If both of us live long enough. Right now, as I have explained, Zoltan and I are both extremely busy. We are in danger, and we need help."

"I understand; we have a bargain, then, and I will do what I can to help you. Tell me, why was the Prince here, so far from home, and with so few attendants?"

Ben hesitated; then he nodded and took the plunge. "The largest of the islands in this lake is, or was, the home of a friendly wizard of great power, allied to the White Temple. His public name is Honan-Fu. In his academy a few select apprentices—"

"I know something about Honan-Fu," Yambu rapped out impatiently. "Go on."

"The Prince wanted to learn something about Honan-Fu's establishment. He thought that by coming here incognito—"

"You need not be so cautious with me, big man. By now everyone knows about Mark's eldest son. Adrian's still only a child—he'd be nine years old now? No more than ten—but blessed with great magic. Or would 'cursed' be a better word for his condition?"

"All right, then. Mark wanted to see the place at first hand, before he sent his nine-year-old heir to be apprenticed."

Yambu was nodding. "That should be interesting —one day to see a true magician-king upon the throne of Tasavalta."

Ben grunted. "As for the Prince being unattended on this trip, well, you see his entire escort before you. Zoltan and I came with Mark down the Sanzu, then down the cliffs beside the Upper Cataract to reach this lake. That part of the route you must have taken yourself.

"We brought no magician with us—a grievous mistake, perhaps. Still, we thought we were headed for a friendly reception in the castle of an enchanter stronger than any we could have brought with us. But from the moment when we arrived on the shore of Lake Alkmaar two days ago, we could tell that there was something wrong out there on the magician's islands. We knew that Honan-Fu had been expecting us in a general way at least, and anyway I suppose a wizard of his stature ought to have known that we were here. But he did not know. At least no boat came for us, and no messages.

"We were suspicious, and hesitated even to go into any of the villages. At last we talked to a few of the fisherfolk who live in isolated huts along the shore. They were reluctant to speak to strangers, but certainly something else besides our presence was bothering them.

"And then this morning, at last, we had our greeting from the island." Ben gestured savagely toward the lake.

The lady moved to stand beside the huge man at the window, and rested one hand lightly on his shoulder, as if to seal a bargain. She said: "I have dealt for many years with magicians—most of whom were far indeed from any alliance with the White Temple. And so I think I know that other kind, know them well enough to smell them when the air is as thick as it is here and now with their effluvium. Sometime during the past ten days, Honan-Fu has been supplanted on his island. How, and by whom, I know not, though the town is full of rumors, and suddenly invading soldiers in gray and red are everywhere. They have little to say about the one they serve. But obviously the new ruler is a wizard of tremendous power, who is no friend of the Prince."

Then with a decisive motion she turned from the window, toward the odd little dragon that still perched preening itself upon its stand. She said: "It will be best, I think, if we dispatch a messenger."

"You said that creature was no messenger."

"I said that it would take no word to Tasavalta for you. But as for bringing help here for the Prince—it may just possibly be able to do that. And the sooner it is dispatched the better, I think, if Mark is not already beyond help."

Moving beside the washstand, the lady whispered a

few words into the beast's small curving ear.

With this the backbone of the dragon stiffened, and its demeanor changed abruptly. It drank noisily from a jar of water beside it on the stand, then hopped onto the lady's wrist. Ben could see semitransparent membranes on its eyes, which he had not realized were there, slide back to leave the orbs a shiny black. The creature had turned its head toward the window, and stared out into the sunlight.

Lady Yambu carried it to the sill and sent it out with a sharp tossing motion. The wings of the small dragon beat rapidly and it rose with surprising speed into the sky.

"What message did you give it?" Zoltan asked. "Where is it going?"

"There is only one message that it will carry. Trust me. I have a reason for not offering you a better explanation now."

Ben, squinting up into the bright sky, presently rumbled an oath. There were a few patchy low clouds above the lake, and out of one of them a set of leathery wings far larger than those of the small dragon had appeared. This creature was not nearly as big as the griffin that a few hours ago had carried off the Prince, but still large enough to be a formidable hunter of game no bigger than the messenger.

Now Zoltan muttered too; a second and then a third of the predatory flyers had come into sight out of the cloud. Their grotesque shapes sped in pursuit of the small dragon.

The issue of the chase was lost in yet another cloud.

# CHAPTER 3

A LITTLE before sunset of that same day, all three of
the predatory flying creatures Ben had watched
returned, gliding, to their new base on the island that
had so lately been the domain of Honan-Fu. On their
return to the magician's castle all three flyers selected
flight paths that would tend to shelter them from observation, and each came down as softly and as unobtru-
sively as possible upon a different high place. For their
final descent they chose a moment when almost all the
human eyes within the castle walls were focused elsewhere.

And, having landed, they avoided reporting to the
Master of the Beasts, or any of their other human
masters, who were the recent conquerors of this island
and the domain around the lake. Instead of delivering
information on potential enemies, on resources discovered, or perhaps news of some prey that had escaped
them—and thereby risking punishment—the creatures
brooded on their perches, waiting silently to be fed, and
dropping dung down the once-spotless walls of the
stolen castle.

Very few of the humans inside the castle walls were
at all aware of the flyers' return. None of the people who
might have seen them were paying the hybrid creatures
any real attention at the moment.

Perhaps the human breeders of the hybrid flyers had

18

made them a touch too intelligent for their intended purposes.

The beasts looked down upon a crowd of several hundred people, mostly soldiers in gray and red, who were gathered in the castle's largest open courtyard. Only days ago this court had been a fair place, bright with flower gardens and musical with fountains. The flowers had all been trampled into mud since the castle's new master had taken charge, and half of the fountains had ceased to run. The pipes were broken in several of the fountains, including the largest, in the center of the court, which had been smashed, the sculpture on its top destroyed. In place of the statue of some otherwise forgotten woodland god, erected there by Honan-Fu because he liked the art and craft that had gone into it, a flat-topped altar had been hastily and crudely constructed, out of beams and slabs of wood laid horizontally on piles of rock and broken statuary.

The slabs that formed the center of the high table were now already dark with drying blood, the human blood of Honan-Fu's apprentices and servants, required for sacrifice to the powers of dark magic.

Upon a balcony overlooking this altar, an improvised throne had been set up. The occupant of the throne sat with his back close to a wall of the keep, and it would have been hard for anyone to approach or even see him from that direction. Nor was it easy for the people in the courtyard below the balcony to right or left to see him because of the tall screens that had been placed at each side of his chair.

Only from directly in front of the man on the throne, where the high altar stood, was anyone able to view him at all clearly. From there it could be seen that the shape of his body was only partially that of a man.

The right hand of the one who sat upon the throne was more plainly visible than the rest of his figure. That hand was extended at shoulder height, and clutched the black hilt of a Sword. The gleaming blade of this weapon, a full meter long, was dug lightly, point-first, into the floor of the balcony at the base of the makeshift throne.

Anyone standing close enough to get a good look at the fist that held the Sword could see that it was gray and taloned, almost as much like a bird's or a dragon's claw as it was like a human hand. Its owner's survival over the millennia had not been easily accomplished, and it had involved him in several compromises, of which the one involving alterations in his physical shape had been only the most noticeable.

The courtyard was nearly quiet now, a deepening pool of shadow as daylight began fading from the sky. Torches were being lighted, and once a long flame snapped like a banner in a gust of wind. But here, inside the castle's outer walls, the wind did not persist.

Only recently, within the past hour, had this quiet been achieved. Some of Honan-Fu's apprentices had fought back against their conquerors even as they were being dragged to the altar, or even after reaching it; and some of those apprentices had been, by any ordinary standard, magicians of considerable strength. But against the powers that had seized this castle from their master, their best efforts had been infantile, completely useless. All of their powers were scattered before the sacrifice, and in the process of the sacrifice itself their bodies were burned and minced, their minds dispatched to meet whatever fate the minds of magicians encountered after death.

The resistance of their master, Honan-Fu, had been more prolonged, but in the end no more effective. He had been overcome in magic, but he had not been burnt in sacrifice. His vanquisher considered that he had better use for him than that.

The still-living body of Honan-Fu was bound now between a pair of tall stakes standing before the altar, and certain human servants of the conqueror were dousing the defeated magician with pails of cold water filled at the pulsing spray of a broken fountain. Magic, the magic of his conqueror, against which Honan-Fu was no longer capable of fighting, was going on him with the water, and his sparse frame and wrinkled face were being rapidly covered with a mail-coat of ice. The crystalline white coat was still thin, and it cracked with his uncontrollable shivering almost as fast as it was formed; but with every pail of water thrown upon him it inexorably grew thicker.

"There will still be room inside your icicle for you to shiver, if not to breathe," called down the one who sat upon the throne; his was a human voice, harsh but not extraordinary. "You will find yourself able to dispense with breathing for a while, at least as long as you are under water. As most of your future existence lies in that environment, I thought it best to arrange something of the kind."

If Honan-Fu had any response to make, it must have been a silent one. He was a small man with wispy gray hair and epicanthic eyes, who had said very little to any of his conquerors since their first onslaught took him by surprise. And perhaps he was silent because by now his ice-encrusted lips had already grown too cold and stiff to talk.

"You will be brought out of the lake from time to time," called down the man—or being—on the throne, "to talk to me. You and I have much to talk about. But I am somewhat pressed for time just now, and our talk will have to wait. Unless there is something you feel you must say to me before you go. Any defiance you feel compelled to offer? Any bargainings you'd like to try? Now is the time, or they will have to wait indefinitely. . . ."

Still, the shivering little wizard had nothing to say in reply. Instead he had one more counterattack to try —magical, of course, —and it was more subtle and ingenious than any he had previously essayed. The man on the throne, despite his own ancient powers, had no inkling that the attack was coming until he was informed of it by a thrum of power in the Sword he held. Only half a heartbeat later did the conqueror's more conventional defenses, his personal spells and demons, come into play; they would have protected him adequately, he was almost sure, but even before they were activated the counterspell of Honan-Fu had been rendered harmless by the Sword of Force.

The man on the throne was surprised and delighted to observe the effectiveness of his latest acquisition.

"Shieldbreaker, hey?" He held the Sword up at arm's length and admired it. It and its eleven fellows were of divine workmanship, he had been told; he had discounted that theory until now. But now, he realized, he was going to have to trace down the truth of their provenance.

"I could feel that power," he said, more to himself than to anyone else. "I like it. This toy is going to remain at my side for some time to come, though as a rule I have a dislike for carrying edged weapons of any kind."

He wondered now, in passing, how effective this Sword might have been in an earlier era of his life, if it were set in opposition to the titanic powers of Orcus or of Ardneh—but those were tests, thank all the gods and demons, that he would never have to face again. The magician on the throne, who had been no more than human in that era, had somehow managed to survive both of those superpowers.

And, from what he had seen of this future world during two years of tentative exploration since his arrival in it, he expected to be able to reign supreme.

Honan-Fu was by now completely encased in ice if still not exactly frozen solid. At a signal from the throne, burly attendants now untied the defeated magician from the tall wooden stakes, and dragged him away to be lowered into the lake. The spot selected was in its own little courtyard, really a grotto, a deeply arched recess in the wall of the keep itself. Behind its gate was a deep permanent well of fresh water, maintained by a direct connection to the lake outside the castle walls. Originally this well, or pool, had been intended to provide easy access to drinking water even during a hard-pressed siege. The grotto holding the well was accessible from the large courtyard through a small gate.

As the former master of the castle was carried through the small gate and out of sight, the man on the throne heaved a sigh, like one who has disposed of yet another dull duty in a busy day. He toyed with his newly acquired Sword, spinning it briefly like an auger, so that light of torches flickered from its brightness, and the keen point bored a very little deeper into the stone floor of the balcony.

And then his whole being appeared to change. Where he had been grotesque, only marginally human, he now appeared as a muscular young man, golden-haired, blue-eyed, and of surpassing beauty.

"Now," he called in an unchanged voice to his chief subordinate, an aging, bulky man in military uniform who stood below. "Bring out this Prince who owned this lovely implement before me. I'd like to have a word with him before he's put away."

"I know him, sire," the man below responded. "And I think he will repay more than a few minutes of Your Lordship's attention."

The officer turned away and made an economical gesture of command. Presently the captured Prince Mark, battered and still somewhat bloody about the face from the morning's fistfight, was brought out of a dark doorway in the lower castle wall, and bound up in the place just vacated by Honan-Fu, between the altar's stakes. The men who bound him, as soon as they were finished, began to fill their pails with water again.

At first Mark, having endured some hours of utter darkness in a dungeon, had to squint even in the faint light of the sunset sky and torches. Looking around him, he could see no sign that either of his Tasavaltan friends were also being held captive. That was faint consolation, but it was all he had.

There was only one face in the hostile throng that Mark could recognize, and he saw it without surprise, though with a sinking in his heart toward despair.

"Amintor," he said through dry lips that were still caked with his own blood.

The military officer, obviously here in a position of considerable importance, returned the Prince a salute, gravely but silently. Mark noted that the aging, portly baron, once a fearsome warrior himself, was limping heavily on his left leg. Mark had no doubt that the limp was a result of their last encounter, two years earlier.

But there was an even worse sight than the face of his old enemy for the Prince to see. Despairingly, Mark identified the hilt of Shieldbreaker, visible in the well-formed fist of his still-unknown chief enemy.

The occupant of the throne now leaned toward him slightly. His harsh voice was completely strange to Mark. "You are another man, Prince, to whom I intend to speak at some length. I believe that we have several matters of some importance to discuss. But alas, conversation must wait. Unless you have something you urgently wish to tell me now."

The first bucket of water splashed on Mark. He shivered involuntarily, though at first the wet chill felt good on his cracked lips and swollen face.

"An indefinite time of discomfort awaits you, Prince. But at least the ice will not be eternal; sooner or later your time in the cold lake will be interrupted. Draw comfort from that fact if you can. But remember that how long you are allowed to spend out of your bath will depend upon how entertaining and informative I find your conversation."

The second pail of water splashed over Mark, and he felt the intense, magical cold of it, deeper even than the chill of ice, and fear and understanding began to grow. Meanwhile the handsome—nay, beautiful—man on the throne was studying him carefully. As if he wanted to watch the details of the freezing process, or perhaps as if Mark reminded him of someone that he had known long ago.

Mark did not utter another word. His captors did not insist. The Ancient One exchanged a few words with Amintor. And soon the two of them were watching Mark, pale and with his teeth chattering, being lowered inside his own maturing icicle to a place in the deep lake beside the wizard Honan-Fu.

# CHAPTER 4

WITHIN a few minutes after Lady Yambu had released her dragon from the window of the inn, she and her visitors brought their conference to an end. It was mutually agreed among the three of them that the less they were seen together, the better.

Leaving the inn by the back door, Zoltan and Ben at once turned their steps uphill and inland, climbing the gullied, unpaved alley behind the inn toward the edge of the settlement, which was hardly more than a stone's throw away.

Their chosen alley led them to an almost deserted street, and the street in turn, still climbing uphill, passed out of town and in a short distance had become little more than a narrow footpath. Turning to look back as they passed the town's last scattered buildings, they found themselves well above most of the settlement they had just quitted. There, standing out among lower and shabbier roofs, was the inn, one of the few two-story buildings. On the upper veranda that ran along its inland side, easy to see from here, was the place where Yambu was to leave a visible signal whenever she wanted another conference with them.

As the two men continued hiking uphill along the path, they debated whether they were going to be able to trust her or not. Zoltan, who knew comparatively little about Yambu, voiced his suspicions. Ben shared these doubts to some extent, but he was more optimistic. He could remember more about the lady than her public reputation of years past.

"She was your enemy then, and Uncle Mark's," Zoltan objected. "Why should we trust her now?"

"Aye, I know she was. But there are enemies and then there are enemies. And whether it was wise or not, we've already made the decision now and it's a case of trying to work with her. We've no other choice that makes any sense at all."

Zoltan had to agree, however reluctantly. The alternative to staying on the shores of Lake Alkmaar and trying to help Mark would be to leave at once for home. Tasavalta was months away, by riverboat until the cliffs were reached, and above them by foot or riding-beast. Doubtless more months would pass before they would be able to return with help. A slightly better choice than that might be for one of them to head back alone —Zoltan would probably be the swifter traveler—while the other one waited here by the lake, keeping an eye on developments as well as possible.

Of course when the Princess in Tasavalta failed to receive a winged courier from Honan-Fu bearing word of her husband's safe arrival, the Tasavaltans would begin to be alarmed and would take action anyway. Their first efforts at probing the situation, by winged scouts and by long-distance magic, would be under way long before either Zoltan or Ben, hurry as they might, could bring home word that help was needed.

Sending a message from Triplicane directly by a flying beast would speed up the Tasavaltan moblization enormously. Ben had hoped to find some such creatures available at the docks, but Lady Yambu had assured him there were none.

Zoltan asked now: "What was that business of hers with the little dragon?"

"I don't know."

"A dragon's not something our people in Tasavalta

would be likely to use, or our allies either. More likely our enemies would use one—have you any hope that anything will come of it?"

Ben trudged on. Eventually he said: "I don't know that either. If you decide to trust someone, then trust them. Or don't. Half measures only do harm."

Scouting yesterday among these hills with Prince Mark, trying to find some native willing and able to tell them what had happened on the wizard's island, Ben and Zoltan had observed an abandoned hut or two, with tattered nets of thin string still stretched outside, suggesting that the dwellings had once been inhabited by fowlers. These huts were now the objective of the two men, on the off chance that there might possibly be someone still living in the area with a flying messenger that could be bought or hired—or stolen—and might make it all the way to Tasavalta in a matter of a few days.

As he went up the hill behind Ben, Zoltan was thinking gloomily that the odds of his uncle still being alive were not good, and they were worsening by the hour. He was also wondering if he, being somewhat faster, ought to suggest that he run on ahead of Ben and search. The trouble with that idea was that neither of them were quite sure where they were going. The supposed fowlers' huts had been on this long and uneven hillside *somewhere*. . . .

Ben, who was still trudging a little in advance, stopped so suddenly that Zoltan almost ran into him.

"What—" Zoltan began, and then fell silent, staring past Ben's shoulder.

An easy bowshot up the hill, Prince Mark, dressed just as they had seen him last, was standing looking down at them.

Mark was poised alertly just off the nearly overgrown path where it ran between two pine trees. Even at the distance, Zoltan could see the marks of the morning's fight on the Prince's face, but he gave no sign of having been seriously hurt. As his nephew and his old friend stared up the slope at him, momentarily too shocked for speech, Mark raised a hand in a gesture that was more a signal of caution than a wave.

Ben started uphill again, almost at a run. And was stopped after only two or three strides by a sudden pushing gesture of Mark's palm.

The Prince, his voice calm, called down to them: "Wait. Not now. Wait for me to come to you."

And then he stepped off the trail and disappeared into the nearby trees.

Ben and Zoltan turned stunned faces to each other. Then, facing uphill again, they stood waiting, still speechless with surprise.

Hardly had they begun to recover from their shock when they caught sight of the Prince again, as Mark became briefly visible through the trees a little way up the slope. He was still moving away from the path and following a course that angled down the hill. He shot a glance downhill and saw Ben and Zoltan watching him. Again Mark paused, just long enough to send them a reassuring wave. He was considerably closer now, and Zoltan could see the marks of the morning's fight more clearly.

And again, as soon as Zoltan and Ben started toward the Prince, he called out sharply to them. "Wait, I told you! Have patience, and I'll be with you shortly." Again his tall form moved out of sight, still on his angled downhill course.

Groaning with a delayed sensation of relief, Ben began to mumble curses. In a moment he had slumped down to rest on a small rock outcropping. But a moment after that he was on his feet again, gazing with impatient curiosity toward the place where Mark had most recently vanished. There was no one to be seen there now.

The two men waited. They looked uphill and down. Heartbeats of time stretched out into minutes, but Mark did not reappear.

Nor was any sign of him to be found when his

nephew and his old friend, stirred into activity again, reached the place where they had seen him last. Except that Zoltan found a small mark, badly blurred but very fresh, in a patch of wet earth exposed on the slope. The footprint, if it really was such, was too vague and incomplete to offer any hope of identification.

Time ticked away. Now Zoltan and Ben began to gaze at each other in fresh bewilderment. Zoltan once stood up and drew in breath as if to shout Mark's name, but Ben, suddenly scowling in suspicion, jabbed at him with a hand, almost knocking him off his feet, to keep him silent.

Zoltan was now trying to recall the exact words Prince Mark had shouted to them. What he could remember was not at all encouraging. Mark's declarations had been vaguely reassuring, but not at all informative.

An effort to find more fresh tracks along the course the Prince had been following downhill soon came to nothing. There were a few old footprints blurred by rain, and the marks of little animals, but nothing useful.

Ben was scowling fiercely. "Had he Shieldbreaker still with him just now? It seems to me I saw a swordhilt at his waist."

"No. No, I am sure that he did not."

Each held to his opinion on that point; though otherwise, they agreed, the Prince had been dressed just as they had seen him last.

"And he told us to wait here. Didn't he? Isn't that what he called to us twice?"

"All right. Yes, he did tell us that. Where did he go, though? Just to run off like that again without a word . . . this is madness."

"He might have got past us and be heading down to the settlement."

"That's just what he did. But why should he do that? Without stopping to give us a word of explanation?"

The two men repeated to each other the exact words they remembered the Prince uttering just a few minutes ago. The differences in their two versions were insignificant. He had really assured them that they did not have to worry about him. And he had ordered them to stay where they were.

Therefore they settled in, howbeit grimly and impatiently, to wait.

Shortly after her two visitors departed, Lady Yambu had gone out of her room, down the upstairs hall, and out onto the upper veranda. She had no particular goal in mind; such little walks had become her habit during the dreary days of her stay at the inn.

Standing on the narrow rustic veranda, looking up toward the hills in the direction that she supposed her new allies must have taken when they departed, she observed a single figure moving, angling down along the partially wooded slope. Somehow, even at the distance, it did not appear to be one of the local people. It was certainly not the bulky form of Ben of Purkinje, and what she could make out of the clothing indicated that it wasn't young Zoltan either. Unless for some reason the youth had changed his garments in the few minutes since she'd seen him last. . . . The distance, a couple of hundred meters, was too great for her to see much more of the figure than the movements of its arms and legs, but there was something about it, some tinge of familiarity, that tugged at her memory. Vaguely uneasy, she remained on the veranda, watching.

Less than a minute later the same figure came into her view again, much closer now. With movements that impressed her as furtive, it emerged from behind some trees and entered the highest street of the town proper. It was a man, she was sure of that now, and he was near enough for some details of his appearance to be observable. Yambu was able to focus on the figure for only a moment before it vanished again, this time behind a building.

That moment had been quite long enough. A wave of faintness came over the lady watching. She, who had once been a queen, was not accustomed to such a reaction in herself, or minded to tolerate it, and she fought against the weakness fiercely.

That she should have a strong reaction was understandable. She had just seen the Emperor, the father of her only child. He had been cloaked in gray and masked in a black domino, as she had so often seen him in the past.

Yambu hurried back to her room. Her hands were shaking as she put on her pilgrim's rugged footgear and her traveling outfit of trousers and cloak. Leaving her room again, she hastened back to the upper veranda, where she set out the prearranged signal, a simple bright-colored rag snagged on a rugged railing, which would indicate to her new allies that she wanted to meet with them at once.

Having done that, Yambu left the building and went out into the muddy street. She climbed through the town to the place where she had seen the gray-cloaked figure pass, on the highest of the town's three streets that ran parallel to the waterfront.

So, the Emperor was here. But what did his presence signify? Years had passed since she had seen him last, and that had been on the night before a battle.

Peering up and down each street as she came to it, she saw only a few of the townsfolk going about their business, and a few of the new garrison of soldiers in gray and red. There was no sign of the Emperor, or any other person or thing of interest. After hesitating briefly at the edge of town, Yambu continued on the path that went uphill, to the appointed place of meeting with Zoltan and Ben. This was well away from the settlement, beside a small stream on the rocky hillside.

\* \* \*

Only a few minutes after she arrived there the two men joined her. When they did, they found her pale but composed.

"We saw your signal—" Ben of Purkinje began.

The lady cut him off with an imperious hand. "Ben."

"Yes, ma'am?"

"You told me that after the stone struck Ariane in the head—down there in the treasure vaults of the Blue Temple—she was still able to move about. For some time."

This was obviously not what Ben had been expecting as an opening to this hastily summoned meeting, and he frowned. But after looking closely at the former queen, he did not protest the apparent wild irrelevance. "That's right," he said.

"And then, some minutes or an hour after being hit, she suddenly collapsed."

"Yes."

"And died."

"And died."

"But are you quite certain that she was dead?"

He looked around at the wet woods and back at her. No, he hadn't been expecting this at all. "Of course I am. She died within a minute or two of losing consciousness —but why do you ask about that now?"

"Because," said the former queen, "I have just seen my daughter." She ignored their brief clamor of questions and pressed on. "On the hillside not far below us here. As if she were just coming up out of the town. I would have gone to her, but she waved me away. And she was smiling. As soon as I recovered from my shock I went to the place where I had seen her, but she was gone."

Zoltan muttered words of astonishment. But Ben had been hit too hard even for that. The color had faded suddenly under the weathered surface of his skin.

Lady Yambu went on. "I should tell you that

despite the depth of my surprise her appearance was not totally unexpected to me. Because I met her father once, years after she was supposed to have died. And on that occasion he assured me solemnly that Ariane was still alive."

Using both arms, the lady made a gesture expressive of both frustration and determination. She went on: "He has, as everyone knows, a reputation for insane jokes; I, who have borne one of his children, can tell you that the reputation is well deserved. But I can tell you also that he was not joking when he told me Ariane was living. To have told me such a thing at such a time could not have been a joke, not even an insane one. No, he was very sober and convincing." She paused. "Still, at the time I did not believe him."

"Why not?" asked Zoltan.

The lady, as he had more than half expected, ignored his question totally. She said: "Also, I thought that I saw him, my daughter's father, walking here upon this hillside only a few minutes before I saw her."

Ben said hoarsely: "Her father was—is—the Emperor."

"So you know that. And presumably you also know something about him—? Good. I shall not have to try to explain that he is not the figure of simpleminded fun that common folktales paint him." Yambu heaved a sigh. "Not that I really could explain that man. Yes, her father assured me that she was still alive, despite what had happened to her down in the treasure vaults. He told me that she had been living with him for several years."

"Living with him." Ben's voice was a hoarse mutter. "Gods and demons. Where?"

"The gods only know that. Or perhaps the demons know. Wherever he chose to live, I suppose."

Long moments went by in which all three of them were silent. Ben was staring intently at the lady. Then at last he said in a choked voice: "You lie. Or he lied to you. I tell you I saw her die."

Yambu appeared to think the accusation too ridiculous to deserve her anger; she only sniffed at him imperiously. "Why in the world should I lie to you? And as for the Emperor lying to me on such a matter—no, I think not. Not on that occasion anyway."

Zoltan spoke up again, after a hesitation but firmly enough when the words came. "Lady, you have told us you did not believe him."

"True, I did not believe him when he told me, or for years afterward. But recently I have been giving the matter much thought. And I know who I saw today."

Ben was staring at her as if there were some truth that he too had to have and by staring he could force it somehow into visibility. He appeared to be unable to find anything to say.

At last Yambu repeated her earlier question to him: "Was Ariane still a virgin when you saw her die?"

Ben was slow to answer, and his voice was low. "We loved each other, she and I. She was very young and very beautiful, and the daughter of a queen, and when you look at me I know it sounds ridiculous to say she loved me. But so it was."

Yambu measured him with her eyes. "I have not said it was ridiculous."

Zoltan, meanwhile, was staring silently at the huge man, as if he had never seen him before. It was quite plain that Mark's nephew had never heard this story before, or suspected anything like it.

Ben, gazing into the past now, went on. "We had only a few days to try to know each other. And not so much as a quarter of an hour, in any of those days, to be alone together. So if it is of any importance to you, yes, your daughter remained a virgin until she died. At the time, the point was of considerable magical importance to the wizards. And so I know that it is true, even though she had been in the Red Temple." Ben jumped up from the rock he had been sitting on. "And if I thought—if I

could believe for a moment—that Ariane was still alive,
I would leave all that I possess to go to her."

Yambu asked him harshly: "Would you leave even
your Prince?"

Ben's enormous shoulders slumped. He said: "That
decision does not have to be made. My Prince, alive or
dead, is here, and here I stay until I have done all that I
can do for him. And your daughter is dead. I tell you
that I saw her die."

Abruptly the three people fell silent; they were all
aware that someone, a single person, was passing on one
of the hillside paths not far away. From behind intervening evergreen shrubs they observed the passerby with
great interest. But it was only some local peasant,
bearing a small load of firewood, and they turned away.

The place where they had met and had been talking
until now was relatively public, and by common consent
they moved to continue their conference at a place
farther from any trail. The new site, also on the hillside,
had the advantage of better concealment, of allowing
them to overlook much of the town, while being themselves screened from any likely observation by a growth
of low evergreen bushes. Zoltan, looking down, thought
that the bunched needles made the town beyond them
look like a drawing half-obliterated by the mad scrawling
lines of some determined vandal.

Their discussion was just getting under way again
when it was once more interrupted. All three of the
people on the hillside saw, at a distance of a hundred
meters or so, a peculiar figure walking in the nearest
street of the settlement below.

What drew their attention to the figure was first the
darting, scrambling way it moved. Second was the fact
that the other people in the street turned to gaze after it
as it darted from between buildings on one side into an
alley on the other. After it had passed, some of the

townsfolk appeared to exchange looks, and perhaps words, with one another before going on about their business.

The three on the hillside studied the figure itself as well as they could at the distance; then they also exchanged glances among themselves. If they had marveled before, they were dumbfounded now.

Ben said: "It was your daughter, walking in the street. And I am going down to her."

"It was she," Yambu agreed in a stunned voice. "I will go with you."

"Wait!" cried Zoltan. His voice was not very loud, but something in it stopped the other two.

The young man looked at them, one after the other. He said: "Lady, I have never seen your daughter Ariane. What does she look like?"

It was Ben who answered. "You could not have missed her just now, among those shabby commoners. Tall, and as strong as most men, but there's no doubt from her shape that she's a woman, and still young. And her red hair, like a long flame down her back. She moved across the street quite near the intersection, jumping over the worst of a puddle. . . ." Ben stopped. Yambu was nodding her agreement.

But Zoltan's face was contorted, his eyes squeezed shut as if he were in pain.

"I did not see her," he announced.

"What do you mean?" Yambu demanded.

"I saw *someone*, a single person, cross the street near the intersection, just as you did, and jump the mud puddle while the townspeople moved away. But it was certainly not a young woman, with red hair or without. It was Prince Mark again, my uncle, whom I know well."

There was a brief silence while the others digested this.

"That red hair!" Ben ripped the words out like an oath. "There can't be any mistake!"

"What red hair? I tell you the one I saw just now

was a man, brown-haired and bearded!"

They all three looked at one another, all of them trying to master their emotions, all trying to think. Yambu said: "Then what we have seen is magic—"

The three of them uttered the word almost in unison: "Sightblinder!"

"Or some spell equally powerful. Yes, that must be it."

They were sitting down again, in the same place, and Ben said those words, and the other two heard them, without conviction. All three of the people on the hillside had handled some of the Twelve Swords at one time or another—it was hard for any of them to believe in the existence of any such equally powerful spell.

"We must investigate," decreed the lady after a long silence, sighing as she spoke.

"Whoever is carrying Sightblinder came down the hillside alone a little while ago," said Zolton. "And perhaps he or she will soon be going up again."

"If not," Ben decided in a heavy voice, "we must go down into the town and search for him, or her. Though for Zoltan and me it would be wise, as we all agreed earlier, to appear there as seldom as possible."

The three decided to wait where they were for a while longer before trying to search the town.

Before an hour had passed they saw a lone figure ascending the path again. And for each, as each whispered to the others, it was someone they loved or feared. This time for Ben it was his wife, who was at home in Tasavalta and in logic could not be here at all.

Firmly disregarding the evidence of their senses, the three moved out of their ambush and closed in, as upon a dangerous armed enemy. Zoltan and Ben held weapons ready. Their quarry, whoever it really was, saw them coming and displayed alarm, and cried out warnings to them, words that reached the ears of each of them in the tone of some voice that had long been loved or feared. It cost each of the three an effort of will to ignore those pleading warnings and close in.

At last, in a brushy hillside ravine well off any of the regular footpaths, they managed to corner their quarry, who by now was moving slowly and erratically, as if nearly exhausted.

Ben saw Barbara, his own diminutive, dark-haired wife, looking at him piteously. Making a great effort, he called to her: "Throw down that damned magic blade, whoever you are—I know you have it there!"

Yambu, this time, saw the Emperor again, turning at bay to face her, and wondered if it was her love for him or fear of him that the Sword played on to cast his image. She too moved forward implacably, though she was unarmed.

Zoltan moved forward against an image of the Prince, his uncle, who now appeared to him with a Sword that might have been Shieldbreaker raised in a two-handed grip.

"Stay back, all of you! I warn you!" called out the one voice that was heard as three quite different voices.

But the three came on.

The wielder of the Sword of Stealth raised it, making a halfhearted and inexpert defense.

Still, it took courage for Ben to swing his staff against a Sword that suddenly looked like Shieldbreaker, gripped in the hands of Mark—Ben had not blundered, there was only a clang, as of hardwood on ordinary steel, and the Sword-holder, mishandling the weapon awkwardly, staggered back. Zoltan sprang forward to grapple with him, or her.

Zoltan in the next moment found himself seizing his own mother's arm and twisting it painfully —somehow the experience was even worse than he would have imagined such a thing would be. It wasn't only that he saw his mother. He felt her tender flesh, heard her soft breath, he *knew*—though no longer quite

with certainty—that it was her. But he gritted his teeth
and persisted while his mother struggled wildly against
him, screaming. Then Ben's hands clamped upon the
foe, and the struggle was over.

There was a clanging thud, as of an arm's length of
steel falling to the rocky ground.

Pinned upright by Ben's grip upon his arms was a
shabby, hungry-looking figure, lean and ill-favored, a
mere boy, younger than Zoltan and not as big or strongly
built. The youth was sobbing now, as with relief.

On the earth at his feet, which were clad in worn
country shoes, lay a black-hilted Sword. But only after
Zoltan's hand had touched the black hilt could he clearly
see the small white symbol of a human eye upon it.

> *The Sword of Stealth is given to*
> *One lowly and despised*
> *Sightblinder's gifts: his eyes are keen*
> *His nature is disguised.*

"Who are you?" Ben was shouting at the boy.
"What's your name?"

The answer came between great gasping sobs. "Arnfinn."

# CHAPTER 5

ARNFINN'S blubbering was not entirely the result of fear. A part of the cause was sheer relief, relief that the strain of the last few days was over. The responsibility of what to do with the terrible weapon he had been carrying had now been lifted from his shoulders. Whatever happened next, at least he was not going to have to support that oppressive weight any longer.

He was sitting where he had been pushed down on the rocky earth of the hillside, collapsed in defeat and futility, while close around him stood the three people who had thrown him down and taken the Sword away from him. And even now, in the depth of his fear, he was struck by what an oddly assorted trio they made. One was the biggest, strongest-looking man Arnfinn had ever seen; the second was an elderly lady dressed in pilgrim's gray; and the third was a young man only a little older than Arnfinn, of sturdy build and rather ordinary appearance.

Or, more exactly, the young man's appearance had been rather ordinary, until he had started to handle the Sword.

As soon as the young man picked up that magical blade, Arnfinn saw him changed into a rapid succession of other people. First came Arnfinn's own father. Then a bully from the village of Lunghai, who more than once

41

had made Arnfinn's existence miserable; and after that a certain lady, really only a girl, the beauty of whose image, however false, could still make Arnfinn catch his breath. One figure followed another, each evoking either love or fear, or sometimes both. The sequence returned at last to Arnfinn's father, who had been dead for years, and Arnfinn buried his face in his hands and wept again.

Meanwhile the giant and the old woman were paying little attention to whatever transformations the Sword might have been causing their companion to undergo in their eyes. Their attention remained thoughtfully fixed on Arnfinn.

When Arnfinn heard rather than saw the young man put down the Sword again, he dared to raise his face once more. These people had not killed him yet, and maybe they were going to let him live.

It was the gray-robed woman, her voice imperious, her accent aristocratic, who shot the first question at him: "What were you doing with this blade?"

"Nothing," Arnfinn responded automatically, defensively, without thinking. That answer was almost the truth, but obviously it was not going to be satisfactory, though so far they were letting him take his time and think about it.

Using his sleeve, he wiped his face of tears and sweat, achieving with the rough cleansing a kind of fatalistic calm. "I brought it here to town to try to sell it."

"Brought it from where?" the young man demanded.

"From my home village. It's a place called Lunghai. About three days walk to the west of here."

"And how came this Sword into your hands?" This was the giant, anger still rumbling dangerously in his voice.

Arnfinn continued the slow process of getting himself under control. "Some children of our village found this weapon—they said they found it under a bush, I suppose they were telling the truth but I don't know how it got there—and they were playing with it. Frightening everybody, and—"

"And so you took it away from them."

"Yes. For their own good. The gods know what trouble they might have caused with it." Arnfinn looked up, appealing to the three grim faces. "I intend—I intended to share the money with them, and with their parents, when I had sold the Sword. Their parents were very much afraid. They just wanted to be rid of it."

Anger still threatened in the huge man's voice. "Who did you think you were going to sell it to?"

Arnfinn gestured toward the water. "I had heard there were good wizards living on the islands in Lake Alkmaar—that's what all the people in my village believed, though our people seldom came here to Triplicane. I didn't mean to do any harm."

"What harm do you think you've done?" This was from the young man. Despite his youth he somehow sounded more like a leader than either of the others did.

Arnfinn shifted his position on the rough ground. He drew in a deep breath and heaved it out again. "I don't know," he said. "I don't know."

There was a pause. Then the woman asked him: "How long have you been here, then?" And the young man at the same time: "What kept you from going through with the sale?"

Now words poured out of Arnfinn in a rush. "I've been here for days. I've lost count how many. When I got here—well, I was carrying the Sword, and so naturally everyone in the town acted strange every time they saw me. The gods only know who or what they saw, or thought they saw, when they looked at me. If there's any way to turn the power of this weapon off, I don't know what it is. And of course I didn't dare to leave the thing anywhere, for fear of losing it. I hardly dared to set it down. So—I haven't had much actual contact with the people here. I've been sleeping out, up there on the hill."

"And you're saying," the lady asked him, "that you never actually tried to sell the Sword to anyone?"

"That's right. I never showed it to anyone, or talked about it."

"Why not?"

"I was afraid to try, ma'am. As soon as I arrived in town, I began to hear that there were strange things going on out on the islands. I could see that there were quite a few soldiers in the town and they had taken over the docks. And there were strange rumors about Honan-Fu and what might have happened to him. The people I talked to were all worried."

"What did these strange rumors say, exactly?"

Arnfinn managed a shrug. "That there were new rulers out there on the island, and they were evil. One man had heard a story about huge flying shapes, reptiles, demons, the gods know what, dropping out of the sky at night over Honan-Fu's castle. And there were stories of how the new rulers had done bad things—even kidnapped a few people from villages along the mainland shore. I didn't want to sell the Sword to anyone like that."

The giant said: "Fortunate for you, you didn't try, I'd say. Well, you won't have to worry any longer about selling the Sword. It's in good hands now."

Arnfinn nodded hastily.

Zoltan looked at his two companions, then back at Arnfinn. He said with authority: "You'll be compensated for it someday. You and the children of your village who found it for you. If your story about how it came into your possession turns out to be true."

"I've told you the truth." At least he had told them a lot of it. What he had held back, he thought, would probably not be of any importance to them; and it was not something he was going to tell to anyone, whatever happened.

Arnfinn wiped his face with his sleeve again. "Now, can I go?" When nothing intimidating happened to him in response to this question, he dared to get back to his feet.

That move, too, was accepted. At least nobody knocked him down again. Instead, the big man pointed a huge finger at the ground, and grumbled a warning at him, that he should stay right where he was; and then the three moved to a little distance, where they could confer without their victim hearing them. Obviously the subject of their conference was what to do about him.

Watching them, Arnfinn could imagine them coming to one of at least three possible decisions. One, they could determine to kill him after all, in which case he ought to be bounding down the hillside right now, running for his life. He wasn't doing that, so it followed that he didn't really believe that he was going to be killed, not after their having talked to him so reasonably. Two, they could try to enlist him in their cause, whatever that might be. Three, they could send him home. In Arnfinn's current mental state he wasn't sure which alternative would be worse.

The three did not take long to reach a decision. In only moments they were coming back, surrounding him again.

The gray-robed woman had pulled out her purse and was counting out some coins. Arnfinn felt a little dizzy; at least they were not going to finish him right now.

"What will you do," the young man asked, "if we tell you you are free to go?"

"I'll go home," said Arnfinn promptly. "I'll leave here this instant, and never come back."

The big man added his endorsement of that plan, emphasizing it with a brutally graphic statement of what would happen to Arnfinn if he did come back.

"I won't."

"See that you don't."

The lady extended the coins to him in her hand, and Arnfinn muttered thanks and took them—he put them into his pocket without counting, but still it looked like more money than anyone in Lunghai except the lord of its manor had seen for a long time.

He turned away. The moment he started downhill toward the town, three voices challenged and warned him.

He stopped and turned again, explaining that his road home led in that direction. "But I'll not stop in the town. I don't know anyone there, and none of them know me." Which was true enough, for none of the folk of Triplicane had ever seen him without the Sword.

The three let him go on, evidently convinced by his fright, which was certainly real enough.

Even though Arnfinn knew no one in the town, and no one in the town knew him, still there was one stop he had to make, someone in the neighborhood he had to try to see. He knew it was mad foolishness, but still he had to try to see her once more, even if he knew it could be no more than one look from a distance. Even if the three came after him and killed him for it.

He kept on going straight through the town, a stranger insignificant and unnoticed, until he came out on its other side. There he presently found himself standing in front of Triplicane's most substantial dwelling. It was a low, sprawling manor house, which was invisible from the road behind high walls and trees. It was obvious that wealth and power dwelt here.

Arnfinn had entered the grounds of this manor before, but now he knew that he would never be able to enter them again. Now, without the Sword of Stealth, the best he would ever be able to do was to wait outside, loitering in the road. If he did that it might be possible for him to see her just once more—perhaps catch a brief glimpse through the strong bars of the gate. It was not much of a chance, but it appeared to be all that he now had left.

The realization was sinking in on him that in losing

the Sword he had lost whatever chance might have remained of repairing the ruin he had managed to make of his life during the few days when he'd had the Sword in hand.

Arnfinn began to weep again. This time his sobs were quieter, slower, and more bitter. Looking back, it was hard for him to see how he might have been able to do things differently.

# CHAPTER 6

HIS journey to sell the Sword hadn't started out in hopelessness. Far from it; in the innocence of its very beginning it had been something of a lark.

The presence of the Sword of Stealth in the village of Lunghai had been kept a secret from the great majority of the villagers, at least up to the time of Arnfinn's departure. The very few people who knew what he was up to, a small group of immediate family and close friends, had seen him off with quiet rejoicing. At the last moment a couple of his relatives had suggested that it would really be better after all if someone accompanied him. But that point had already been discussed, and really settled. Everyone else in the little group of people who knew about the Sword had work to do in the village, work it would be impractical for them to leave. Arnfinn would have little work to do until the harvest started, and he swore he would be back before then. And if Arnfinn went alone, taking the Sword with him, it was possible no one else in the village would know about the real purpose of his trip until he was back with the money he had realized from its sale.

The day of his departure was fine and promising, in the lull of work before the harvest began in earnest. Arnfinn, riding a borrowed loadbeast, took pleasure in the sheer novelty of the journey. And not long after he had left his own village behind him, he began to appreci-

48

ate the possibilities of fun in the miraculous power of the weapon he was carrying.

A pair of poor farmers, one of whom Arnfinn recognized when he chanced to meet them on the road, suddenly put on unintentionally comical expressions and cleared themselves hastily out of his way. This pleased him disproportionately, and he tried in vain to imagine who, or what, the Sword had made them see. At the next tiny hamlet that Arnfinn came to, shortly after his encounter with the farmers, the peasant women who saw him pass ran from their huts to grab up small children and bring them inside.

Arnfinn, grinning as he tried to guess in what image, terrible or awesome, the Sword had presented him to the women, rode past all of them on his phlegmatic borrowed loadbeast and said nothing. Whenever he cast his eyes down at his own body, even if he did so at the very moment when people were retreating from him in fear, he saw only the same poor clothes as always, covering the same scrawny and unimpressive frame. Only within the past year, after his sixteenth birthday, had he begun to admit to himself the possibility that he was never going to grow much bigger than he was, never going to be huge and powerful.

Even earlier in life he had been forced to concede in his own mind that he was never going to be handsome. His face had never actually frightened anyone—not until the magic of the Sword of Stealth had begun to alter it in the sight of others. But with his nose and Adam's apple standing out like brackets above and below the bony projection of his chin, his was a countenance that had provoked more than a few jokes.

After passing through that first hamlet Arnfinn came to a long stretch of road where there were no more villages. Nor, for the time being, were there any other travelers for him to meet. In solitude the loadbeast kept plodding methodically forward. The sun turned through a sky hazed lightly with the onset of autumn.

And, he kept thinking to himself, he hadn't even *drawn* the Sword to frighten any of those people. Sightblinder—that was what it had to be—was just hanging there in its fancy scabbard, from the fancy belt that had been with it when the children found it. Belt and scabbard alike were skillfully sewn of fine sturdy leather, and both were mounted with what Arnfinn assumed were real jewels; he suspected that those decorations might be treasure enough in themselves to enrich the village of Lunghai considerably.

Or, perhaps, more than enough to get the whole village into trouble. Even in Lunghai people had heard of the Twelve Swords, magical weapons forged by the gods themselves more than thirty years ago. If Arnfinn and his people hadn't known of the good wizards on their island, he wouldn't have any idea of where to go to try to sell this marvelous blade. But Honan-Fu the wizard was known to be a good man, kindly to the poor, and trustworthy in all his dealings; not that Arnfinn himself had ever met him, but all the common folk who had met him said so. The good wizard would advise Arnfinn on what to do, and not cheat him out of the village treasure that had been entrusted to him.

The next village that Arnfinn came to was totally new territory to him. He had never in his life before traveled so far in this direction. And this village saw the end of the lightheartedness with which he had begun his journey.

The road passed directly through the small village square, a plot of brown grass and a few trees. A woman who was seated on a bench at one side of the square stared at Arnfinn as he approached. Her face grew pale, very pale. And then, jumping to her feet and giving a cry suitable for a death or a birth, she appeared to go mad.

Arnfinn, already alarmed, panicked now and kicked his loadbeast to make it go faster. But the woman overtook the trotting animal and then ran beside it, clinging to Arnfinn's knee, entreating him to stop. She kept calling him over and over by some name he could not understand, one that he had never heard before. The woman's cries resounded, bringing people out of the little houses around the square. She was not young. Her graying hair fell in disheveled curls beside her weathered cheeks. Her eyes, enormous with emotion, never left Arnfinn's face.

Arnfinn, in his embarrassment and growing fright, was unable to imagine what might happen if he did stop and try to talk to this screaming madwoman. How could he explain? That would mean giving up the treasure of the Sword, if only for a moment, trying to demonstrate its magic. And to give it up was something that he dared not do.

Obviously the woman thought that he was someone she had deeply loved, someone she had not seen for many years—perhaps someone who was dead. Unable to remain silent in the face of her clamoring entreaties, he made abortive attempts to reassure her, to explain, to somehow shut her up. But despite his stumbling efforts, all she could see and hear was her loved one, inexplicably riding on, refusing to stop for her. Some of the other people of the village, this woman's neighbors and perhaps her relatives, were looking on aghast, though they made no move to interfere. Eventually, Arnfinn thought, even as he struggled to get away, they will be able to help her. Because each of them will have seen me as a different person, and sooner or later they will all realize that what has ridden through their village was an enchantment. Then soon they will all get over this.

And how could Arnfinn stop? What could he have said to her, what could he have done for her if he did stop?

At last he clamped his own lips shut and kicked the loadbeast into a run. This too, at first, only seemed to make matters worse. The woman's grip on the loadbeast's saddle was brutally broken when the animal began to run. But she still tottered down the road after Arnfinn. For a long time she kept up the hopeless pursuit, begging him to come back to her. It seemed to him that he had to ride for an hour, sweating in the chill air, trying to shut his ears, before the sound of her cries had faded entirely away.

When night came he slept in the open. And for a day or two after that incident he avoided villages altogether, making a long detour whenever a settlement of any kind came into sight ahead.

He could not avoid encountering other travelers now and then. Inevitably they displayed either one of two basic reactions, and Arnfinn wasn't sure which one was worse: the fear or the strange, puzzled love. Puzzled, he supposed, because the loved one was behaving so strangely, offering no recognition.

But Arnfinn no longer found anything enjoyable in either reaction. And so he ceased to wear the Sword. Taking off the belt and scabbard, he wrapped them in his only spare shirt, making an undistinguished-looking bundle, and then contrived to tie the bundle onto the loadbeast's rump along with the rest of his meager baggage.

On the following day he was traversing a particularly lonely stretch of road when two men suddenly appeared out of the scrubby forest no more than an arrow's flight ahead of him.

More to reassure himself that his treasure was safe than to seek its protection, Arnfinn reached behind him and felt inside the bundle for the hard hilt of the Sword. And the moment he touched it, his perception of the two men changed.

In Lunghai, robbers were very rare indeed. But stories about them were common enough, and many of the village men were reluctant to undertake even necessary journeys on these roads, except in groups. Arnfinn, listening to the stories, had mentally allied himself with the braver village men, and had tended to dismiss such fears as a sign of timidity. Now, however, matters suddenly wore a somewhat different aspect.

There was no obvious reason to assume that these two men were robbers. But Arnfinn, from the moment he touched Sightblinder, was certain that they were. When they looked toward him, and then started in his direction, he stopped his mount, then turned it off the road at an angle, urging it to its greatest speed. It was a young animal, and healthy enough, but the healthiest loadbeast was not a riding-beast, and certainly not a racer.

Behind him now the men's voices were hailing him, in friendly tones, but Arnfinn ignored the call. He steered his animal among trees, and forced it through a thicket, trying to get himself well out of their sight.

Halfway into the thicket his mount rebelled against this strange procedure, and came to a stubborn halt. He saw, through a thin screen of dead leaves, the two men on their swift riding-beasts go cantering by on the road he had just left. They were a savage-looking pair now in their anger, muttering curses as they rode, and Arnfinn noted with a feeling of faintness that they both had drawn long knives from somewhere. Robbers, no doubt about it. Murderers. He twisted in his saddle as soon as they had passed, and with shaking hands he started to undo the bundle that held the Sword.

His fumbling fingers let the burden go, and with a noisy crash it fell from the animal's rump into the dry twigs of the thicket. At once one of the robbers' voices sounded, startlingly near; they must have already turned, they were already coming back to kill him.

Jumping, almost falling, from his saddle after the Sword, Arnfinn, praying to all the gods whose names he had ever heard, scrambled after Sightblinder on the ground. At last he reached it. Unable to get the bundle open quickly, he thrust his right hand inside and grasped the Sword's hilt, and felt the full power of it flow into his hand. That flow was not of warmth, nor cold, it was of something he could not have described, but it passed through the skin as cold or heat would pass.

He was still in that same position, crouched awkwardly on all fours almost underneath his puzzled animal, when the two men on riding-beasts came crashing into the thicket after him.

As soon as they saw Arnfinn both of them reined in their mounts so suddenly that one of the riding-beasts tripped and almost fell; and the alteration in the two men's faces was immediate and remarkable. Arnfinn was reminded of the first two farmers he had encountered on the road.

One of the bandits looked down at his own drawn blade as if he were surprised beyond measure to find it in his hand; then, favoring Arnfinn with a sheepish effort at a smile, he sheathed the weapon and turned, and rode away even more quickly than he had approached. His companion meanwhile had been trying to find words, words that sounded like a terrified effort at an apology. Then he too put his knife away—he had to thrust with it three times before he found the opening in the unobtrusive sheath—and turned and fled.

Slowly Arnfinn regained his feet. He stood there beside his loadbeast, listening to the crashing sounds of the enemy's retreat. It sounded to him as if they were afraid he might be coming after them. Soon the hoofbeats sounded more solidly on the road, and soon after that they dwindled into silence.

Arnfinn stood there in the middle of the thicket a while longer, his eyes closed now, his right hand still gripping Sightblinder's hilt. His shivering fear, even before the tremors of it died out in his arms and legs, had almost entirely transformed itself into something else. Before his eyes opened, he had begun to smile.

He had never seen Lake Alkmaar before, but when first he came in sight of the broad, shimmering water there was no doubt in his mind that he had found it. He stopped and dismounted, letting the beast rest after the long, slow climb up the landward side of the hills. Arnfinn remained standing on the tortuous road for some time, petting his mount absently and looking down.

Well below him, and still at some little distance, lay the biggest settlement Arnfinn had ever seen, which had to be the town of Triplicane. Even now, in the middle of the day, the smoke from more than a dozen chimneys faintly marked the air. At the lakeside docks in this town, his advisers in the village had assured him, he would be able to find a boat that would take him out to the castle.

He raised his gaze slightly. There, on an island out near the middle of the lake, was the castle, looking appropriately magical, just as it had been described to him. The home of the benign wizard Honan-Fu himself.

The wizard, Arnfinn had been told, was a little old man with a wispy beard and a kindly manner. He tried now to imagine what it might be like to talk to such a powerful man, and what the good wizard might be likely to offer Arnfinn for such a Sword.

But now, for the first time, Arnfinn felt a stirring of reluctance to give Sightblinder up, even at a price that would have made the people of Lunghai very happy.

Frowning slightly, he remounted his loadbeast and started down the road to town.

As he passed to and fro along the windings of the descending way, the landscape below him changed. The far end of the town came briefly into sight, bringing with it his first glimpse of the roofs and grounds of an extensive lakeside manor.

Arnfinn had scarcely given that house a single conscious thought during his journey, but even before he had started he had known of its existence. And he knew the name of the person who was said to live there, who must be grown-up enough by now to have her own establishment apart from her father's. Only now, when he was actually in sight of the place, did the idea suggest itself to him that maybe, on his way to sell the Sword, he might just dare . . .

To do what? He wasn't sure exactly. But what harm could it do to simply go out of his way a little bit, enough to ride past that manor house on the road that ran directly in front of it. If he were to do that, then maybe, just possibly, *she* would see him from a window. See him not in his scrawny, ugly, ordinary body, but transformed, if only for a moment, into what he would wish to be in the eyes of such a lady. Even if he became something that frightened her, for just a moment . . .

Twice already in his young life, Arnfinn had seen Lady Ninazu. The first time had been five years ago, when he was only twelve and she apparently no older. At that time she, already well on the way to becoming a great lady, had happened to pass through Lunghai, escorted by a troop of the constabulary who served her father, Honan-Fu. Important-looking men, though the wizard himself was not among them, had surrounded the half-grown girl on every side. The appearance even of her escort in their uniforms of gold and green had been fine almost beyond belief in the eyes of poor country folk like Arnfinn and his neighbors. And as for the young lady herself . . .

Until that moment the boy Arnfinn had never dreamed such beauty could exist. He remained staring after her helplessly, until people began to make jokes and poke him to rouse him from his trance.

She was, his fellow villagers told him in response to his questions, the only daughter of Honan-Fu himself, and she lived with her father in his island castle.

The insistent routines of village life soon occupied Arnfinn's attention again, but he did not forget the young lady and what he considered her transcendent beauty.

He did not start to dream about her, though, until he had seen her again.

That had happened only a little more than a year before Arnfinn undertook his trip with the Sword. The place was a larger village than Lunghai, where folk from all the district round were gathered to see a traveling carnival in one of its irregular local passages. Again Arnfinn caught only a brief glimpse of the daughter of Honan-Fu. She had grown and changed, of course, though not as he had changed, for she had only become more beautiful. Her beauty was now less childlike and unworldly, more womanly. This time he asked no more questions about her; he could see very well that there was no point in asking.

Now, when he was about to ride into Triplicane for the first time with Sightblinder at his side, Arnfinn hesitated at the last moment whether to wear the Sword into town, regardless of the sensation that might produce, or bundle it up again behind his saddle. After some hesitation he decided to continue to wear it. If lonely roads were likely places to encounter robbers, big cities, at least in all the stories that he had heard, were notoriously worse. Arnfinn supposed that Triplicane was not really a big city. But to him it looked more than big and strange, and impressive enough to make him wary.

There were so many streets in this town that he could not immediately see how many there were, enough to make the passage through it somewhat confusing. Though Arnfinn kept as much as he could to the less traveled streets, still everywhere he looked there were more people about than he was used to seeing in one place.

To his surprise, many of those who passed him in the street did not appear to notice him at all, even though he was wearing the Sword. He was sure its power was still working, because many did stop and stare at him. But then, most of those who stopped soon went on again about their business, as if perhaps they thought they had been mistaken at first in what they had seen.

The modest stock of food Arnfinn had brought with him from home was running out, and with his few coins in hand he went into a store. He hoped also to be able to learn something about transportation to the castle on its island.

He dared not leave Sightblinder on his loadbeast tethered outside, and so he carried it into the store with him. He could only hope that a storekeeper in a city like this one might be ready to ply his trade in spite of marvels, as capable of indifference as some of the passersby appeared to be.

But that was not what happened when he entered the dim shop that smelled of leather like a harness shop, and of food like a pantry. Instead, the young woman behind the counter turned pale with her first look at Arnfinn. "You've come back!" she breathed.

"I only want some food," he answered, having come in stubbornly determined to stick to business no matter what.

She looked quickly toward the curtain that closed off the back of the store. "My husband—" she began.

At that point a burly, bald man appeared from behind the curtain, as if on cue, or as if perhaps he had been waiting there, listening suspiciously, from the moment Arnfinn entered. At the sight of Arnfinn, fear and hatred filled the shopkeeper's face, even as a more mysterious excitement had filled that of his wife. But then the balding man was quick to mask his feelings. He stood with folded arms, waiting silently for what Arnfinn might say or do.

Silently Arnfinn played the role of customer, picking out bread, sausage, and cheese. The woman served him, gathering his choices on the small counter.

Suddenly she burst out with a question, as if she could contain it no longer: "Does Honan-Fu still survive?"

Arnfinn was sure that he had heard her question clearly, and yet it made no sense to him at all. "Why should he not survive?" he countered, trying to sound confident.

At that the goodwife relaxed somewhat, and even the man's tension seemed to ease a trifle. "I was sure," she said to Arnfinn, "that you must be with them. The new masters out there. Do you suppose you could put in a good word for us? We have no finery for sale here, and their soldiers wear their uniforms, but still they'll want to buy something, won't they? And they'll all be having to eat like anyone else."

"I'll do my best," said Arnfinn. At that the man actually made himself smile, though he was sweating with the struggle he had to make against his fear. And even in his presence his wife looked at Arnfinn with open invitation in her eyes.

Speaking together, man and wife refused his coins when he would have paid them for the food.

Arnfinn did not insist. He feared that he might need the money. Slowly he moved out into the street again, where he stood munching bread and sausage as he watched the endless parade of passing strangers. He puzzled over what the people in the shop had said to him. Why should not Honan-Fu survive? He was going to have to find out.

The most direct route from his present location to Lady Ninazu's manor, as Arnfinn calculated it, lay through a busy-looking part of the town. But he felt that he was beginning to grow accustomed to his situation with the Sword. And he wanted to talk to someone. Someone would have to tell him what had befallen the good wizard.

Passing through what he thought was probably the busiest street, Arnfinn was suddenly accosted by a young girl who bore a baby in her arms. It was obvious from the girl's first words to him that she saw Arnfinn as her former lover, the baby's father, and demanded some acknowledgment of responsibility from him.

Then she fell back a little, as if amazed at her own temerity in accosting him thus. He remained silent, trying to think of what he ought to say. Meanwhile the girl's baby, looking at Arnfinn, displayed the greatest curiosity and delight.

Then suddenly the infant, still looking at him, screamed in terror.

Taking advantage of the distraction, he broke away from the girl, and moved on at a fast walk, leading his loadbeast, the sheathed Sword banging against his leg. People scattered at his approach.

The girl followed him a little way, then gave up, screaming some despairing insult. When he was sure that she had abandoned the chase, Arnfinn paused for breath. To a small boy who stood staring at him he spoke, asking directions to the docks. And was promptly hailed by an old man who, with tears in his blind, staring eyes, groped his way with trembling arms to Arnfinn, and seized him in a hug.

"Come home with me now, Will! You're mother's there. She'll be so glad to see you're safe after all—"

Arnfinn, his control deserting him, broke free from the old man's grasp and ran again. He rushed like a madman through the remainder of the town, looking neither to left nor right. When from behind him he heard yet another cry, as of despair, he did not stop to see whether it was directed at him or not.

Dusk was coming on when at last he found himself standing at the edge of open country, in front of the manor house where he was certain *she* must live.

Arnfinn stared at the closed heavy grillwork of the tall front gate leading to the grounds. He was physically very tired after his day's journey, and also worn by the strain of all that had happened since his arrival in the town. But now he found that he could not rest until he had managed to learn something more about *her*. Could she be safe, if there was doubt as to whether the powerful wizard, her father, was still alive?

Not even with the powers of the Sword in hand did he dare to simply present himself at the gate of the manor and ask—or demand—to be admitted. There would be guards and attendants there, and the gods only knew who they would think he was. They would let him in, by reason of love or fear; of that much Arnfinn felt certain. But what then? What would he say to the people he encountered inside?

What could he say to *her* if she appeared?

Trying to make up his mind as to what to do next, he circled the manor at a little distance, staring at the high stone wall that ringed it in. He was at some distance from the road, in an empty field that sloped down to the shoreline of the lake, when he heard the music of a lute, coming from somewhere beyond the wall. A moment later he heard the voice of a woman singing, and he imagined that that sweet voice must be hers.

There was another, smaller gate in the wall back here, and this one was standing open slightly. Looking through it, Arnfinn could see that it led to stables. There was a soldier slouching against the wall just outside the gate—Arnfinn knew little enough about soldiers, and could not have identified the red and gray uniform worn by this one even if it had occurred to him to try.

But the soldier was looking in his direction now, and he was going to have to do something. He walked forward, wondering what he was going to say.

The soldier snapped silently to attention, saluted, and drew the gate wide open. Arnfinn walked through, leading his loadbeast with him—the music of lute and voice seemed to draw him like a spell.

Just inside the gate he handed his animal's reins over to one who reached for them with quiet efficiency. Then he walked on, unopposed, into the grounds. There were scattered trees, neat hedges, and broad lawns, now turning brown with autumn. And in the middle of one of those grassy spaces an arbor that must have been a pleasant shady place in summer, overgrown as it was with vines. But the leaves on the vines were dead now, and the oncoming night was already turning chill.

But she, the young lady Ninazu, was there anyway, sitting in the arbor, dressed as gloriously as he remembered, though in different garments. At her first glimpse of Arnfinn, even in the failing light, she jumped to her feet, letting her lute fall with an unmusical thud to the wooden floor of the summerhouse.

"By all the gods," she said to him, and her voice had in it such soft intensity that his own voice, despite all that he could do, almost broke out, stuttering a protest. "By all the gods," she breathed, "it's you, and you have not forgotten me. My crystal foretold that I would see you soon."

And for once the emotions written by Sightblinder upon a human countenance were too complex for Arnfinn to interpret.

But the girl had jumped up from her seat and was running toward him. And in the next moment he was being passionately embraced and kissed.

# CHAPTER 7

"**A** PIECE of good luck for us at last," said Ben, looking at the Sword, complete with belt and sheath, where Zoltan had dropped it on the ground at their feet. The three had brought Sightblinder back with them to their hillside observation post, which lay behind a screen of low evergreens through which it was possible to watch much of what went on in the town below. The youth from whom they had taken the Sword of Stealth had already completed his hasty descent into the town, had appeared briefly in those streets below, and then passed out of their sight. Already Ben, at least, had almost forgotten him.

Zoltan now put out his hand and stroked the hilt of Sightblinder again. As he did so, he momentarily became Prince Mark in the eyes of his two companions. Then Zoltan drew back his hand and squatted, gazing silently at the Sword of Stealth.

Ben went on: "But even the best luck is no good until it's used, and we must find the right way to use it."

"We must also keep in mind," said Lady Yambu, "that Shieldbreaker is almost certainly on the island now, in the hands of the one who sent the griffin to carry away your Prince. And the person who carries it will doubtless be the most dangerous enemy with whom we shall have to deal. Whoever has the Sword of Force in

63

hand will be immune to the powers of Sightblinder or any other weapon."

"And so far we have no idea who he is. Or she," Zoltan put in. He got to his feet and stood staring toward the islands.

"I have been here in Triplicane eleven days," said Yambu, "listening to the rumors that pass among the townsfolk. And I can give you an answer to that question. The new ruler of that castle in the lake is called the Ancient One, or sometimes Ancient Lord. He . . ." She fell silent, observing Zoltan's reaction.

"If that's his name I have seen him once before," said Zoltan. "And I was lucky to survive."

Ben, looking at him, nodded slowly. "Two years ago, or thereabouts, that was. Well we remember it, in Tasavalta. But we still know little of this Ancient Lord. Our ignorance about the enemies we face here is certainly enormous." The big man turned to the lady. "I wonder what Sightblinder would show the new ruler of the magician's island if one of us appeared carrying it, and if its power were not blocked by Shieldbreaker?"

"An interesting question," Yambu acknowledged, "even if not immediately pertinent. What, or whom, does this Ancient Master of evil fear above all else? It is probably pointless to try to imagine anyone whom he might love."

Ben nodded. "But as you say, those questions will have to wait. Now we face others that must be answered. Two or three people cannot share the powers of this Sword. One of us must take it to the island, and use it to look for Mark. Now, which of us carries it? And what do the other two do to help?"

"The question of who takes the Sword must lie between you two, I think," said Lady Yambu. "Because I ought to be perfectly able to visit the mysterious islanders without its help." Reading the question in her companions' faces, she explained: "Why should not I, as a former queen, pay a courtesy call upon whatever power now rules those rocks?"

Ben ruminated on that idea. "We certainly don't have to tell you how great the risks might be. Are you really willing to accept that danger, to help a former enemy?"

The former queen spoke sharply in reply. "You certainly do not have to tell me about the risks, especially now that you have already managed to do so. We have made an agreement, you and I, and I intend to abide by it. And remember that in my day I have faced the Dark King himself; so I feel no uncontrollable trembling at the prospect of encountering this usurper; let him be as ancient as he likes."

Zoltan was nodding. And Ben, after a little more thought, nodded his approval too. "All right, my lady. Make your visit to the island as you wish, if you are able to arrange for one. Meanwhile the Prince's nephew and I will somehow settle between us the use of the Sword. But I have one more question for you, my lady, before we wrestle with that decision."

She returned him a look of cool inquiry.

He asked: "About that little dragon you dispatched. What result may we expect from it, assuming that the creature was not devoured in midair?"

"If I were you," the lady answered, "I should expect nothing. We must do what we can on our own." Then she softened a trifle. "I have good reason for keeping silent, I assure you."

The men exchanged a look but said no more on the subject.

"You have a means of transport to the island?" Zoltan asked the lady.

"I have said I do not expect much trouble in arranging that."

Ben shrugged, and said: "It is agreed, then. We will make our separate ways out to the castle on the island, and meet and communicate with each other as best we can when we are there." He paused, considering. "A mad-sounding plan, if it can even be called a plan at all. But we lack the knowledge to make plans with any greater intelligence, and I for one cannot simply sit here and wait."

"Nor I," Zoltan put in quickly.

"Then it is agreed, as you say," Yambu answered firmly. "And now, gentlemen, I bid you good-bye for the time being. And good luck."

A few minutes later, Ben and Zoltan were making their way along the shoreline of the lake, heading east, in the direction away from the town. Zoltan carried Sightblinder, balancing in one hand the belt, the jeweled sheath, and the blade that it contained.

Their tentative plan, which they were trying to put into a more solid shape as they walked, was to commandeer a small boat somewhere along the shore—given the Sword's powers, there should be no great difficulty about that. Once in possession of a boat, they would make their way out to the islands. Whether there would be any advantage in waiting for darkness before they set out across the water was something they had not yet decided.

"I should be the one to carry Sightblinder when we go," said Barbara, Ben's diminutive, dark-haired wife, walking now beside Ben where a moment ago Prince Mark had been striding blithely along. Then Barbara turned her face toward Ben, grew in stature to his own height or a trifle more, and suddenly possessed blue eyes and long hair of a flaming red. He had to look away.

"You'll be my prisoner," his companion went on, now speaking to Ben in a voice Ben had never forgotten, that of Yambu's daughter, Ariane. "No one will try to stop us on the way to the island dungeons—every castle has a dungeon, doesn't it?—and that's where we'll find Uncle Mark. There should be no problem unless we run directly into whoever now has Shieldbreaker—what's the matter?" The speaker's voice abruptly deepened at the end.

Ben dared to turn his head for another look, and saw Prince Mark walking beside him again, engaged in plotting his own rescue.

"Therefore," said Ben, "we must take care not to run into him." He nodded grudgingly. "The plan you propose has some merit. Not much, but perhaps more than any other we are likely to be able to devise in the small time we have to work with."

Striding around the shoreline of a cove, they passed a small wooden dock, on the verge of total abandonment if not already past it. The only vessel at the dock, a small rowboat, now rested half-sunken in the shallows, where, if moss and discoloration were any evidence, it had been resting for a long time. A couple of meters inland stood an upright post, which had probably once supported a partial roof over the facility. Stuck lightly to this post, and stirring in the breeze as if to call attention to itself, was a torn and shabby paper poster. Ben, driven by a vague though desperate yearning for any kind of information, paused to peel the loosened paper from the wood—it was an advertisement for what sounded like a traveling carnival, described in large, crude printing as the Magnificent Traveling Show of Ensor.

Still clutching this piece of paper absently in his hand, Ben walked on. Zoltan, now wearing the aspect of Ben's young daughter Beth, walked at his side. Ben looked down at the sturdy, half-grown girl taking her short steps, and said to Zoltan: "Did your uncle Mark ever tell you how he once played a role in a small traveling show? I was in it too. Probably this one is much like that one."

"He's mentioned something about it," Prince Mark said, taller than Ben again and taking long strides, longer than Ben's, beside him. "You were the strongman, of course?"

"No," the huge man answered vaguely. Again becoming aware of the paper still in his hand, he looked at it. "'The next performance in Triplicane,'" he quoted, "'will be at the time of the Harvest Festival.' Which must be rapidly approaching in these parts, I suppose, though there can't be much growing on these rocky slopes for anyone to harvest."

"Unless they're counting the lake's fish as the main crop. And I thought I saw some indication of vineyards on the high slopes there, farther on." It was Ariane who gestured at the hills.

Half an hour later Ben and his variable companion were still walking along the shore, having had no success in finding a suitable boat, when with little warning a small cloud of fierce flying creatures fell upon them from the clouded sky.

Ben fought back with his staff, and Zoltan raised the keen-edged Sword. But in a matter of moments they realized that they were not under attack at all. The strange hybrid flyers were not coming to tear them apart, but to offer service. They circled nearby, then landed on the ground, wrapping themselves in leathery wings; they recoiled from the blows of Ben's staff, not as attackers would dodge back but cringingly, jaws closed and ears laid back in submission, like beasts trying to avoid punishment.

"What dolts we are!" said Ben. "It is the Sword, of course. They take you for someone else, some human lord that they are bound to serve." He spoke openly, having no fear that beasts like these would be able to understand more than the simplest words of human speech.

"Of course," said his wife, Barbara, and lowered Sightblinder's keen steel. "What do we do now?"

Before Ben could decide upon an answer, a new factor had entered the situation. A griffin descended from the upper air to circle majestically, looking the scene over. Presumably it was the same creature that had carried off Prince Mark—even in the stories there was never more than one griffin at a time—but it was now equipped with a saddle, saddlebags, and stirrups.

After circling round the two men several times at low altitude, making the smaller flyers scatter in excitement, the griffin landed near Zoltan, who recoiled somewhat in spite of himself. The creature crouched there with its great wings folded, its eagle's eyes staring at him over one feathered shoulder. When he did not move, it backed toward him a short distance and crouched lower.

Ben edged away a little. The griffin ignored him totally.

"Ben?" Zoltan's voice quavered slightly. "I think it expects me to get on and ride it."

Somehow the dignity of the beast's gaze made it look more intelligent as well as larger than any of the more ordinary flyers—not a difficult standard to surpass.

"Ben? Magicians do ride them, don't they?"

Ben opened his mouth and closed it. He didn't know what to advise.

The griffin was looking at Zoltan as an intelligent riding-beast might have looked, waiting patiently for its master to climb into the saddle.

"I'm going to do it," Zoltan decided.

"Maybe I should be the one to ride it," the big man muttered, but even as he spoke he was edging away from the griffin a little more, and he was unable to muster any great enthusiasm behind the words.

"You obviously can't—you weigh a ton and a half, to begin with."

"I doubt that would matter much to a griffin. From all I've heard, they fly more by magic than by muscle."

But Zoltan, though showing signs of trepidation, was already climbing aboard the half-feathered and half-furred creature's back. In a moment his feet were in the stirrups and he was as firmly in the saddle as a man could be. Now it was apparent that there were no reins to grip.

All was not well, however. The great beast clamored and snarled, and breathed out other noises less definable. It moved on its feet and stretched its wings, but it did not take off. Instead, with Zoltan helplessly on its back, it stood up on its two mismatched pairs of legs and turned toward Ben. Awkwardly it walked closer to him, still making unearthly noises. When its beak opened, there were no teeth to be seen, but the beak itself looked as dangerous as a scimitar.

"I think," Ben said, gripping his staff, "it doesn't like me."

"Maybe it recognizes you somehow as an enemy. Might the problem be that it doesn't want me to leave you here unguarded?"

"That's an idea, but I don't know what we can do about it. Chop my head off before you go."

Meanwhile the squadron of lesser flyers, apparently taking a cue from the griffin, had reformed itself in the air and was fluttering around Ben, cawing and snarling menacingly. The moving circle of the creatures tightened on him. His repeated gestures of submission had no effect, nor did Zoltan's tentative efforts to take command.

Neither man had any idea of how to go about giving these creatures orders, beyond shouting human speech at them, and making crude gestures. Zoltan tried these methods now, to no avail.

"Wait, I have an idea," Zoltan announced. He shouted at the beasts until their clamoring had stilled to some degree. Then he spoke to Ben. "See that shed over there?"

Ben turned to look. There was some fisherman's outbuilding, big as a small house, dilapidated and by all appearances long-deserted, but intact in basic structure.

Zoltan went on: "I'll lock you up in that. What do

you think? Close the door on you anyway. At worst it shouldn't take you a minute to kick your way out again, once we're, uh, out of sight."

Ben got the idea, and walked ahead when Zoltan, once more dismounted, urged him along with an imperious gesture. In a few moments they were at the shed. When Ben pulled open the ill-fitting door, the interior proved to have two rooms. The floors in both rooms were of earth, and both contained piles of crates and other fisherman's gear, looking long disused. And a good part of the back wall of the building was actually missing; there were holes in it through which a man would be able to crawl out any time.

Such niceties were evidently beyond the understanding of the small flyers who were circling the building now. These happily abated their clamor as soon as Ben had gone inside the shack and passed out of their sight. Meanwhile the griffin, maintaining its dignity, remained in front.

With a sigh of relief Ben moved through the first room, on into the room that was farther from the door. There, a narrow space between the rough planks of the wall facing the beach offered a chance for him to observe what happened next.

He could hear Zoltan stumbling around somewhere in the first room, behind him; there was a slight delay before the young man appeared in the doorway to the second. There he stood, regarding Ben with a rather odd expression.

Ben demanded: "What's the trouble? If you don't want to trust yourself to that thing in flight, well, I don't blame you. But I'll give it a try if you don't."

"Never mind," Zoltan answered after staring at him a moment longer. "Here I go." He turned and left the room.

And a moment later Ben, looking out through the crack between the planks, saw Prince Mark stride out to greet the waiting flyers, and Barbara vaulted again onto the griffin's back. In a moment the whole flock was airborne once again. And only moments after that they were well out over the water, fading rapidly into the dusky sky.

Yambu, after bidding her new allies a farewell on the hillside above the town, had returned directly to the inn. There she quickly hired a man to transport her modest luggage down to the docks—she might easily have carried the few things herself, but now it was time to consider the matter of status once again. As she was paying her bill at the inn the proprietor told her that the *Maid of Lakes and Rivers* had arrived at last. She took the news as a good omen.

In another few minutes she was at the docks. There the captain of the newly-arrived riverboat made an effort to intercept the determined-looking lady before she could step onto his deck. He told her that if she was the passenger he had heard about, the pilgrim lady who wished to go far downriver, she would have to wait. He had already been summoned out to the island, with his boat and entire crew.

That was news to Yambu, but she would not admit it. "But of course, my man, I want to go to the island. You may cast off as soon as my luggage is on board."

A moment later, Yambu was standing on the deck. And the captain was at least half-convinced that her wish to visit the island was the real reason he had been ordered to take his boat there.

The dirty deck and modest deckhouse offered no spot suitable for a lady to sit down, and so she stood, with dignity. Her attire of course was far from queenly; but then it was the dress of a pilgrim, and even a queen, once she put on the gray of pilgrimage, might become hard to distinguish from a commoner.

Yambu was still waiting on deck for the short voyage to begin, gazing unseeingly at the remnants of a white poster of some kind affixed to a nearby bollard, when a high, wild, inhuman cry, faint with distance, made her look up into the darkening sky.

The moon, near full, was newly risen; and as she watched a dark shape passed across its disk, as of a flying creature that bore a human being on its back.

# CHAPTER 8

EMERGING cautiously from the shed into the rapidly thickening dusk, Ben looked out over the lake. The islands now were no more than ghostly little clouds, almost invisible in the last light of the sun and the rising glow of the newly risen moon.

He wished Zoltan well.

He began moving carefully eastward along the shore, still determined to gain possession of a boat if it was humanly possible to do so. With the Sword gone to where it was more urgently needed, he might need to use craft or violence to achieve his purpose. But he was determined that somehow, before the dawn—

He had proceeded for no more than about twenty paces along the shore when a sound behind him made him whirl. Out of the ruined shed a figure staggered, then turned through the dusk toward Ben. It was holding one hand to the top of its head.

Ben raised his staff to guard position and moved to meet the apparition. In a moment he dropped his weapon, recognizing Zoltan.

"Gods and demons! Why aren't you—?" Helplessly Ben shifted his gaze out over the darkening lake; the griffin and its passenger had long since passed out of sight. He turned back to the swaying form before him.

Zoltan sat down with a crunch in the rough, damp shingle that made up the shoreline here. "I'm not out there, if that's what you're asking, because I'm still here. I was just on my way into the shed for a last word with you. . . . Someone must have hit me over the head. I'm getting a lump the size of an egg."

"Hit you? Hit *you*? Then who in all the hells was *that*, astride that flying thing?"

"It was whoever hit me, I suppose. How the hell should I know? I couldn't see him."

Ben closed his eyes. In memory he could see how Zoltan had come from one room of the ruined shed into the other. And he, Ben, had seen Zoltan as Zoltan, not as Mark or Barbara. "I should have known," the big man muttered to himself, and opened his eyes again.

His fears were quickly confirmed. There was no longer any swordbelt at Zoltan's waist. No jeweled scabbard, and, of course, no Sword.

Again Ben turned his gaze again out over the darkening lake, then back to Zoltan. He said: "Whoever it was, it seems he has taken Sightblinder with him."

Zoltan nodded, then paused for a few breaths to deal with whatever was going on inside his skull. Then he asked dazedly: "What do we do now?"

Ben swore a few more oaths. Then, in a quiet voice, he said: "As soon as you're able to walk a straight line again, you can help me find a boat. What else?"

The wind from the south side of the lake was picking up, distant thunder also rumbling from that direction, and the surface of the water was growing choppy when the *Maid of Lakes and Rivers* under light sail eased up to the small docks at the foot of the castle. The small stone docks seemed pinned down by the frowning mass of those high, gray walls.

Basket torches, hanging from those high walls, and mounted in several places on the docks themselves, made the immediate surroundings very nearly as bright as day. Lady Yambu, still intent on reestablishing her rights as a person of importance, froze the captain and some crew members with a single glance, and was allowed to be the first to disembark once lines had been secured. The captain even bowed his head in her direction as she stepped ashore. She felt inclined to pardon his earlier lapses in matters of protocol, as doubtless he had other matters on his mind that he considered much more important. Yambu had heard him talking to his mate during the brief crossing, both men were worried that their boat was going to be seized by the new masters of the lake and islands, and what would happen to them and to their crew in that event they did not know. Still, they had not dared to refuse the summons to come here.

Quite possibly, thought Lady Yambu, they were too much afraid of demons to do that.

She herself, during her years of power, had had too much experience of those inhuman entities to fail to sense their spoor now. It was not an immediate presence, but still the subtle sickness of them hung about this castle like a polluted mist.

Behind the lady, as she stood on the dock waiting to be noticed by someone in authority, the riverboat's crew had begun a hasty unloading of her cargo, apparently in obedience to orders already received somehow from within the walls. Whatever part of the lading the new masters of the castle might find valuable would doubtless go no farther.

She took note that several beautiful sailing craft, as well as vessels of a more utilitarian nature, were already tied up at these docks.

On the mast of one of the sturdy cargo boats nearby was stuck a poster; the torchlight Lady Yambu could read its largest print, advertising the forthcoming return of the Magnificent Show of Ensor, whatever that might be.

And now her presence had indeed been noticed by someone in authority. And the first decision regarding her had already been taken. A man in a uniform she took to be that of a junior military officer appeared at an open gate, and with a few words and a deferential gesture indicated that he was ready to conduct her within the walls.

They passed in through a postern gate that was doubly guarded, and after, a brief passage between tall stone walls, beneath a narrow strip of clouded sky. Then they entered another door. This led them to a dark chamber furnished with several benches, worthy to be the anteroom of a prison. Lady Yambu was invited to take a seat, then left to wait alone.

Again she chose to remain standing. Her wait had lasted only a few minutes when another official, this one obviously of higher rank, appeared. This man, bowing low, announced that the Ancient Master was willing to see the great Queen Yambu at once.

"Queen no longer," she declared.

But the elegantly dressed courtier, holding the door open for her now, might not have heard her objection. He led her from the anteroom and along a different passageway. Soldiers in uniforms of gray trimmed with red, a livery she had seen in the town but still did not recognize, opened door after door for her, offering salutes. Torchlight showed the way, indoors and out, but the castle as a whole was now too deeply bound in darkness for her to form any estimate of how strongly it might be defended—making such assessments was a habit that had stayed with her, it seemed.

At one point she passed a descending stair, ill-lighted, that looked to her like a way down to a dungeon. Yambu made a mental note, as well as she was able, of the stair's location.

She was making swift progress, she believed, toward the Ancient Master, whoever that might be. Evidently no games of power and rank were going to be played in the nature of keep-the-old-lady-waiting. Probably the new lord of the castle was something of a stranger to this part of the world, and he expected, or at least hoped, that she might be able to provide him with some useful information. Well, perhaps she could.

It was good that she was not going to be kept waiting. Still, she could almost have wished for a few hours' delay, to give her two allies time to get to the island.

It seemed oddly reasonable and natural to Yambu that she should be here, inside a castle again, with men of rank bowing deferentially before her, and events of great moment to be decided. Suddenly she found herself wondering how far she really would be willing to go to help her old enemy, Prince Mark. And what had happened to her search for truth? Only hours ago she had been serenely convinced that finding some abstract truth was all that mattered to her any longer.

But that, of course, had been before another Sword had touched her hand.

She had just finished congratulating herself on her swift progress toward her meeting with the Ancient One when she was made to wait once more, this time in a more comfortable place. Hardly had she settled herself to inspect the artwork on the walls—left over, she supposed, from the days of Honan-Fu—when a door opened and a man entered, dressed in rich garments and wearing a jeweled collar. He was a large man, aging, scarred, and somewhat overweight, and he limped heavily on his left leg.

"Amintor," she said, surprised—but then on second thought she was not really all that surprised. This man had served her as a general, years ago. And more than once during those distant-seeming years he had also shared her bed.

Amintor bowed. "The last time we met, my lady, you were certain that you had withdrawn from the world."

"I have discovered no other world but this one in which to live." She looked him up and down. "You seem to be prospering, Baron."

"Indeed, fate has been kind to me of late."

They chatted for a few moments, of old times, mostly of inconsequential things. Presently Amintor turned her over to the guidance of another officer, who led her out into the corridors of the castle again.

Following her new guide, she climbed steep stairs.

They emerged from these stairs onto a balcony overlooking a central courtyard of the castle, an enclosure much disfigured by what must have been quite recent vandalism. A crude new construction, looking like a sacrificial altar, occupied the center of the space. But she had little time to look at this, or the rest of the setting—the figure that awaited her on the balcony demanded her attention.

This figure was manlike—with some surprising qualifications—and as the former queen drew near, it rose from its throne as if to greet an equal.

The torchlight here was adequate, and her first good look at the Ancient One, his vestigial wings and certain reptilian attributes, afforded Her Ladyship something of a shock. But Queen Yambu had seen strange things before, and she was not going to show that she was shocked unless she chose to do so.

The formalities of greeting were got through routinely, despite the no more than half-human aspect of her host. In a minute Yambu found herself seated near the throne, on a chair almost as tall as it was, and of fine workmanship compared to the crudity of the throne itself. No ordinary throne would have done for this particular ruler, Yambu realized; there was the problem of accommodating his tail.

But she had to pay attention. Her host, in his harsh and somewhat absentminded voice, was declaring that the fame of Queen Yambu, great as it doubtless was in these regions of the world, had somehow escaped his ears until very recently. The implication seemed to be that until very recently he had been far away, in some other part of the world altogether. But he did not say where he had been.

She asked: "And where, my lord, are these remote areas, in which I am unknown?"

He chuckled. "It is not a matter of *where*, so much, dear lady, as of *when*. But that doesn't matter now." He paused. "My leading counselors inform me that you are an old and bitter enemy of Prince Mark of Tasavalta."

"Indeed, sir, until now my relationship with the Prince has been conducted almost entirely across battle-fields."

"And I am given to understand that you are also an old acquaintance of Baron Amintor, my military commander?"

"I am more than an old acquaintance, I should say. He is a skillful officer, and served me well."

"Ah, my lady, I could wish that I had met you sooner—I wonder how many more of your former associates I am likely to encounter in these parts?"

Already Lady Yambu was morally certain that this man knew something of her meeting in the inn with Mark's two companions. She said: "I myself have seen one other, during the past two days. And with him was one who was presented to me as a nephew of the Prince—but I cannot vouch for the truth of that relationship."

"Ah." The beast-man did not sound surprised. "And your old friend was—?"

"Hardly a friend of mine. An interesting fellow, though—Ben of Purkinje is his name. Which way he and the princeling nephew went after I had terminated our meeting, I have no idea."

"And in what way—if I may ask—is this man interesting?"

"You may ask of me whatever you like, dear Ancient Master—is that title an appropriate one for me to use to you?"

"It will do, Your Ladyship, it certainly will do."

"Good . . . an interesting man, then, and I do not mean only in physical terms—I suppose you will have heard about his remarkable strength. He was presuming rather desperately on his status as an old enemy, to ask my help."

"An intriguing thought." The tailed creature shifted on its throne; for just a moment Lady Yambu had the impression that it, or he, was flirting with a change of shape into a much more fully human aspect. "And what did you tell him, dear lady, if you do not mind sharing your discussion with me?"

"I do not mind. The idea of helping an old enemy —at least some old enemies—might have its interest. But I have other interests now. Ben was disappointed when he learned that my status as a pilgrim is quite genuine."

"Your status, then, is *still* quite genuine? Your pardon, Queen Yambu, I did not mean to question your sincerity. But I thought that you might now be in the process of returning from some spiritual quest, and therefore ready to replace your gray robe with something more—well, more regal."

"Alas, no. My pilgrimage, though it is several months old, can hardly be said to have begun as yet."

"I see. A difficult venture, then. I thank you for interrupting it to visit me. And what god or goddess is its object, estimable lady?"

"The goddess Truth, Your Ancient Lordship."

The figure on the throne threw back its head and gave vent to an honest laugh, which gave the impression, if not the look, of greater humanity. "I do not know that goddess yet. But then I have been absent from the world's affairs for a long time."

"I do not know her either," Yambu admitted readily enough. "Oh, once or twice in my life I think that I have seen her, passing through the air above a battlefield; but never did she linger there for long." And now the tone of Lady Yambu's voice changed suddenly; a certain dreaminess appeared in it, as if in anticipation of a pleasure. "And now, sir, I have a question of my own. I would like to know what you have done with Prince Mark."

"I have done that which ought to please any old enemy of his." Having said that, the Ancient One paused for a moment as if in thought. "He is another interesting man, this Mark. They tell me he is a child of the Emperor, though I am not sure in what sense that description is to be taken. The expression is new to me, a part of this new world in which I find myself. Proverbially, it would mean anyone subject to great misfortune, would it not?"

"Something like that, sir. But in Mark's case I think it is meant in a literal sense. There really is an Emperor, you know."

"There were those who claimed that title in the world from which I came. Perhaps they had earned the right to it. But I understand that this Emperor is something different." The Ancient Lord's eyes, purely reptilian for the moment, probed at Yambu. "They tell me further, Your Majesty, that when you were only a girl yourself you bore the Emperor's girl-child. At that time, apparently, he was still considered a person of some importance."

"He was so considered by many people. Yes." There was much more that Yambu might have said on the subject, but she saw no reason to enter into such a lengthy discussion now.

"Interesting. But not a matter of vital concern, I think. Rather an example, it sounds to me, of a potentially important power whose day has already come and gone." The grotesquely misshapen man stroked his chin—more precisely, his lower jaw—and said to her: "Of much greater interest to me in this new world are the Swords—all the more since I have seen what one of them is capable of doing."

And with a flourish the figure on the throne leaned forward slightly, into fuller torchlight. The Ancient One's right hand brought forward, where Yambu could see it, a black-hilted weapon that she was sure must be Shieldbreaker, though just now whatever symbol might be on the hilt was covered by a clawlike hand.

The man who was holding the Sword said to her: "I have heard that the adoptive father of Prince Mark was the smith who actually worked at the forge to make these twelve fascinating toys."

She shook her head. "Look at the workmanship, dear Ancient Lord. If that is even an adequate word for it. I think it transcends workmanship; it almost transcends art. Can you believe that it is merely human? Even Old-World human? No, it was Vulcan, the god, who forged these blades. But I believe there is some truth in the story, that the man called Jord was also there, pressed into providing some kind of assistance —and Mark was born to Jord's bride less than a year thereafter."

She had made sure to register restrained surprise when first the Sword was shown to her. And now she let herself react again, when her host suddenly leaned the cruciform hilt a little closer to her, and moved his claws to let her see the small white hammer-symbol on the black.

Yambu said: "I have, at one time or another, held others of the Twelve in my own hands. But never this one."

As if he suspected that she yearned to hold it now, its present owner drew it back. He asked: "You would agree that this is the most powerful Sword of all?"

The lady smiled at him faintly. "All twelve have great magic. And also little tricks. The most powerful Sword of all is that one whose powers happen to be required at the moment."

"Well answered, Queen Yambu!"

"Queen no longer, as I have already told your people."

"But queen again, perhaps, one day."

She wondered suddenly if this man might really be

anxious to recruit her to his cause. If all this part of the
world was truly new to him, it might really be hard for
him to find trustworthy and capable subordinates—that
was hard enough to do at any time.

She said: "I think not, Lord of the Lake—but that
sounds too small a title for a man of your obvious
accomplishments."

"Oh, it is, Your Ladyship, far too small. I mean to
be Lord of the World one day—one day not too far
distant." He sounded calmly confident.

He drank wine then, and suddenly arose from his
throne. A rich cape, which had been draped behind the
chair, now fell about his body, covering most of the
deformity from the shoulders down. Standing, the Ancient Lord was taller than Yambu, somehow considerably taller than she had expected.

Around his upper back his cape bulged out, a
symmetrical enlargement quite unlike the deformity of a
hump. And as Yambu watched, the bulge stirred lightly,
giving her the sudden idea that rudimentary wings
might be enfolded there. Wings on a man, she thought,
would make no sense at all; but they would not be the
first thing about this one that did not make sense.

He said: "Come with me, lady, and I will show you
what has happened to Prince Mark."

They descended the interior stairway from the
balcony, and this time turned out onto the courtyard
and across it. On its far side a postern gate let them out
through a comparatively thin interior wall. The place
they entered was more a grotto than a courtyard, a
narrow space surrounded by high walls, in which a
narrow rim of paving surrounded a well or inlet of dark,
chill water. On the far side of the well a low arch of stone
covered the entrance to a watery tunnel under the castle,
which was defended by a heavy steel grillwork against
any commerce with the lake outside.

Standing on the narrow stone rim of the pond, Lady
Yambu watched as attendants took hold of a heavily

secured rope and hoisted an ice-encrusted form, in human shape, out of the water in which it had been shallowly submerged. Lake water, she thought, oughtn't to be quite *that* cold, not at this time of year anyway. Magic, of course.

Two of the soldiers who had done the hoisting held the bound form up between them, while another leaned forward and struck it where the face ought to be. The blow seemed impersonal, as if he were trying to get a good look at a frozen fish. The soldier's fist shattered the white integument sufficiently for Yambu to be able to recognize the features of Prince Mark. The Prince's battered face was blue and gray with cold, and there was bright blood around his mouth, as if he might have bitten his tongue with the violence of his shivering, perhaps, or in some effort not to cry out. But Mark's eyes were open, and alive, and when they rested on Yambu she thought they recognized her.

A moment later she had taken a step forward, and swung her own arm. It was more like a warrior's blow than an old woman's slap, and the Prince's helpless head bobbed sideways with the impact.

Yambu stepped back with a sigh. "I have long dreamed of doing that," she assured her host. And in the privacy of her own thoughts she marveled at this strong new evidence of how suddenly and completely her dedication to the abstract truth seemed to have evaporated. Evidently some things, after all, were more important.

"Is there anything else that you would like to do?" her host inquired. When she turned to face him she saw that his reptilian aspect was entirely gone, and the wings too; in place of the grotesque creature she had been talking to now stood a fully human man, young and strong and of surpassing beauty. The rich cape hung now in different, straighter folds. Golden curls fell to the young man's muscular shoulders; his clear blue eyes regarded her.

"Not at the moment, Your Lordship," she replied, and bowed her appreciation of his magic.

At a nod from the lord of the castle, the Prince was allowed to splash back into the lake. He sank like a stone, his rope tugged taut again.

Then Yambu gestured toward the second rope nearby, which presumably led to another submerged form. "And who is our dear Prince's companion, Ancient One?"

"None other than this castle's former owner, my dear queen. Another acquaintance of yours, perhaps—? No? Well, no one can know everyone of importance in the world. I should like to try to do so, though."

Interruption in the form of a flying messenger spiraling softly down between the grotto's walls came at that point to cut their conversation short. The Ancient Lord, having heard the message that the beast had come to hiss into his ear, announced as much, with what seemed genuine regret.

"But we have much more to say to each other, dear Yambu. I insist that you remain here as my honored guest for some time before you resume your pilgrimage."

She would not have dreamt of trying to decline.

# CHAPTER 9

ARNFINN awoke, on that unreal morning after his first arrival at Lady Ninazu's manor, into what seemed at first a gloriously prolonged dream. He was lying naked amid the marvelous white softness of her bed, and he thought the place was still warm where she had lain beside him. Even after he had experimentally cracked his eyelids open, it was perfectly easy to believe that he was still dreaming. This world in which he found himself this morning seemed to bear but small resemblance to the ordinary waking universe in which he had spent his life before encountering the Sword of Stealth.

It was in fact the nearby voice of the young lady herself, raised in shrill and ugly tones as she berated one of her servants, that convinced Arnfinn of reality.

Turning his body halfway over amid the bed's incredible luxury, he lifted himself up on one elbow and surveyed the room in which he had awakened. Lady Ninazu's voice sounded from beyond rich draperies concealing a door, and for the moment Arnfinn was alone. His own clothes, the few poor garments he had worn upon his journey, made a crude and grimy scattering across the floor's thick bright rugs and colored tiles. But the Sword of Stealth, with sheath and belt and all, was with him in the bed. Even at the peak of last night's excitement he had remembered to make sure of that. If the lady had been at all aware of Sightblinder's presence between her sheets, she had been diplomatic enough to say nothing about it.

She had said several things, though, that were already, despite the considerable distractions he now faced, coming back to Arnfinn's thoughts this morning.

For example, at one time last night she had said: "I am surprised, lord, that you have come to me alone and unattended." Only to amend that a moment later with: "But then I suppose a wizard with powers like yours is never really unattended anywhere."

Last night Arnfinn's attention had been consumed by other matters. But this morning that last statement struck him as important. He could not help thinking that it could be of great importance indeed to know exactly which wizard Lady Ninazu thought he was.

It appeared that he was going to have a few moments longer for reflection; Lady Ninazu was still out of sight behind closed and brocaded draperies, tongue-lashing her servants in the next room over some female triviality of hairdressing or clothing. He shifted again in the bed, marveling anew at its whiteness and softness. He had never really imagined that anyone lived like this.

And now another memory of last night came back: Her Ladyship, unbelievably naked, incredibly lying in bed with him, sleepily clasping Arnfinn's workworn, underfed arms and shoulders in her hands, and murmuring, without the least trace of mockery in her voice, about how marvelously muscular he was.

And again she had declared, in a voice soft with passion, "I sometimes wonder, lover, whether I fear you or I love you more."

And again: "It is now, as you must well remember, two years since we first met—a little more than two years. And yet sometimes I feel I don't know you at all."

And yet again, in what now seemed to Arnfinn her most mysterious utterance of all: "I have heard from others that there are times in which the appearance of your body changes. I hope that is only a lie, spread by your enemies."

"Changes?" Arnfinn had dared to ask. She wasn't, at least he hoped she couldn't be, talking about the changes wrought by the Sword of Stealth—but if not that, what?

And that was the only moment during the night in which the lady had apparently come close to being disconcerted. With lowered, fluttering lashes she had murmured: "I meant no offense, my dread lord."

"It does not matter," her supposed dread lord had responded awkwardly, not knowing what else to say, having no idea of how a real lord might have phrased the thought. And the lady had looked blank for a moment, as if something in her bed-partner's speech or manner puzzled her. But still the power of the Sword prevailed; whatever else the victim of its deception might suspect, the identity of the person who held Sightblinder was usually the last thing that the victim could be made to doubt.

After that exchange of words Lady Ninazu had busied herself again with dedication to Arnfinn's pleasure, and he had forgotten her words until now.

And now he forgot them again, for the draperies opened. The lady, wrapped in a loose garment of white fur, stood in the doorway smiling down at him for a long moment before she closed the curtains behind her again and came over to the bed. On her way toward it she paused to wrinkle her pretty little nose at some of the disgusting peasants' clothing on the floor, and kick it out of her way. "Where can *that* have come from?" she murmured crossly to herself.

But she was smiling again by the time she reached the bed. "I am very pleased," she said, "that my lord, who for a thousand years, or perhaps ten thousand, has had his choice of women, continues to be pleased with me."

Arnfinn, who had had exactly two women in his

lifetime previously, without the idea of choice having really entered into it on either occasion, swallowed. "How could I not be pleased?" he responded.

The lady curtsied, a small movement that flirted with mockery while still managing to give an impression of humility; but at the same time he, even Arnfinn the innocent, could see the calculation in her eyes, and the fierce pride.

She whispered: "And will I continue to please you?"

Despite the enchantment of her beauty, there was something . . . Arnfinn could feel a wariness developing in him. What would a real great lord have said in response to her question? "You will always please me. But there are many demands upon my time."

"I am sure that there are more than I can possibly imagine. But now you have at least established firm control of my father's stronghold. Tell me—that bothersome man—my father—I take it he is no longer in a position to bother anyone?"

Moment by moment the dream was developing imperfections. There was something in the way this girl spoke of her father that began to curdle both lust and satisfaction.

"No," Arnfinn answered, going along with what she evidently wanted, again not knowing what else to say. "He is not." This, then, he was thinking, was a daughter of Honan-Fu. And a daughter who rejoiced in her father's downfall. Once again Arnfinn knew the beginning of fear. Without really understanding why, he could feel a disagreeable knot beginning to form in the pit of his stomach.

Approaching the bed, the lady sat down close beside him. Then, as if it were a gesture requiring boldness, she reached out to put her hand on her dread lord's arm.

"And"—her voice dropped; something of great importance was about to be said—"my twin brother. How is he?" Lady Ninazu seemed to be holding her breath as she awaited her wizard lord's answer to that. Her eyes were enormous.

The lady was hanging on Arnfinn's response so raptly that it almost seemed that she had ceased to breathe. The rise and fall of her breast was almost suspended. Arnfinn could feel the knot in his own gut grow tighter in the presence of this intensity of will and of emotion, neither one of which he understood.

What to say?

"He is as well as can be expected," Arnfinn replied at last. "Under the circumstances."

"Ahh!" It was more an animal's unthinking snarl than it was a word. Her eyes blazed at him fiercely, though what the passion was that made them blaze he could not tell. "What does that mean?"

A moment ago this girl had been all fluttering subservience, and now she was almost threatening. The fear induced in her by Sightblinder had been and continued to be genuine, though she was keeping it under control; what could bring her to raise such a challenge despite her fear?

Arnfinn's own fear awoke again, as if in sympathy with hers. He knew that if he once allowed himself to give in to his own timidity in this situation, terror could overwhelm him. Instead he forced himself to sit up straight on the edge of the bed—making sure that he was still touching the swordbelt with one hand—and to stare at the woman with as much regal authority as he could try to mimic.

She quailed at once; before he had to say a word, her eyes fell before his gaze.

"Oh, well," she murmured. "If you will not answer." Then, to Arnfinn's amazement, a tear appeared in the corner of Lady Ninazu's eye. She folded her arms in the sleeves of her white fur robe and rocked back and forth in the immemorial way of women grieving. Her voice dropped so low that he could barely hear it. "It has been more than two years since my brother and I have been allowed to see each other. Since that day on which we served you so well, master, he has not even been allowed to see the light of day. And year after year, day after day, my father has treated him so cruelly. He was still like a child two years ago; and anyway what we did was right—Kunderu and I opened the way for you to come into this world, didn't we? Isn't it wrong, isn't it monstrous, that his punishment should have gone on so long?"

"Your twin brother," Arnfinn muttered to himself, gaping at the lady, trying to understand. It was the first time he had ever heard of the existence of any such person.

"My dread lord, do not toy with me!" The words burst from the lady's lips, though a moment later she would have bitten them back. Arnfinn had never seen anyone so gripped by emotion—not even the madwoman in the village, though she had been much noisier.

In the next moment Lady Ninazu had fallen on her knees before him. "My brother, Kunderu. Why cannot you let me see him now? Even though he is a great wizard himself as you well know, all power is in your hands now. Can you not at least allow me to see him? If I could see my brother again, if I could know that he is free, and happy—for two years now I've lived for nothing but that. Oh, great lord, oh, great lord, help me!"

The world was beginning to turn gray in front of Arnfinn. Shame and love and guilt and fear swept over him together. He had all that he could do to keep himself from leaping up and running from the room, even as he had run from the poor people on the roads and in the town, the deluded fools who had thought that he was the most important person in their lives.

"I will be your loyal slave forever," she implored him. "What does it matter to you now that he once angered our father? Unless—unless, oh, gods, unless you have some agreement now with Honan-Fu—?"

It was like that woman in the first village all over again, only a hundred times worse. Like the girl with the baby in the town square, only a thousand times more terrible.

"I will do what I can!" Arnfinn barked at last, almost shouting. At the same time he jumped to his feet, and even as he jumped his left hand went out and grabbed the jeweled belt, dragging the Sword with him. It came with him as inexorably as some prisoner's chain. With muscles energized by desperation, he pushed the lady violently away from him.

Ninazu cried out in pain as her body crumpled to the floor on a soft rug.

Arnfinn stood momentarily paralyzed. Now, on top of everything else, he had hurt her, bruised her physically. He stood in the middle of the room, eyes shut, hands clenching his head, one arm looped through the sword-belt, holding it to him, in agony lest in his own fear and torment he should commit some greater violence that would hurt her yet again.

But Lady Ninazu was not much hurt. She scrambled to her feet, and in a moment was at Arnfinn's side again, murmuring in his ear, soothing him when she saw that he appeared to be stricken. It seemed that she had made an amazingly swift recovery from her grief and pain. Now she moved lightly about Arnfinn, talking, almost as though a moment ago she had not been on the verge of hysterics.

And Lady Ninazu must have given some signal to her servants, for now some of them were entering the chamber, pushing before them a cart that rolled on large silver wheels and was topped with a golden tray. The metal part of the cart looked like solid gold to Arnfinn, and it was laden with food on golden plates. He could recognize none of the dishes, but the aromas reminded Arnfinn, even in his distress, that he had not eaten for many hours.

Despite his ravenous hunger, he had to get away. He could no longer face the lady, knowing how he had deceived and cheated her. Her every worshipful glance accused him. Her beauty and her tears had become more than he could stand.

He kissed her once more, hopelessly and chastely this time. To her look of astonishment he muttered half-incoherent promises of return and promises of help. Meanwhile he was busy pulling on his clothes, going through contortions in the process so that the Sword of Deception should remain always close at his side.

Then he fled, at the last moment grabbing up some food from the cart to eat on the way. When Lady Ninazu called after him, Arnfinn only roared at her and rushed on, as he had run from one woman in the small village, and from another in the streets of Triplicane.

He was out in the grounds of the manor, heading for the rear gate where he had come in, when he encountered one of the stable's supervisors, who dared to speak to him.

The man bowed nervously. "It's about the, uh, the griffin, my lord."

"The griffin."

"Sire, the steed on which you arrived last night. If it needs care, feeding . . . I confess that none of us this morning are able to see it as anything but an ordinary loadbeast." And the man smiled, shaking his head in humble awe at the power of the lord's magic.

"Then care for it as you would a loadbeast. I will return for it later." And Arnfinn stalked on.

He wasn't going to need the loadbeast now because he wasn't going home. He couldn't go home now. . . .

On foot he wandered despairingly back toward the town. He was hopelessly, cruelly, insanely, suicidally, in love with Lady Ninazu. And in trying to love her, taking advantage of her, possessing her so falsely, he had wronged her terribly. If she were ever to find out how he had tricked her with the Sword . . .

But worse than her revenge, infinitely worse, would be the fact that then she would know him as he really was. The contemptible, vile, ugly, scrawny, cowardly, deceitful wretch he was—

Arnfinn sobbed as he walked, almost staggering with the burden of his guilt and his remorse. Not knowing, hardly caring, where he was going at the moment.

It seemed to him inevitable that he would be found out. And when he was, the lady, or the powerful wizard who must be her real lover, would have him cut up into small pieces, and the pieces burned. But no, before it ever came to that, he would kill himself out of sheer shame. It was impossible that he could ever find a way to make amends for what he had done to her—

*If I could see my brother again, if I could know that he is free, and happy . . . I live for that.*

Arnfinn could feel the terrible weight of the Sword dragging at his side. With such a weapon even a coward might be able to accomplish almost anything.

Between the lifeless trees of autumn he could see part of the lake, and the castle on its island.

Kunderu, she had said the man's name was. Her twin brother, held prisoner out there for—how long, two years?—in punishment by their father, the oh-so-kindly Honan-Fu. In punishment for what? Arnfinn wondered briefly. She had said, implied, something about how she and her brother had helped the wizard she now called her dread lord. . . .

But then that thought was pushed aside by another. Everyone ought to have known better, thought Arnfinn, than to believe that such a powerful old man as Honan-Fu could really be as benevolent as the stories painted him.

Arnfinn found a quiet place on a hillside, a little off the road, where he could sit down with his Sword and stare out at the castle. He had decided that he was ready to lay down his life, if need be, for the lady he had so cruelly wronged. He would find her twin brother, if the man called Kunderu was still alive, and he would release him.

The trouble was that Arnfinn had no idea of how to begin to go about performing such a feat. Except that he would have to take Sightblinder to the island, and somehow use its powers to achieve his end.

He would have to go out there to the castle ruled by the commander of the soldiers in red and gray, who had all the folk of Triplicane terrified. Out there into the den of the murderers and torturers. He, a country yokel—he knew what he was—would have to stand alone among them. Even if he did have one magic Sword, a weapon whose powers he scarcely understood—

Arnfinn was trying to picture himself where he had never been, in a world that he had never seen and could not very well imagine. In his imagination the parts of that world that he could not see clearly quickly filled up with terrible shadows.

Suppose, just suppose, that he were standing there now, in the great hall of that castle, making demands of one who sat there upon a throne—of one who was in all likelihood the real and jealous lover of Lady Ninazu. In a great hall with columns taller than the trees of the forest, and filled with people, crafty and deadly people, devious magicians and brutal warriors who did not know what it meant to be afraid, men and women whose business had been plotting and uncovering plots almost from the day that they were born.

If he, Arnfinn, who now feared to cross the town square because of the strangers who might accost him, were in that castle, what would he be able to do there?

Assuming that the magicians on the island were as subject to Sightblinder's powers as the peasants along the road—but how could he even assume that?—then what would happen? What image would those wizards and clever warriors see when they looked at Arnfinn?

When no two of them, perhaps, saw him as the same person, how long would it take them to understand what was happening?

For an hour he sat brooding on the hillside, the drawn steel of Sightblinder in his hands, digging little holes in the earth with the god-forged point of it and cutting up twigs with the almost invisible keenness of its edge.

Fear receded gradually. His breathing grew easier, his heartbeat slowed and steadied, and the knot in his stomach began to untie itself. Because he wasn't going to start for the island this moment. No, he saw now that he couldn't do that. This was going to require some planning.

Later in the day, wandering hesitantly among the hills at the far end of town from the manor, unable to make up his mind on any decisive course of action, Arnfinn came upon a deserted hut. The shack stood at some distance from any of the regularly used paths and roads that crossed the landscape. The hut provided him with partial shelter, and that night and on succeeding nights he slept uneasily in it, with an intermittent drizzle penetrating the overhanging branches and the ruined roof. At least he felt secure that no one was going to bother him here.

Each night, after a day of aimless wandering and scrounging food, he dozed off in the hut, hoping that no one would find him—and hoping even more fervently that no wild beast was going to come along, indifferent to the personal identities of its human victims as long as they had flesh and blood to eat. But in his cooler moments, Arnfinn supposed it unlikely that any such large predator would lurk so close to a large town.

He was still living in that hut three days later, scrounging food in and near the town as best he could, avoiding human contact as much as possible, and trying to nerve himself for the attempt to do what Lady Ninazu wanted done, when the three ill-assorted strangers way-laid him and took his magic Sword away from him.

And an hour after he had lost the Sword, rousing himself from his hopeless vigil across the road from the gates of Lady Ninazu's manor, he moved and thought with a fatalistic calm. There was nowhere in the world for him to go, nothing else that he could do, until he had retrieved the Sword—somehow—and used it as he knew he must, to try to make amends to the lady he had so cruelly wronged.

When, later, Arnfinn saw the huge man and the shifting form of one who must hold the Sword, walking together along the shore of the lake, he stalked them.

# CHAPTER 10

AGAINST this terror, the Sword of Stealth was as useless as a pin. Riding the griffin high above the lake, Arnfinn gritted his teeth to keep himself from screaming in dread of the sheer drop below him. In the distance, the last tinges of the sunset were reflected in the water, but directly underneath him there was nothing but an incredible gulf of air with black water at the bottom of it.

In the next moment he had to close his eyes as well. But even with his eyes closed he could still feel in his stomach that he was aboard a flying creature, with only a vast emptiness beneath. Even the escort of small creatures with which he had left the shore had now been left behind.

He remembered once, when he was a small boy, seeing a small flying predator struggling terribly to lift a half-grown rabbit, and in his guts he could not really believe that this beast beneath him could go on from one moment to the next supporting his weight.

Arnfinn's right hand was entwined in a deathgrip in the long hair of the griffin's leonine mane, while his left hand, close beside the right, was having trouble finding a solid grip. It grabbed at one tuft after another of what felt like eagle feathers, which pulled loose every time his fingers clamped upon them. He opened his eyes long enough to shift his grip, getting a firm hold with both fists on the hairy mane.

If this had been a riding-beast or a loadbeast Arn-finn would have felt reasonably confident of being able to control it, even without reins or saddle. But he was totally ignorant of the proper way to give this creature orders. He wondered if it was interpreting his efforts to cling to its back as some kind of commands.

That possibility was unsettling enough to force Arnfinn's eyelids open again. This latest terrified glimpse suggested to him that he had now reached an altitude almost equal to that of the surrounding distant hills. On the positive side, he made the reassuring discovery that if he did not look straight down, he could keep his eyes open.

Presently he was sure that the griffin was now descending gradually, in almost a straight path toward the approximate center of the watery plain ahead, where from an island there arose the shadowed shape of the dark castle, marked here and there with sparks of torchlight.

Arnfinn had not appreciated how swift the griffin was, until, unbelievably, the castle was already very close beneath him. And then the creature was down, achieving a soft and springy landing. In a moment Arnfinn slid from its back and once more had solid rock beneath his feet, though he was still high above the surface of the surrounding lake.

Here, atop the highest tower of the castle, was an aerie the size of a small house, a place set aside to serve the arrivals and departures of aerial spies and messengers, and to provide the beasts with living space as well. Right now most of the roosts and cages stood empty. Whatever birds had once been kept there by Honan-Fu were dead now or departed, and evidently most of the reptilian and avian creatures serving the new masters of the castle were out on patrol.

The newly landed griffin, bulking larger than a

riding-beast when it spread its wings, dominated the space. The few smaller creatures present were sent flapping and fluttering out of its way, making noisy cries of protest.

Arnfinn, once he had slipped gratefully from the creature's back, lost no time in getting clear of it altogether. At the moment he scarcely cared where his feet were taking him, as long as they were firmly on solid ground again.

But even as the griffin moved away, walking somewhat awkwardly on its two mismatched pairs of legs, Arnfinn realized that a pair of human observers had witnessed his arrival. One of these men was standing by with a broom in hand, while the other held a small measure of grain. They were obviously low-ranking beastmasters, handlers and caretakers of the creatures here.

It was equally obvious that the two unquestioningly accepted Arnfinn as a person of overwhelming importance, for they bowed themselves immediately out of his way, one of them spilling the grain from his measure in his haste to do so. Behind them as they moved, Arnfinn observed the upper end of a ladder. When he had scrambled down it he saw the head of a descending stair.

Flames in wall sconces of twisted metal burned at intervals on the way down, set close enough together to let him see the footing. After two turns of the spiral, when Arnfinn had reached a place where he was for the moment sheltered from all human sight, he paused. Leaning his back against the wall he took a few deep breaths. Clutching the talisman of his Sword with one hand, Arnfinn used the tattered sleeve of his free arm to wipe sweat from his face, despite the chill draft blowing down the stair.

He had done it now. He was really here.

The next question was, where would an important prisoner like Kunderu, a wizard and a wizard's son, be likely to be hidden? Though Arnfinn had never been inside a castle before, he like everyone else knew that they were supposed to have dungeons underneath them. But he had also heard an old story or two in which prisoners of high rank and deemed especially important, or for some other reason deserving of special treatment, were kept locked up in high towers instead.

Anyway, since he had arrived atop the castle's highest tower, he might as well begin his search efforts at the top.

There was another problem, which only now occurred to Arnfinn: once he had located Kunderu, and somehow secured his release, how were the two of them going to return to the mainland? Briefly he toyed with the idea of persuading the magically powerful griffin to carry two passengers at once. The flight had been a hideous experience, and he had no wish to repeat it, but it had the one blessed advantage of being quick; either he and Kunderu would promptly effect their escape, or else they would be promptly killed. The alternative to using the griffin would be to commandeer a boat. . . . Arnfinn decided he wasn't going to make his choice just yet.

At the next landing down the tower stair, about twenty steps down from his first rest stop, he came to a narrow window through which he was able to survey the deepening night outside. Light enough remained for him to see that his griffin-mount, along with an escort of smaller flyers, had just taken off again, evidently heading out once more on patrol.

One question settled. He and Ninazu's brother were going to have to get away by boat, and that in a way was a relief. He would not have to fly again.

Arnfinn moved on down.

Presently, now only moderately high in the castle's architecture, he came out on a small terrace. This would be a good spot, he thought, from which to try to see what might be going on below, where parts of several open courtyards were visible. There were several lighted windows, as well, at his own level or a little higher, which he thought might repay investigation. He stood there beginning a survey.

Some time ago, Lady Yambu had given up listening at the door of the apartment to which she had been conducted as a guest. It was a comfortable enough place, even somewhat luxurious; but she was quite sure that if she left, or tried to leave, there would be a confrontation. She was effectively a prisoner. It was no more than she had expected.

Is this how I search for truth? she thought. But if I were not here, if I had determined to persevere very strictly in my pilgrimage, where would I be? Back at that damned room at the inn, probably, still waiting for another boat that might or might not be willing to take me down the Tungri.

Looking out from one of her gracefully thin windows—these quarters were certainly quite a change from her room at the inn—she saw, on a balcony at a slightly lower level, the figure of the Emperor. He was wearing his gray cape and a clown's mask, and looking tentatively about him. In that first moment of recognition, despite her experience only hours ago, she had no doubt that it was really the Emperor she saw.

Only when she saw him inexplicably turn into the hideously pallid figure of the Dark King, dead now these many years, did Yambu suddenly realize that this must be Zoltan or Ben. One of them at least must have managed to reach the island with the Sword of Stealth.

Lady Yambu brought a candle over to the window, and began some cautious signaling.

Arnfinn's attention was drawn to one window by the tiny movement of the flame inside it. The window was not many meters away, and despite the poor light, he at once recognized the gray-haired lady as one member of the infamous trio who had assaulted him and taken away the Sword. He was more than a little surprised to see her here. What she and her companions had said when they took his Sword away had made him think that they were not connected with the new lords of the lake and islands.

But, who was she seeing when she looked at him? Obviously not someone she greatly feared.

Arnfinn waved back, a slight, cautious gesture, and then began to work his way nearer her apartment, a task made considerably more difficult by his complete ignorance of the interior layout of the castle. Traveling through corridors that were almost completely dark, he found his vision somehow enhanced, he thought, by Sightblinder. What little was shown him by stray glints of light was easier to interpret in terms of real surfaces and distances.

He came out on another untenanted small balcony, from which he hoped to be able to see the window, and found to his satisfaction that he was closer to it. Taking a shortcut that involved some risky climbing—by this time risks were assuming a different proportion—he soon found himself standing on yet another balcony, near enough to the lady's window to allow them to conduct a quiet conversation.

"Who is it?" she whispered out to him, the imperious tone that he remembered still lingering in her voice. "Zoltan or Ben?"

Arnfinn, trying to understand that question, wondered if the lady could be speaking of a pair of twins, so that she did not know which one she thought she saw. Or, were Ben and Zoltan two different people, and had she seen him as first one and then the other as he approached?

"What does it matter?" he whispered back. Then,

bluntly: "I must know. Where are the important prisoners being held?"

He could see her shake her head impatiently and blink. "Prisoners? I know where the one of most importance is, at least. If you can get me out of this comfortable cell, I'll take you directly to him."

# CHAPTER 11

AS soon as Zoltan felt steady enough on his feet to travel, he continued with Ben along the shoreline in the direction away from Triplicane. They met no one as they walked. From time to time Ben cast a glowering look out over the lake, but the griffin, along with its unknown rider, and their flying escort of lesser creatures, had all disappeared into the distances of the darkening lacustrine sky.

Still Ben and Zoltan moved on. As the dusk deepened around them they stumbled around and over two more deserted docks, but except for one half-sunken hulk there were no boats of any kind to be discovered.

By this time both men were almost staggering with weariness. Abandoning their efforts for the time being, they sought shelter in a small hillside grove of evergreens, only a stone's throw from the water. There, on ground softly carpeted with needles, they slept until it was almost dawn.

Zoltan, who was the first to come fully awake, immediately set about scrounging up some breakfast. Seldom had he ever undertaken a journey of any length without bringing along a fisherman's line and a few hooks, and this trek to Alkmaar had been no exception. He could hear the downhill rush of a small stream that ran nearby, screened by trees. The underside of a log yielded a few juicy grubs for bait. Meanwhile Ben, groaning himself awake at last, came up with the flint and steel necessary to get a fire started.

Zoltan's skill, aided by moderate good luck, soon provided a few fish. As the two men breakfasted, discussing their problems and peering out over the lake, a pair of large rowboats came into sight through the usual sunrise mist and the accompanying strange optical effects. The boats, filled with soldiers uniformed in gray and red, were following the shoreline from the direction of the town.

Ben cast a quick glance upward, making sure that his small fire was producing no visible smoke. But the soldiers in the boats were not scanning for evidence of campfires. A little farther along the shore, in the direction they were going, stood a small fisherman's house, dark and deserted-looking in the dawn. But the house proved not to be deserted. When the big rowboats grounded in front of it and the troops poured ashore and into the building, screams and cries for mercy followed quickly.

Soon the soldiers were dragging a woman out of the house, while screams in a man's hoarse voice went on inside. And now they were bringing children out.

Zoltan, young as he was, had seen bad things before, but still he could not watch this. Instead he moved to a little slope facing away from the house, where he sat with his fingers in his ears.

Ben, his ugly face looking as if it were carved from stone, the breeze from the lake ruffling his graying hair, sat watching through it all. He wanted to know all that he could about the enemy. Even at the distance he tried to pick out individuals among them, for possible future reference.

The officer in charge of the troops, a red-haired man with a penetrating voice, looked on indulgently during the rape and killing. When that had been concluded, he ordered a few of his men aboard the single small fishing boat tied at the dock beside the house. The little craft appeared to be leaky—Ben could see the prize crew bailing industriously before they put their oars into the locks. Soon all three boats were rowing back in the direction of the town.

Ben swore gloomy oaths. He said to Zoltan, who by now had rejoined him: "One of the things the bastards are doing, then, is rounding up all the available boats. No wonder we couldn't find one to borrow last night."

"If we'd just kept going a little longer we might have had that one," Zoltan grumbled, watching it disappear. He was still pale from listening to the screams, and now and then he touched the place on the back of his head where he had been hit.

"And it's small wonder, too," Ben went on, "that we have seen practically no people on the shore. The fisherfolk all around the lake, or this end of it anyway, must be abandoning everything and moving out."

"So what do we do now?"

"I don't know."

Zoltan turned his head. "Sounds like someone coming. Uphill, that way."

There was a path in that direction, not very far away, but pretty effectively screened by evergreens. And now there was a lone man, in drab civilian clothing, walking on the path.

"Shall we keep quiet, or say hello to him?"

"Let's ask him how the weather's been."

When they appeared suddenly on the path, one in front of the man and one behind him, he collapsed at once in a terrified heap, signing that his pockets were empty and he had nothing to give them. But he was quickly convinced that they were not robbers and meant him no harm. Then he became willing to talk; indeed it was almost impossible to stop him for long enough to get a question in.

He was a wiry man of middle size, with bushy black eyebrows starting to turn gray. His name, he said, was Haakon, and he was, or had been, a part-time weaver of

fishing nets, as well as a former member of the constabulary serving Honan-Fu. It had not been a very energetic
or well-disciplined outfit, according to Haakon, and now
he, like the other members that he knew about, was lying
low and had even burned his old uniform.

Haakon went on to relate how, at the time of the
takeover a few days ago, he had seen a small army of the
invaders come down one of the small rivers that emptied
into the lake, and approach the castle. He estimated now
that there had been about two hundred soldiers, in ten
or twelve boats.

"You and your constabulary made no resistance?"

"We weren't even called to duty before it was all
over, the castle lost, and Honan-Fu dropped out of sight.
Anyway, it would have taken us days to mobilize effectively."

Ben fixed his eyes on the man in a steady gaze. "I
think it's time you got together now. Going by what you
say yourself, there's no huge army occupying the castle
—not yet anyway. It could be retaken, if you didn't
advertise that you were coming."

Haakon appeared to consider that. "Well—there
could have been other troops arrive that I didn't see.
And I'm not one of the constabulary officers."

"Then find your officers, man. Or choose new ones.
Did you see what just happened to that family of
fisherfolk down there? Where is the rest of this constabulary now?"

"I don't know. Scattered about." Haakon obviously
was beginning to regret that he had spoken so openly to
these strangers on the subject. No, he had no idea as to
where any boats could possibly be found now. The
invaders had been gathering them all up.

"And where," asked Zoltan, "can we find you if we
should want to talk to you again?"

The man looked from one of them to the other.
"They know me at Stow's shop in Triplicane," he said at
last. The information was given out so reluctantly that

Ben and Zoltan, exchanging glances, both believed it was the truth.

Presently, after making their informant a present of the single fish left over from their breakfast—a gift he accepted gratefully—and wishing him good luck, Ben and Zoltan walked on.

When the two were sure they were alone again, Zoltan asked: "We are going to keep on looking for a boat? Despite the evidence that there aren't any available?"

"Unless you have a better idea."

"We could have a try ourselves at raising this constabulary that our friend talked about."

Ben shook his head. "If they can't raise themselves under these circumstances, we wouldn't have much chance. We're outsiders, strangers. They'd never be willing to trust us in time to do Mark any good."

Zoltan trudged on another score of paces before he spoke again. "We could remain in hiding until night falls again, and then swim out to the castle on a couple of logs."

"That's crazy. But all right, we're going to have to do something. And what we're doing now is getting us nowhere."

"Look out."

The soldier who had just appeared on the slope ahead spotted them an instant after Zoltan had seen him. His bold command to halt was directed at their fleeing backs.

A moment later a whole squad of voices had joined in the clamor. There would certainly be pursuit. The two who fled had not much of a start, and each glance back showed soldiers coming on in energetic fashion. And now, to make matters worse, a couple of enemy flying scouts had ceased their observant high circling out over the water and joined in the chase across the land.

When these creatures, emboldened by their gathering numbers, dared to dive within range, Ben beat at them with his long staff and drove them off. After that the flyers stayed at a safe altitude, circling and cawing raucously to guide the soldiers in the right direction.

The chase went on, with the enemy gaining slightly. Their gasping quarry climbed a difficult rock slope, and clambered down another, getting a little farther ahead again.

Zoltan, when he had time and breath to spare, threw rocks and curses at the flyers, and prayed to all the gods and demons for a sling. But he had no sling, and none appeared.

The moments in which the two fugitives dared to pause for rest were rare. And now, slowly, they were being forced back in the direction of the town.

One of the flyers suddenly broke away from the circling flock above and flew in that direction.

"The people chasing us have signaled it to call for reinforcements," Ben grunted. "They'll try to pen us in between the patrol that's following us and troops come out from the town."

But no reinforcements appeared, and still the two Tasavaltans were not caught. The chase continued in zigzag course; the day wore on until the sun had turned past its high point. Here and there a rill of water, tumbling from broken rock, offered the fugitives a chance to get a drink. As for eating, they had no time.

Either the flyer had had trouble in locating a responsive officer in town, or the enemy were beset by other difficulties and had none readily available. All day long the hiding and chasing continued inconclusively. The sky turned gray, and a fine, misting rain began to fall.

At last Zoltan, crouched wearily in a dripping thicket, could say to Ben: "Another hour and it'll be dark."

And then somehow, at last, it was dark, and they were still alive and free. Now the chance existed for the two of them to slip away, get through the hills and on the road back to Tasavalta.

"Not that they mightn't catch us tomorrow," Zoltan qualified in a weary voice.

But Ben had a different idea. "I think that we ought to go into town instead."

Zoltan raised an eyebrow, considering. "Well, they won't be expecting us to do that."

"No, they won't. And there'll be boats there, we can be certain of that much. Guarded, no doubt. But hanging around out here in the hills, we have small chance of staying alive, and no chance of accomplishing anything useful. I say it's either go into town or head for home."

"If we were going to run for home," said Zoltan, "we would have done it long ago."

At least the rain had stopped again, and their pursuers had apparently given up for the night. After an hour's sorely needed rest, Ben and Zoltan ate such scraps of food as they still had with them, and then made their way slowly and cautiously toward Triplicane and into its streets.

But hardly had they got well in among the streets and houses when there sounded a renewed outcry and pursuit.

They ran again. A dark alley offered a moment's respite, but there were all too few dark alleys in a town this size. Ben grunted. "We must split up, it's our only chance."

"And meet where?"

"At the castle on the island," Ben answered grimly. "When we can. Or in the next world if there is one."

Zoltan looked at Ben as if he would have said some kind of a farewell. But then he only nodded, and, with lots of running still in him, went dashing swiftly away.

Ah, youth, thought Ben with heartfelt envy. He slumped down quietly where he was in the shadows, and just sat there for a few moments regaining some breath and energy while he listened to see if Zoltan should make good at least a temporary escape.

Before distance had entirely swallowed the sound of the young man's running steps, they broke off in an indeterminate scramble. Ben strained his ears, but he could hear nothing more. There were no cries of triumph, or other indication that Zoltan had been killed or taken.

He could, of course, proceed himself in the same direction and try to investigate. But, no, whatever had happened, the two of them had split up. One of them at least had to get out to Mark, on the island. The damned island; it was beginning to seem half a continent away.

When Ben moved again it was in the opposite direction from the one Zoltan had taken.

He went down the remaining length of the original dark alley, and then was pleasantly surprised to see the mouth of another one just across the street. After that alley there came another. When he had progressed for some distance in this fashion, he dared to cross a space of open moonlight. He was heading as best he could toward the water, where surely there would be boats, even if they were guarded.

Then again there were torches behind Ben, and voices, and he thought he heard a warbeast snarling, or perhaps it was only a dog. A good tracking dog would be bad enough. That was all he needed on his trail. He had to have the water now, and no question about it.

A street went by him, an alley, and then another street. And presently, now on the very edge of town, he found his way blocked by a high stone wall. As far as Ben could tell in the darkness, it extended for a long way in both directions.

Ben was much better at climbing walls than his bulky shape suggested. The mass of his huge body was very largely muscle, and now his great strength served him well, letting him support himself wedged in an angle of the wall, where enough little chips of stone were missing to give fingers and toes a purchase. Tall as the wall was, he got himself to the top of it and over.

It was almost a four-meter drop into complete darkness on the other side, but fortunately his landing was in soft grass.

He crouched there, listening for news beyond the weary thudding of his own heart, trying to tell whether or not his arrival had been noticed. So far there was no indication that it had. Silence prevailed, except for the usual night insects, and darkness extended almost everywhere. It was broken only by the concentrated glow of a couple of ornate lanterns that shone on latticework and barren vines a modest arrow-shot away.

Getting to his feet, Ben stole as softly as he could toward the lights. He saw now that the vines, leafless with autumn, wreathed and bound a summerhouse of latticework, built larger than a peasant's cottage. The lanterns glowed inside.

Ben circled close to the arbor, meaning to go around it. He did not see the young lady in almost royal dress who was seated within, against all likelihood in the chill night, until she had raised her own eyes and looked directly at him.

"I see you," she announced in a firm voice. "Come here and identify yourself."

# CHAPTER 12

WHEN the soldiers sprang upon Zoltan in the streets of Triplicane they kept their weapons sheathed and were obviously determined to take him alive. His arms were pinned, and before he had the chance to draw his own weapons they were taken from him. He struggled fiercely as long as he thought he had the slightest chance of breaking away, but when he found himself in a completely hopeless position, he let his body go limp and saved his strength.

His captors, working with quiet efficiency, bound him firmly, while at the same time they took care to cause no serious injury. They had nothing to say to him beyond a few passing comments on his ancestry, but Zoltan gathered from the few words they spoke among themselves that they considered him a catch of some importance.

Bound hand and foot, and aching from the blows he had received during the struggle, he was carried through the streets and conveyed quickly to the docks. There a command post had been set up, and he heard a couple of officers exulting over his capture before one of them ordered him placed immediately in a small boat. From what Zoltan could hear of the officers' conversation it was certain that they knew he was Prince Mark's nephew.

The only consolation Zoltan could find was that

Ben was not in the boat with him, and that the soldiers, from what he could overhear, were still pressing an urgent search for someone.

Whatever might have happened to Ben, it now appeared that he, Zoltan, was going to get to the island after all.

As soon as he had been tossed into the boat, Zoltan wriggled and turned until he was lying on his back near the prow, his head and shoulders sufficiently elevated to let him see out over the gunwales. He was facing the backs of six soldiers, who now bent to their oars, and the sergeant on the rear seat was facing Zoltan along the length of the boat.

At a word from the sergeant the backs of the rowers bent in unison, and oars squeaked in their locks. The lights of the docks and the town began to move away. Staring out over the darkening face of the lake, marked here and there by a few lonely sparks of fires upon its distant shores, Zoltan pondered a temporarily attractive scheme of trying to roll himself out of the craft once it was well out into deep water. If he could manage to drown himself, tied up as he was, he would at least have succeeded in avoiding interrogation.

The moon was coming up now, its light beginning to make things ghostly.

For two thirds of the distance to the castle, the boat made uneventful progress, the sergeant only now and then growling a command, the men rowing steadily and in near silence.

But at that point in the journey, just as the craft was about to pass between two of the smaller islands, Zoltan observed something strange. It was as if a piece of one of those islets, which was some forty meters or so distant, had detached itself from the main body—detached itself, and was now drifting silently through the gloom toward the boat. A tiny, moving islet, whitish in the darkness and the peculiar moonlight. His imagination suggested something out of a story of the far northern seas, a drifting floe of ice, which might perhaps be big enough to let a desperate man use it for a raft. Zoltan watched it as if hypnotized . . .

Because the appearance of the thing gradually convinced him that it was neither a drifting island nor a chunk of ice. It possessed too much mobility, and it changed shape. It was alive.

Zoltan had once seen a living dragon that was bigger than this mysterious object. But this was no dragon, though it had eyes. Eyes the size of plates, reflecting impossible colors from the night. And fur, a pale silvery mat that became visible for what it was, roaring a cascade of water back into the lake as the thing began to rise out of the shallowing water with the nearness of its approach.

For long seconds now every soldier in the boat had been aware of this bizarre apparition. One after another the men had ceased to row; and now, as if a signal had been given, they all started shouting at the same moment.

Their shouts had no effect. The furry mass was wet and dully glistening, and the moonlight seemed to play strange tricks of light within its surface as it rose higher and higher, the top of it now three meters above the lake. Atop the silvery form Zoltan could now distinguish an almost human head, manlike but gigantically magnified, supported upon almost human shoulders.

And now there were two arms. Limbs quite unbelievable in size, but there they were. And now one of those arms was reaching with its great hand for the boat.

Long moments had passed since the soldiers had ceased to row. Uttering cries and oaths, they had begun to scramble for their weapons. Now one of them, the sergeant, swung with an oar against that reaching hand; the wooden blow landed on a knuckle, with a sound of great solidity, and had not the least observable effect.

The huge, five-fingered hand was thickly covered with the same strange fur as the rest of the creature's body. The hand was big enough to enfold a man's whole body in its grasp, bigger probably, but still it was very human in its shape. And now it had clamped a hard grip on the nearest gunwale, and Zoltan could hear the planks of the boat's side grind and groan and crunch together.

The boat was tipping now, the side held by the great hand rising, about to spill its contents into the lake on the side away from the silver monster.

By now most of the soldiers had their swords in hand. But they were too late to use them—if indeed such puny weapons could have done them any good. Everyone aboard the boat, Zoltan included, shouted aloud as it went over.

Zoltan had just time to close his mouth before the splash and grip of icy water claimed him. His bound feet touched bottom, less than two meters down, and he twisted his body in the water in an effort to stand erect, or at least float with his head up, so he could breathe. But he need not have made the effort. A hand as big as the one that had tipped the boat closed gently around his body, and he was lifted from the lake almost before its chill had had time to penetrate his clothing. He was able to catch one glimpse of the crew of military rowers, all floundering to swim or stand or cling to their capsized boat, the men in neck-deep water just starting to get their feet under them, before he was borne away.

He was being carried by the being who had over-turned the boat, and who was now wading away from it through water no deeper than his thighs, though already quite deep enough to drown a man. The giant's two columnar legs sent up their roaring wakes in alternation, making speed away from boat and islands into water that was deeper still; the bottom dropped off sharply here.

Meanwhile, one of the giant's hands still cradled Zoltan, while the fingers of the other plucked with surprising delicacy at the cords that bound him. One after another, like withes of grass, those strings popped loose.

In the next moment Zoltan, his arms and legs now free, had been lifted up to ride like a child sitting on the giant's furry shoulders, astride his neck. Meanwhile his savior, almost chest-deep in the lake now and rapidly getting deeper, continued to make impressive speed away from the shouted outrage of the soldiers surrounding their tipped boat.

By using both hands to cling to silvery fur, Zoltan managed to keep his seat. He delayed trying to speak; the noise made by the great body beneath him in its splashing passage would have drowned out any merely human shout. But presently the splashing quieted almost completely as the giant began to swim. Zoltan's small additional weight upon his neck apparently made little difference to him in this effort.

At last, in the lee of another of the smaller islands, Zoltan was set down upon a sandy shore. The tipped boat was hundreds of meters distant now, and the castle even farther away, beyond the boat.

As soon as he had solid land under his feet again, the young man made a low bow to his rescuer. He said: "My lifelong gratitude, Lord Draffut."

"You know me, then." The giant still stood erect, surveying more distant events from his six-meter height; the voice from that great throat was manlike, except that it was deep as any dragon's roar. Then he looked down. "But I do not recognize you."

"We have not met before, my lord. I am Zoltan, nephew of Prince Mark of Tasavalta."

"Ah." Draffut now squatted in the shallows, bringing his head down closer to the level of the man's. "And where is the Prince himself tonight?"

Zoltan turned briefly and raised a hand toward the torch-sparked castle and its reflection in the lake. "In there, somewhere, I am afraid. If he is still alive."

"Ah. And was it he who sent the little flying dragon

to find me, bearing the only message that it could, that my help was needed?"

"Lady Yambu did that," said Zoltan, feeling suddenly guilty for his past suspicions. Then he hesitated. "Did she know, when she sent the dragon, that it would bring you?"

"Doubtless she at least hoped that it would. Fortunately I was already traveling this way when the message reached me, on my way to Tasavalta from the far south. I bear grim news, and the Prince is one of the people that I meant to see—but that can wait. How strongly is the castle defended?"

"I have heard an eyewitness account of the arrival of about two hundred troops." And Zoltan explained what little he and Ben had been able to learn on the subject.

Draffut was just about to respond to this information when he suddenly raised his head, gazing up into the night sky. Zoltan, looking up also, saw that one of the small flying scouts from the castle had discovered them in the moonlight and was circling overhead.

As soon as the flyer began to clamor its discovery, Draffut emitted a startlingly shrill cry from his own huge throat. It sounded like the flyer's own primitive form of speech, and it had an immediate effect.

Draffut had called the creature, and it came spiraling down to him—and he caught it gently as it came down, much as a man whose hands were quick enough might have snatched a small bird on the wing.

Then for several minutes the Beastlord held conversation with the little flyer, while it remained perched on one of his fingers. Draffut managed to match the sounds of its voice so perfectly that Zoltan, looking on in awe, was often unable to tell which shrill tone proceeded from which throat.

Then suddenly the conversation was over, and Draffut tossed the flyer lightly back into the air. The small winged thing silently flew up and away, headed now for the dark shoreline in the opposite direction from the castle.

"Now it will no longer serve our enemies," said Draffut. He went on to explain that since his arrival in the vicinity of the lake he had already persuaded a number of nonhuman creatures to abandon their service to the new ruler of Honan-Fu's domain. He had convinced them that they would be better off to desert that unnatural cause, allied with demons as it was, and adopt a way of life more in keeping with their own true natures.

Then he shook his huge head, as if at some unpleasant memory. "I regret to say that some of them would not listen to me."

"What happened then?"

"I wrung their necks—that, you understand, is an option I do not have with humans who are determined to persist in evil. My own nature forbids that I should harm any human."

Zoltan looked back toward the tipped boat. Other craft, with torches, had come from the castle and were now approaching the scene of the disaster to find out what had happened and rescue those still in the water.

Draffut was smiling. "I wanted to ask questions of a soldier. Or better yet, ask them of the soldiers' prisoner, once I saw that they had such a person in their boat. But before I tipped the boat I had first to make sure that the water there was shallow enough for the men aboard to stand in. Some of them might have been poor swimmers."

The young man shook his head impatiently. "I was beginning to hope that you could even force your way into the castle, and its dungeons. My uncle Mark is there."

Draffut shook his head in turn. He drew back his lips in what might have been a smile, displaying carnivorous-looking fangs that would have served a dragon. "If there are human defenders on the walls, as I am sure there must be, I cannot attack them. Nor could I do much damage to the demons who would be called up to help those men, though in the case of demons it would not be for want of trying."

"Ben and I are both determined to get into the castle." Zoltan thought of trying to explain his own reason. But then he just left it at that. He gestured toward the town. "I don't know if Ben's still living either."

The Lord of Beasts gazed at him in silence for a moment. Then Draffut said: "I can probably create enough of a distraction for you to get into that castle, if that is what you really want. But before you do, you ought to know what kind of an enemy you are going to face there."

"I'm sure he's formidable. And whatever he is, he now also has Shieldbreaker in his hand—but still I must go."

"I understand that men are sometimes willing to go to almost certain death, and that Ben of Purkinje would feel so. The Prince has saved his life more than once."

"And my uncle has saved mine also."

"Very well. But even if the one who rules in the castle now did not have Shieldbreaker—you should know something of his nature before you go to face him."

"Is he called the Ancient One? If so, I have seen him once before." And Zoltan shivered. The night was wearing on and growing colder.

"That is the name by which he is called now," said Draffut quietly. He drew a deep breath into the cavern of his chest and let it out again. "Thousands of years ago, when Ardneh was alive upon the earth, this same man walked the earth as a servant of the evil emperor John Ominor. He was named Wood, then—that at least was his public name—and his body was more fully human then than it is now. You said that you have seen him?"

"Yes. About two years ago." And Zoltan shivered again.

"Then there is much that I need not try to explain. In olden times his mind and soul were more fully human too, though nonetheless evil, I suppose. For about two years now he has been here, active in our world. How he can have survived until now I do not know, except that he must have made a pact with some unknown evil that allowed him to traverse the ages swiftly, or lie dormant through them. And the pact has changed him for the worse. . . . I was certain that Orcus, the grandfather of all demons, had slain him, even before Ardneh died."

All this was beside the point as far as Zoltan could see. He quickly brought the discussion back to present problems.

"Lord Draffut, what can you do to help Prince Mark? And our companion, Ben of Purkinje. It would be a great help to me to know whether he's still alive or not."

"I am going to do what I can to help the Prince. First we must be absolutely sure that you are still determined to get into the castle where he is."

"I am determined," said Zoltan.

And he thought that with those words he had spoken his own doom.

# CHAPTER 13

THE young lady who confronted Ben under the glowing lanterns of the autumnal summerhouse was of slender build and considerable beauty. The soft appearance of her hands, the length of her well-cared-for fingernails, the royal elegance of her clothing, all indicated that she had led a sheltered and wealthy life. But despite the sophistication of her manner and her clothing, Ben judged that she was really no older than Zoltan.

There was a certain natural alarm in her eyes —along with other things less easy to read—as she gazed at this giant and uncouth intruder. But there was less alarm than Ben would have expected; certainly there appeared to be very little chance that this particular lady was going to scream or run away in panic.

Still Ben moved very slowly, doing his best not to alarm her any further. Shuffling a step or two closer to the pavilion, nodding and smiling subserviently as he moved, he allowed her to see him plainly in the lantern light.

He topped the performance with a little touch of his forelock. "Begging your pardon, ma'am, I don't mean any harm, I'm sure. They were after me with dogs and such out there—don't know why, I'm sure." And he went through the humble little routine of bowing and nodding and smiling again.

The girl, still seated but now holding herself very

erect, was swiftly becoming even more judgmental and less alarmed. "Who are you?" she demanded. The question was deeply suspicious, and she was looking down at him like a magistrate from the slight elevation of her chair on the raised floor of the arbor.

"Name's Maxim, ma'am." Inspiration had come seemingly from nowhere. Some of the best ideas, Ben had noticed, arrived in such a way. "They call me Maxim the Strong. I'm with the show, ma'am. Magnificent Show of Ensor. We'll be coming to Triplicane again soon for a performance, and they just sent me on ahead. To put up a few posters, like, ma'am, and just kind of look things over in the town."

"Ah!" the lady exclaimed, as if his answer had enlightened her on some subject of great importance. "The *show!*" And it was as if the mention of the Show of Ensor had given her, or at least suggested to her, some profound idea.

"Yes'm, that's it. The show." Ben bowed again.

She relaxed a little, leaning back in her cushioned chair. He still had not been able to think of any good reason for this attractive young girl to be sitting alone in this chill place in the middle of the night. Unless it had something to do with magic.

Meanwhile she went on: "And you have come to Triplicane to put up posters—tell me, Maxim the Strong, have you been to visit the castle yet? Out on the island?"

"Oh, I know where the castle is, ma'am. But, no, ma'am, I haven't been out there yet. Not this trip."

"But you are going out there." It was an eager assumption.

Ben took the cue. "Yes, my lady, I expect so. We've always been welcome at the castle in the past."

"True. True. My father"—and here the young lady's eyes blazed for an instant with some inward fire—"always enjoyed your *shows.*" This time the last word held unveiled contempt. One of her small hands, resting on the table before her, clenched itself into a white fist.

"Very true, my lady." Ben decided to risk dropping some of the peasant speech and mannerisms. They had been natural to him at one time early in his life, but he was no longer sure he could maintain them steadily.

At the same time, after hearing that "My father" he was wondering if this could be the reclusive daughter of Honan-Fu. The evidence of wealth tended to confirm the suspicion. If so, he supposed she might be expected to welcome and help any enemy of the new regime. But Ben prudently withheld any announcements along that line until he could be sure.

The lady gave no sign of noticing any alteration in his speech. "So you do intend to go out to the castle? How?"

"I—don't know, precisely, ma'am. I was noticing that boats do seem hard to come by in the town."

"A boat can be arranged." Again she leaned forward, and this time lowered her voice. "But you must take me with you. And we should go now. Tonight. At once."

Ben opened his mouth, then closed it again.

His grand hostess, who Ben now thought must be even younger than Zoltan, stood up with a graceful and decisive movement. "There is someone out there whom I must see. And—they don't call you Maxim the Strong for nothing, do they? How are you at fighting, Maxim?"

"Fighting, ma'am? Can't say I care for it at all. But I can do it when I must."

"Yes, you look like you can. There might be one or two people here at the dock who wouldn't want us to take a boat. But you can deal with them, can't you? Especially if I can bring them to you one at a time, and unsuspecting." Her gaze ran appraisingly over Ben's shoulders and down his arms.

Ben was thinking furiously—or at least he was furiously trying to think, despite a feeling that his tired brain was getting nowhere in the attempt. "I—I—I'll do the best I can, my lady, of course. But—"

"Excellent!" The young lady's eyes flashed again, appraising him. "Maxim the Strong—yes, excellent. Yes, I am guarded, Maxim. But I'll have a gold piece for you if you can row me out to the island at once. The boats are just outside that gate back there." And with a motion of her head she indicated a direction in the darkness.

In a moment she had left the arbor and the lantern light and was walking with deliberate, regal speed in that direction. Ben hastened to follow, keeping a couple of paces behind her in the darkness, his feet moving through well-kept grass that was wet with the recent rain. Apparently the young lady had eyes like a cat. Ben couldn't see much of anything for forty paces or so, but then a high stone surface loomed ahead of them again, and presently they stood facing a small closed wooden gate that pierced the outer wall of the manor grounds.

The lady wasted no time. With word and gesture, she made Ben flatten himself against the wall, where he would be within reach of the gate, yet almost out of sight to anyone looking in. Then she rapped sharply on the wooden portal, using the massive rings on her soft hand, and called in an imperious voice.

Presently a small grating high in the gate, something like the spyhole in a prison cell, slid open, and a man's voice outside mumbled something.

"What do you think I want?" the lady shrilled. "I want you to open up this gate, you fool! I cannot speak to you like this."

There was another mumble, sounding disgruntled. But a moment later there was a rattling sound, as of bars being taken down. The gate opened and a guard, wearing the gray and red of the castle soldiers, stuck his head in.

"I want a boat," the mistress of the manor demanded sharply of the sentry. "I want it now."

"Oh, yeah? Really?" The man, with an insolence that Ben found utterly surprising, started to look around. "Is that all you made me open the gate for, to start that again? Because if—"

Ben had not lied about his dislike of fighting, but he had long ago trained himself not to be not in the least squeamish when violence became essential. In a brief flash of his mind's eye, even as his hands reached out for the man's neck, he saw a poor fisherman's house, dark and quiet in the early dawn.

"Very good, Maxim!" the lady exulted almost silently, but with high good humor like a schoolgirl on some lark. "Oh, you are marvelously quick and efficient!" At her feet the uniformed body twitched once more and then was still, and Ben thought for a moment she was about to give it an exuberant kick.

But instead she went to peer cautiously out through the opened gate. Ben could see now that it had been strongly barred on the outside, as if to prevent a determined effort at escape, with less concern for entry. She said: "Evidently there was only one on guard tonight, I see no one else around. They've been so busy—come along, now we can get a boat."

Then she turned back, gazing down at the dead man. "Bring him out, Maxim. We'll stuff a rock into his jerkin; that'll make him sink."

That sounded like a practical idea to Ben; and he had known too many ladies, young and old, of high rank, to be surprised that one of them should demonstrate ruthlessness and efficiency. He scooped the body up.

The small docks that served the manor directly were just outside the gate. In the distance the castle on its island was speckled gaily with flecks of torchlight. The lady moved with Ben, guiding him through the darkness toward the little boathouse. Her clothing, a long, delicate-looking dress and frivolous shoes, wasn't what he would have recommended for a night row across the lake, but this girl, whoever she was, was apparently as ready to ruin her finery as she was to kill, and Ben wasn't going to be the one to bring the subject up.

The dead guard, duly weighted, went off the dock into what was probably reasonably deep water with only a small splash. They might think, when they found him, that he had broken his neck accidentally. Ben supposed they would have to be pretty stupid to think that, but the possibility couldn't be ruled out.

There were two small rowboats waiting at the docks. Ben found a pair of oars just where his guide said they would be, inside the little boathouse, and started to put them into one of the boats.

His hostess meanwhile stood idle, waiting like a true lady to be helped into the boat when the time came. But before Ben could get to that, there were voices coming through the night across the water, and the sound of more than one pair of oars in locks.

She was as fiercely alert as he. "They're coming right from the castle. Quick, Maxim, back inside!"

Muttering powerful but silent curses, Ben got back through the gate with his new young mistress, and pulled it shut and latched it on the inside. The real bar, the one that had been on the outside, of course could not be replaced. The implications of that were not too good. In a minute or two, boats, more than just a couple of them by the sound of it, began to arrive out there. So far there were no sounds of alarm, and Ben could begin to hope that he and the lady had not been seen out on the dock. Quite possibly the boathouse had screened them from the approaching craft while they were disposing of the sentry.

But that the men outside would not even notice the absence of their sentry was too much to expect. Soon there came a hearty pounding on the gate, and soldiers' voices murmuring questions to each other. Ben waited, looking to his hostess; it was up to her now to come up with some cleverness. But she continued silent and passive; then she turned her head back toward the manor house, and there were small sparks as of torches reflected in her eyes.

A man, by the look of him a steward or something of the kind, was hurrying out from the house. He was being lighted on his way by torches in the hands of a couple of lesser servants.

When the steward came close enough to get a look at Ben he stared at the big man uncomprehendingly, even fearfully; but he asked no question and made no comment. It was as if he feared to question any presence that the lady obviously accepted. A moment later he had shifted his hopeless gaze toward the gate, where the soldiers' knocking continued with grim patience.

"Never mind that noise," the lady snapped at him. "What have you come out here for?"

"There has been—an arrival at the front gate, my lady."

"What sort of an arrival? Speak up!"

The man gestured helplessly. "First, a number of wagons, Lady Ninazu. Half a dozen of them at least. It is the Show of Ensor. And then a—a crowd of soldiers."

"Ah!" she cried with delight, and looked at Ben. "Come with me!"

For a moment Ben considered trying to vanish into the orchard, but the lady's imperious eye caught him and dragged him along. He consigned himself to the fates, and followed with a sigh. His only hope was probably her protection anyway, he thought.

Maintaining a respectful interval, he followed her into the house and through its splendors. This was a very long, wide structure, all or very nearly all of it built upon a single level. When they had passed outside again through the front door Ben could see the front gate of the grounds standing open some thirty meters ahead of him. Beyond the open gate more soldiers were milling around.

Lady Ninazu hurried eagerly toward the gate, but he hung back.

Then he saw something that made him advance until he was able to see a little more. Outside the gate, soldiers were indeed arriving, and nonmilitary wagons too, a poor-looking little train of them with crude signs blazoned on their canvas sides. The Magnificent Show of Ensor.

The lady turned and beckoned Ben impatiently, signaling him to join her outside the gate. Slowly he complied. Amid a sudden new prodigality of torches, which were rapidly being lighted at the orders of the lady of the manor, Ben moved outside the gate, where he gazed with dull wonder at the five or six poor wagons, being pulled by tired-looking loadbeasts into camp position.

"Ho, there!" One of the officers in red and gray, who appeared to be in charge of the milling troops, bellowed impatiently toward the wagons. "Who's the boss of that flea circus?"

At once the driver of one of the wagons waved back energetically. He reined his animals to a halt and jumped down from his high seat. Ben, staring at him, felt something in his heart almost stop; and then his blood was pumping steadily again, a little faster than before.

Meanwhile the officer had turned away, to deal with some evidently more urgent problem just brought to him by a noncom. The proprietor of the show had changed course and was now coming straight for Ben.

Ben waited. It seemed that there was nothing else that he could do.

The proprietor of the show was a middle-sized, sturdy-looking man clad in nondescript gray, with a short cloak to match. Dark hair, showing no sign of gray, curled crisply. The only remarkable feature of his attire was a magnificently painted clown's mask that covered his own face completely.

He approached Ben with the familiar manner of an old friend—or perhaps an old military commander. He said, in a pleasant though undistinguished voice: "Maxim! I'm glad to see that you have found the right place."

"Uh, yessir."

"Between us, Maxim, no formalities are necessary." And the masked man reached out with one hand to clasp Ben familiarly by the arm.

No one else, for the moment, was paying the least attention to their conversation. Ben licked dry lips. He said: "We have met before—I think. You are the Emperor."

The other nodded. "Of course. And we *have* met —but you had no way of knowing me then. I sat on a hillside overlooking the sea, and greeted you as you climbed past me. You answered, but you were not minded to stay and talk to me that day."

Ben swallowed and nodded. Since that day years ago he had learned a great deal, about the nature of the world and the powers that moved in it, and now he felt relief almost as at the arrival of a friendly army. And yet at the same time he felt newly uneasy, even somewhat fearful, in this man's presence.

"Will you join us for the evening?" the other went on in his mild voice, gesturing toward his wagons. "Or for longer, if you like."

"I . . . for this evening, certainly, if you wish it."

"I think it would be a good idea. Each member of my little troupe here must be ready to play his or her assigned part. Tonight I have the urge to be a clown. Often I have that urge, and give way to it. A little joke or two, here and there, hey, to lighten up the world?"

Ben nodded again. "Your son," he said, choking a little, "Prince Mark, is out there on the island. I mean, I don't know if he's—"

"Oh, he's alive," the Emperor assured Ben quickly. "Not as fully and pleasantly alive as he has been, or ought to be, but . . . it is not easy to kill one of my children." The eyes behind the clown's mask glittered out at Ben. "My daughter Ariane lives also. You may see her again, one day, when both of you will have to make great decisions."

Ben could not speak.

The smaller man clapped him reassuringly on the arm again. "Come, strongman. Did you see which wagon I was driving? Hop up into it, and put your costume on. You'll find it there. Then be ready to use your strength to help your Prince."

Feeling somewhat dazed, Ben walked out among the wagons. Momentarily he felt now as if he had returned to the days of his youth. He had spent years then in the carnival with Barbara, the dragon-hunter Nestor, and later with Mark himself, long before there had been any suspicion in Mark's mind that he might one day occupy a princely throne.

Glancing in under the canvas of the other wagons as he passed them, Ben saw in one a small mermaid coming out of a bathtub-tank. She looked like one of the creatures that Zoltan had described to him, who could be found rarely in the rivers hereabouts, and somewhat more commonly farther south. This one was certainly not an animal captive, but another member of the small troupe, chatting with a woman in pink tights who was now handing her a towel.

Outside the next wagon were a couple of young men in the tight costumes of jugglers or acrobats, looking enough alike to be a team of brothers. And there, a pair of short-skirted dancing girls who resembled each other even more, enough to be twins.

He came to the indicated wagon, found a step, and hopped right aboard, pulling back the canvas flap. His weight made the light frame tilt strongly on the wooden springs. Someone's cramped living quarters, perhaps those of the Emperor himself. No one else was in it now. Hanging on a prominent peg was a large garment of some leathery animal skin, with spots of fur still on it, and on the floor below it waited a pair of buskins sized for large feet.

Ben changed quickly into the costume, which fit him well. Meanwhile he wondered how in all the hells the Emperor had known to greet him as Maxim. Ben had made up that name on the spur of the moment—or he thought he had.

Might he have seen it or heard it somewhere else? He couldn't recall doing so. But that problem, like some others, would have to wait.

A couple of minutes later, when he rejoined the Emperor and the other members of the troupe in the field outside the front gate of the manor, the process of setting the show up for a performance was already well under way. Little had to be done, beyond arranging some scantly decorations to mark out a portion of the field in front of the manor as a circus ring, and moving a couple of wagons to provide wings behind which it might be possible to organize something approaching a theatrical entrance.

Already the audience too was more or less in place. It was bigger than Ben had expected, certainly over a hundred people. Most of them were soldiers, with servants from the manor and a random scattering of other civilians attracted by the assembly. There were of course no seats, and the soldiers in particular were not settled in to watch. Whatever they had originally come here for, they were only pausing as their officers had paused, to see what might be interesting about this motley group of fools who had come to put on a show.

It was not the kind of audience Ben would have chosen, but he had already decided to obey orders. "What am I supposed to do?" he demanded loudly of anyone who would listen to him. He could see no weights, no strongman paraphernalia anywhere. And even as he spoke, the clown passed right by him, apparently ignoring his question completely. No one else paid him any particular attention.

Next, the clown, having reached the approximate center of the open field, assumed the role of ringmaster. He made a short speech, punctuated by exaggerated bows and obeisances, which earned him a faint titter of laughter from the civilians in the crowd—only a few hoots and muttered curses from the soldiers. Giving a very good imitation of terror, he scampered back behind one of the wagons.

A moment later, to the music of simple drum and flute, the two dancing girls came prancing out from behind the other wagon. It was a simple dance, more comic than erotic. But the assembled soldiers greeted it with a roar of serious lust.

The girls had barely reached the center of the ring when the first of the soldiers rushed from the sidelines to grab at them. One performer was whirled around in a helpless parody of a dance; the other, pawed by a dozen hands, already had part of her costume torn off.

The two victims were able to escape only because fighting broke out almost immediately among the soldiers. As an officer shouted into the confusion, the dancers made good a quick retreat, their faces pale, holding their ripped costumes about them as they ran.

Naturally the dancers were frightened. No, thought Ben as they passed him, it would be more accurate to say that they looked as if they had been frightened, even terrified, a moment ago. But now already they felt safe. They had managed to escape from the small arena, and with monumental trust they were ready to leave their problems in the hands of the clown.

Ben had already moved a step forward. But against a hundred soldiers his interference on the dancers' behalf would have been hopeless; and now it appeared that it might not be necessary.

The clown, enacting a parody of bold defiance, had sprung forward from somewhere to confront the armed mass of the soldiers.

The masked figure had drawn from somewhere a rusty, toy-sized sword, and he waved this weapon wildly as in a thin, hopeless, angry voice he challenged the whole garrison of the town to come against him.

The soldiers laughed. At the beginning it was almost a good-humored sound.

One of them, not bothering to draw a weapon, came at the clown with fist uplifted, ready to knock this preposterous obstacle out of his way with one half-drunken swing. But he couldn't do it, couldn't hold himself together long enough.

Helpless with laughter, the soldier staggered around the clown, who continued to challenge him, and halfway across the ring toward the waiting girls. But before he reached them he had to give up and sit down, abandoning himself completely to hilarity.

The laughter had spread quickly through the military audience, and it was growing steadily louder, though the clown was doing nothing to enlarge his simple routine. The officers, their next reaction anger, the instinct to maintain discipline, were soon as badly infected as the men.

Men and officers alike, they roared, they bellowed, they guffawed. They shrieked and screamed and howled. The noise they made was rising to an unnatural level. Officers abandoned their dignity entirely. Choking helplessly on their own mirth, they rolled on the ground.

The lady of the manor had come to stand beside Ben, watching, waiting.

Turning, looking until he caught Ben's eye, the clown made a sign, a gentle push as of dismissal. It was an expressive gesture, and Ben knew it meant that he and Lady Ninazu were now free to be on their way.

# CHAPTER 14

ONCE again Draffut hoisted Zoltan to his shoulders. Then, swimming and wading, the giant carried the young man with him through the lake, back in the direction of the castle.

When they reached the area of shallower water that surrounded some of the smaller islands, the Beastlord enjoined silence, then set his passenger down again on a dark beach. Some of the victims of Draffut's attack had evidently reached a different island, where they were waiting in hope of rescue; their mournful voices carried through the night.

Draffut crouched beside Zoltan and together they awaited the approach of the next boat.

"What if there's no more traffic on the lake tonight?" Zoltan whispered.

"I think there will be. Even before I tipped that boat, something was stirring the soldiers to activity, in the castle and in the town."

Looking in the direction of the castle on its island, Zoltan found something dreamlike in the appearance of the structure, with the multitude of tiny flames that were trying to light it all reflected in the water. Even more lights had appeared in the stronghold in the few minutes since he had taken his last deliberate look at it. And the docks at the foot of those high walls displayed increased activity. Miniature human figures could be seen swarming over them, though at the distance it was impossible to see just what they were about.

Draffut, who had been peering in the other direction, toward the town, now hissed softly, signaling for renewed silence. Crouching lower, the Beastlord whispered: "Another boatload of soldiers is coming in our direction—no, I think there are two boats this time." Draffut's whisper was a peculiar sound, like the rushing of an almost silent breeze across the night.

Very soon Zoltan, peering over the low, dry elevation of the barren islet, was also able to hear the oars. And shortly after that he believed he could tell that there were at least two boats approaching.

Tugging childlike at the half-luminous fur of the crouching giant beside him, he whispered very softly: "Ben might be on one of those."

The Beastlord nodded his great head once. "When we approach these boats, I'll signal with a roar if I see that they carry no prisoners. Then you can go on to the castle, as you are determined to do, if fortune grants you the chance. But if I am silent, then there are prisoners, or at least one, and you should probably wait to confer with them first."

"I agree."

Presently Zoltan was able to see the dark shapes of the slow-moving boats intermittently silhouetted against the twinkling lights of the distant town.

Moving his lips closer to Zoltan's ear, Draffut whispered a last question: "Are you a good swimmer? Good enough to reach the castle from here, in water as cold as this?"

"Good enough."

"Then do what you must do. And the help of all true gods go with you."

With that Draffut slid away, moving in eerie silence, and, almost without causing a ripple, submerged himself to his neck. In this position he began to swim very quietly toward the two approaching boats. Zoltan, still fully clothed, moved after him.

In only a few moments the Lord of Beasts had reached the boats, and once more the night erupted in clamor and confusion. Once more the giant reared his full height out of the water, and closed his grip upon a wooden gunwale. And in rapid succession these craft too were tipped and emptied of their screaming rowers. Again the men in the boats had scrambled to grab up their weapons and use them against this incredible apparition—only to find themselves in the water, struggling just to breathe and find their footing, before they could even attempt to fight.

Draffut was roaring now, giving the signal agreed upon that there were no prisoners here for him to rescue; and Zoltan reacted accordingly. He, unlike Draffut, was under no compulsion to avoid harming the enemy. Swimming methodically into the tumult of bobbing heads and thrashing limbs, Zoltan picked out his target quickly. Close ahead of him the faint glint of moonlight on partial armor showed him a foe who was ill-equipped for watery combat.

Approaching this man from behind, Zoltan struck silently, taking his victim around the neck and thrusting him under the surface. The bubbles of the man's last breath came up unnoticed by any of his struggling comrades.

A few moments later Zoltan was fumbling under water to lift the helmet from the lifeless head, and pull the drowned man's short cape free at the neck and shoulders. The remaining armor, he thought, ought to be enough to weight the body down.

With the helmet now jammed uncomfortably on his own head, and the waterlogged cape trailing behind him, he waited his chance to seize one of the drifting oars. Once he had this minimum of support in hand, he struck out through the cold water for the castle, paddling with his free hand and kicking briskly.

In the water around him, on every side, others were making progress in similar ways. None of the soldiers were now close enough to Zoltan to get a good look at him, or exchange conversation. He did his best to maintain this situation, preserving a certain distance.

The cold was numbing, but his steady efforts gradually brought the castle nearer. Looking up at those stone walls and towers from the very level of the lake, Zoltan saw them grow more and more intimidating. But it was too late now for second thoughts about his plan; he doubted that he would be able to reach the distant mainland from here by swimming, and there was no telling where Draffut might have got to now.

By now he was close enough to the castle docks to get a good look at the soldiers there. But their activities were not that much easier to comprehend. People appeared to be getting into boats and out of them again. Perhaps some large exchange, as of entire companies, between the castle and the town's garrison had been in progress when Draffut began to disrupt traffic.

Whatever orderly process had been going on had been disrupted, and small wonder, with all the screams and havoc out on the darkened lake, and now with half-drowned, half-frozen refugees swimming in. By now the officers on the dock must have communicated with their superiors, and there would be a discussion going on of what had happened, and whether it was necessary to involve the next higher layer of authority. There were more torches now than ever on the docks, and by their light men were trotting to and fro, into the castle and out of it again.

Zoltan, swimming now within a few meters of the dock—and really sure for the first time that he was going to be able to reach it—took note of what was happening as one man and then another climbed out of the water ahead of him. He rejoiced to see that these arrivals were going almost unnoticed. And now a further distraction for the officers on the dock—out of the darkness behind Zoltan another burst of distant oaths and splashing. Draffut, in timely fashion, had evidently found yet another boat to capsize.

No one on the docks paid more than momentary attention to Zoltan as he, in his turn, scrambled up out of the water, shivering and gasping, to crawl across the stones. No one came forward to help him, any more than they had helped any of the half-dead stragglers who lay wheezing and quaking on the paving blocks around him. Those men who were able to stand up immediately after their swim were being ordered on into the castle through the small connecting gate that now stood open. A sergeant who stood beside the gate was bawling something about a formation in a courtyard. Deeper inside the castle, bugles were sounding, and drums beating; it was evident that at least a partial alert had been declared.

Trying to jam his ill-fitting helmet more securely on his head, Zoltan got quickly to his feet and hurried in through the gate. Here there were fewer torches, and he paused to try to wring some of the water from his cape, meanwhile looking about him. So far, in the semidarkness and confusion, no one had noticed that his clothing under the cape was not a uniform.

Water splattered from the cape as he squeezed and twisted its rough fabric. Not far ahead of him, framed by another gateway, Zoltan could see a large courtyard aswarm with military preparations. It was from there that the drums and bugles sounded, and it was there that he particularly did not wish to go.

On his right, a darkened stairway offered the most obvious opportunity to turn aside; Zoltan seized that opportunity, and went trotting lightly and silently up.

On the first dim landing he paused briefly to listen and look back, trying to make sure that no one below had noticed him slipping away. Then, deciding that he had already attained a level comfortably above most of the lights and activity, he started out to explore.

Exploring in darkness, through totally unfamiliar territory, was slow and difficult work at best. Presently, seeking to find an area in which he could at least see where he was going, Zoltan took another stair upward. This ascent was a narrow and winding one, and proved longer than he had expected. When at last he came to a window he was able to see, on the tower levels of the castle that were higher still, more lights and several sentries. These guards were standing at attention or pacing slowly, and appeared calmly unaffected by the turmoil among their comrades at ground level.

Zoltan stepped back from the window, drawing a deep breath. Slowly an unwelcome fact was impressing itself upon him: now that he was here, he had no plan of what to do next. It had been easy enough to say, at a distance: find Prince Mark. But if Mark was here, and still alive, where was he being held?

Doing his best to think constructively upon that point, Zoltan decided that any prisoner so eminent and important would more likely be locked up in one of these towers than in a dungeon. He had of course no real evidence to support that point of view; but now it crossed his mind that Lady Yambu, assuming she had been able to reach the castle and was still here, would probably also be housed in one of these towers. He could not really picture her being thrown into a dungeon whatever happened. And if Zoltan could reach her, she might be able to help him, or at least provide him with some information about Mark.

After another pause, to squeeze more water out of his uniform cape and other clothing, Zoltan began trying to work his way toward the base of one of the towers that he considered promising. Since he was totally unfamiliar with the layout of the rooms and corridors here, and having at times to grope his way through almost total darkness, a number of false starts and detours were inevitable. At one point, alerted by approaching torchlight, he took shelter in a darkened niche as a youth he took to be a messenger went trotting by.

Pausing in yet another darkened passage, trying yet again to press more water from his garments, the shivering Zoltan wondered whether he ought now to dispose of helmet and cape, and try to pass himself off as a servant or some other civilian worker. He had seen a few such, at a distance, since entering the castle. But he supposed that if he did that his wetness would draw more attention. His clothes were not going to dry quickly on this chill, damp night. Until he could manage a total change of clothing, he had better stay as much as possible in darkness.

He moved on slowly, looking for an opportunity to change his garments. Here was a row of doors, and some of them opened willingly enough when he pushed on them—these were small storerooms, but either empty or filled with moldering, useless junk. It seemed that Honan-Fu, or someone in his household, had been unwilling to throw anything away.

It appeared that nothing so convenient as a clothing store was going to present itself to Zoltan's need. When he had moved past the last of the storerooms, more windows showed him another tower, a good part of it lighted. In one of those high rooms, he thought with a shudder, his archenemy himself might well be quartered. He who called himself the Ancient One might even be peering out of one of those high windows at this moment, while receiving reports from his officers on the disturbances in the lake below. Zoltan shuddered once again, remembering his one contact with that man—if indeed he could be called a man—some two years ago.

Zoltan moved on from the windows. At last, in a disused closet, he found some garments hanging on a row of pegs along a wall. There was a dry, shapeless, almost sizeless smock, which hid most of his own clothing when he put it on. Concealing the helmet and the still-dripping cape behind some junk in a dark corner of the closet, he at last felt ready to try to pass among the enemy.

He would have to be one of the lower class of servants now; no one else would wear a garment so disreputable as this smock. Acting on an inspiration, Zoltan grabbed up a pot sitting on the closet floor. The vessel looked as if it might once have been used to carry water, or grain; he would take it with him. Looking as if you were already busy was the best protection against the curiosity of authority.

Now he could postpone the real search for his uncle no longer. Ready or not, he was going to have to let himself be seen.

He made his way, with some difficulty, from the area of the storerooms and closets into the base of one of the lighted towers. Zoltan could curse himself for not having foreseen the complexity of this place; but he had not, and the only thing to do now was try to get on with the job. Still, it was beginning to seem to him that the job of finding his uncle must be a hopeless one.

Then he urged himself to get a grip on his nerves. Surely it would not be necessary for him to search everywhere inside the castle. The number of apartments in this particular tower was certainly quite limited, and when he had somehow eliminated all of them he would move on to the next—

Rounding a sharp corner, Zoltan unexpectedly found himself confronting two figures in the corridor just ahead of him. The taller was a being with reptilian attributes: short, leathery wings, and a face no more than halfway human. In an instant he knew that he was facing, for the second time in his life, the terrible wizard known now as the Ancient One.

Zoltan recoiled, his hand going to his side in search of a weapon that was no longer there, that had been taken from him when he was captured. A weapon that would have been useless in any case, because—because—

The horror in front of him was standing still,

looking at him, saying nothing. But over its bestially deformed shoulder there appeared another face, calm and recognizable, that of Lady Yambu.

She said: "Zoltan, you need not be afraid. This is not who you think."

Zoltan sagged against a wall. "Ben?" he asked softly.

The horror shook its head. "I am not Ben," it informed him.

# CHAPTER 15

THE fastest and most direct route from the front of Lady Ninazu's manor back to the docks lay through the grounds rather than around the outer wall. Ben, half-urging the lady, half-towing her with him, was moving from the arena where the performance had taken place back toward the main gate. He was about to reenter that gate and then cut through the grounds to reach the boats when he was accosted by two men wearing rough civilian garb.

He might have pushed them aside, but at the last moment he recognized the younger one as Haakon of the bushy eyebrows, who had once introduced himself as a member of Honan-Fu's constabulary.

Ben stopped. Haakon and Ben gazed at each other for a moment in silence. Both of the local men ignored Lady Ninazu completely. On the field in front of the manor, meanwhile, the laughter was becoming louder, more certainly hysterical.

Raising his voice to make himself heard above the noise, the man who was accompanying Haakon said to Ben: "Haakon tells me you are no friend of those rats who have moved in on the island. Well? Quickly, we have no time to waste."

"Well then, Haakon is telling you the truth. What of it? I'm in a hurry too."

Lady Ninazu did not appear to be offended by the

fact that the men were ignoring her. She stood waiting patiently for the moment, looking from one to another of the three men as if trying to gauge the truth about them.

"Nor are we friends of this invader who calls himself the Ancient One," said the speaker to Ben. He was tall, with brown skin, white hair, and a grave manner. "I am Cheng Ho, and I was once a captain in the Triplicane constabulary." He jerked his head toward the Emperor, who was still cavorting down at the far end of the field while waves of noise, noise that could no longer be called merriment, surrounded him. "Who is this man in the clown mask? We have served Honan-Fu for years, and have seen the magicians who visited him, and their contests; and yet we have never seen wizardry like this."

Suddenly Lady Ninazu seemed to awaken. She was impatient to be gone, and not about to allow Maxim the Strong to waste any more of his time with this riffraff.

Ben didn't want to lose her, or offend her either, and so he had to be quick. He said to the two local men: "All I can tell you in a few words about the one in the mask yonder is that you should trust him, if you are no friends of the invading soldiers. That is what I am doing now, trusting his advice. As far as I know, he is a magician without equal—and certainly he can have no love for those who now occupy the castle on the island."

Haakon and Cheng Ho had both taken notice of the lady now, and it seemed to Ben that they were about to speak to her—or to him about her. But her brief interval of patience was evidently exhausted. She would brook no further delays, and Ben allowed himself to be towed and ordered after her.

The uproar made by the soldiers in the field behind them went on without pause as Ben and the lady passed through the unguarded gate and reentered the manor grounds. Taking a last look back Ben could see that the great majority of the civilian audience had already departed. A few of the soldiers were still on their feet, and appeared to be running aimlessly about. But the ground was covered with bodies in gray and red, kicking and convulsing.

The sounds made by the Emperor's enemies followed Ben and Lady Ninazu all across the darkened grounds. Again she led him at a fast walk, as if her vision was indeed keener in the dark than that of any ordinary girl or woman. Or perhaps it was only that she had spent so much time in these grounds that she knew the location of each tree. Presently they were moving past the arbor in which Ben had first encountered her, its lanterns now burning low; and now they were once more approaching the gate that led out to the boathouse and the docks.

Together they listened carefully at the portal before Ben opened it. All was quiet outside, and when Ben swung back the gate there was no one there. Probably, he thought, all the soldiers had gone round to the front of the manor, attracted by sounds the like of which they had never heard before.

Those sounds, not much diminished by the modest distance and the intervening walls, were still a great deal louder than he would have preferred.

The oars that Ben had begun to put in place were still where he had dropped them, in the bottom of the little boat. There was no one to stop him now as he handed the lady down into the boat, and saw her seated in the stern, wearing an attitude of somewhat precocious dignity.

"You are a worthy servant, Maxim." She gave the pronouncement a judicious sound.

"Thank you, ma'am," Ben returned. *And I may at last prove myself a worthy friend*, he thought, *if I can still get out to that demon-damned island in time to do the Prince some good.* And he told himself, for perhaps the thousandth time since Mark had been taken, that whoever had taken him was not likely to have killed him as quickly as this, or even to have harmed him very much as yet. They would be hoping to learn too much from him to do that. Hoping to learn too much, and also to collect a royal ransom.

Ben cast loose the boat, and then settled himself on the middle thwart, and with steady, powerful strokes of the oars he began to propel himself and Lady Ninazu toward the glittering, magical-looking castle on its distant island.

He rowed and rowed, but for a long time the terrible laughter of the stricken soldiers, like the dancing reflection of the manor's lights, continued to follow them over the water. Plainly all of the townspeople of Triplicane, from one end of the settlement to the other, would be able to hear that sound. Those who had been present would spread the story. All who heard the sound or the story would marvel, and some of them would be brave enough to investigate to find out what was happening. Before morning the great bulk of the local population would be aware that the invaders had been dealt a serious blow. Ben had not stayed long enough to be sure exactly what was happening to the garrison, but he suspected that a good portion of their fighting force was being effectively wiped out.

If the lady, seated on her cushions in the stern of the rowboat, had any thoughts at all about the horrible laughter and what might be happening to those who laughed, she kept those thoughts to herself. It was rather as if she was almost entirely caught up in the anticipation of reaching some long-desired goal, and that goal involved her getting to the castle. Holding herself elegantly erect, she leaned forward slightly on her seat, staring into the night past Ben. Evidently she was feasting her eyes upon the torchlit structure ahead of them as his efforts slowly but surely brought it nearer. From time to time, in crisp impatience, she uttered a sharp word or two, urging Ben to greater efforts at the oars.

He responded with eager nods and smiles to these commands, and continued to set his own pace, which was already about as brisk as he felt capable of keeping up across the distance without exhaustion. He expected that he might well need some reserves of strength and wind when he arrived.

Facing the stern of the boat as he rowed, Ben observed how the dark bulk of the manor and its surrounding walls and trees still hid the continuing performance of the Show of Ensor from his sight; a concealment for which he continued to feel grateful. Even with his own immediate fate to be concerned about, along with Mark's and Zoltan's, he still found even the sounds of that performance to be unpleasantly distracting. There were stretches of time as Ben rowed, sometimes periods of several minutes, in which the cacophony of that murderous laughter seemed to be abating not at all with the increasing distance.

Only in Ben's imagination could he now see what might be happening in the arena of the performance; and that uncertain vision showed him the Emperor still playing his own kind of joke, still cavorting in the guise of humility and humor even while the ground around him was littered thickly with his victims, who one after another expired in purple-visaged chokings.

There was no wind tonight to blow those sounds away, and sound as always traveled far over water. At least what slight current there might be in the lake appeared to Ben to be favorable, bearing the rowboat on toward its goal.

Ben rowed, and in the midst of his rowing there came a noisy but more natural-sounding disturbance from some distance in the darkness to his left. He looked in that direction, but the faint glow of moonlight on the broad expanse of water showed him nothing helpful. Now the noise came again, of men's voices shouting raggedly, followed by a heavy splashing as if a boat might have been somehow overturned. Ben altered his course a trifle, intending to give a wide berth to the trouble, whatever it might be.

"What are you doing, Maxim? You are turning off course."

"Beggin' your pardon, ma'am, but it sounded like some trouble off that way. Drunken soldiers or whatever. We don't want to be stopped now, we want to get on to the castle without any interference."

"You have a point there, Maxim. Very well, you may deviate. But not too widely."

Again the lady sat gazing at the faerie structure ahead, all faint moonlight and mysterious shadows punctuated by sparks of flame. "That is my home, Maxim. And now at last, after many years, I am going there again." Suddenly she fixed Ben with a sharp look. "You have never seen my twin brother, have you? The young lord Kunderu?"

"No, ma'am. I haven't had that privilege."

"You are right to put it in those terms. He is, you know, more like a god than like a man, more beautiful even than . . . and when I think of what our father has done to him—I do not see why the new lord of the castle refuses to set him free."

Ben had no ideas on that subject, and in fact he judged it best to keep as silent as possible on all matters political and familial. He grunted and wheezed a little, to demonstrate that he was going to need all his breath just to keep up the pace at which he continued to row. And in truth he was in a hurry. Looking at the stars and estimating the remaining distance to the castle dock, he judged that they would do well to complete the trip within an hour.

Briefly he considered whether he might do better to pull all the way around the island, and try to come ashore on the side opposite the castle docks. But there might well be no way to get into the castle on that side. And besides, the lady's growing tension as they approached the island convinced him that she would stand for no further detours without a very vigorous protest. There would be screaming, at the least.

So far the wench had said no more about her father. Even stranger than that, perhaps, was the fact that her father seemed to have had her under long-term house arrest, in her own house—and still more curious, the new regime had evidently continued the confinement.

What would be the reaction of the soldiers on the docks when they saw that the daughter of Honan-Fu had been rowed out to them? Surely she had at least some arguable right to visit the castle, and so a simple, bold approach would be the best. As for Ben himself, particularly in his strongman's costume of animal skin, with arms and legs left bare, he was probably not the most convincing personal attendant for a lady of high rank. But he was committed now to playing the role—and the Emperor had seemed to think he was capable of succeeding in it.

By now, at last, those horrible sounds from the mainland had faded to the point where they could only intermittently be heard at all. Chances were that the people in the castle would not have heard them, and very likely they would not know that anything untoward had happened to their garrison ashore.

Such was the continuing confusion on the docks as the little boat approached that its arrival was scarcely noticed. One large rowboat appeared to be loading with soldiers, at the direction of a shouting sergeant, while another one unloaded. And all the time occasional swimmers came straggling in, some supporting themselves on oars or bits of driftwood, others relying upon no more than their limbs and lungs. Some of these attempted to cling to the boat that Ben was rowing as he drew near the dock, but at a sharp command from the lady he beat them off with an oar. When he saw that they were castle soldiers he had no reluctance to do so.

As soon as they touched at the dock, Ben jumped out briskly and tied up. Then he turned to offer proper assistance to the lady. She accepted his arm, as impersonally as she might have gripped a ladder's rung, and stepped ashore to face the blank stares of a pair of officers in red and gray. By now these men had become aware that this arrival represented something unusual, even for this night, and they had suspended their argument over some other matter to see what the lady's presence might portend.

Confronting these officers with her best regal stare, Lady Ninazu demanded: "I am the daughter of Honan-Fu, and the twin sister of your prisoner Kunderu. You will take me to my brother at once!"

The officers exchanged wary glances with each other, then turned back to this demanding woman. Ben reflected that it was probably not strange that they should not recognize her—they were doubtless as much outlanders here as he was himself.

At last one of the men replied, with cautious courtesy: "I know of no such person in this castle, lady."

"Oh, do you not? Then I will see to it that you soon learn. Take me at once to your lord, the Ancient Master. He will teach you to speak to me with more respect!"

That set the pair of them back a little. After a brief whispered conference their next step, as Ben had already foreseen, was to summon a superior. Meanwhile Ben himself stood back as much as he could on the small dock, trying to be as unobtrusive as his size and costume would allow, a model slave or servant. If the superior when he arrived should happen to be one who happened to be able to identify the much-sought Ben of Purkinje at a glance . . .

But the fates were kind, and it was a total stranger. This man, bowing lightly to the lady, took charge of the situation skillfully. Treating her with soothing words, he got her to follow him, telling her that in a minute or two all would be arranged just as she wished.

Ben, feeling impossibly large and conspicuous to fit his chosen role of shadowy attendant, nevertheless fell in behind. He would seize the first chance that presented itself to let him slip away.

Before that chance came, he and the lady were led into a kind of waiting room, grimly furnished, and the door closed behind them. Lady Ninazu, trying to open the door again to shout some demand at the men, discovered that it had been not only closed but locked. Immediately she was outraged; but her shouts and her pounding on the wooden panels went unheeded.

# CHAPTER 16

A RNFINN, having as he did the powers of the Sword of Stealth at his command, had experienced no difficulty in obtaining Lady Yambu's release from her comfortable confinement. He had not even found it necessary to speak to the guards who flanked her door. The moment he appeared in the corridor before them they had bowed themselves out of his way.

Stepping forward, he reached for the handle on the door, found that it was unlocked, and went on in. The lady, wearing her pilgrim's gray, was standing in the middle of the room looking at him with an air of confident expectation. And there was something stranger than that in her expression. Arnfinn thought it was almost the same look she had worn at their first encounter, when she and her two friends had taken away his Sword.

Gripping Sightblinder's hilt tighter than ever, Arnfinn moved backward a step to stand against the door as he closed it behind him. He thought to himself: *If those other two are here now, and they try to do that again, I'll kill them. I'll hack them to bits.* Even his untrained hands could feel that, apart from magic, this weapon had just the edge and weight needed to do that kind of work. And no one was going to take it away from him again.

But no men came rushing at him from concealment among the draperies, or leaped up from behind the furniture in ambush. Instead there was only the old lady, who stood alone in the middle of the floor and faced him calmly. Still looking at Arnfinn rather oddly, as he thought, she repeated her earlier question: "Is it Zoltan, or Ben?"

By now, Arnfinn thought he could guess who Zoltan and Ben must be. He said: "I am neither one of them. They are not here to help you now."

For a moment the lady's calm wavered, and she almost stuttered: "If it is—if you are—"

"I am a friend of Lady Ninazu, and also of her imprisoned brother. Who are you?"

The lady seemed to find the question reassuring. Her face assumed a sort of friendly blankness, and for a short time she was busy with her thoughts. Then she said: "I am Lady Yambu. I do not know the lady you speak of, or her brother either. What is his name?"

"His name is Kunderu, and they are twins, the daughter and son of Honan-Fu the wizard. Tell me where Kunderu is being held, and nothing bad will happen to you." Gripping the great Sword with both hands, Arnfinn swung the blade a little, suggestively. But the old woman's eyes did not follow it; as like as not, he supposed, the image she saw of him would not be bearing a weapon.

If she was aware of the Sword in Arnfinn's hands she was managing to ignore it. All she said was: "I have not heard of either of them."

"I tell you Kunderu and Ninazu are the old wizard's children." Arnfinn could not escape the sudden feeling that this woman was making a fool of him again, or at least there was great likelihood of her doing so.

"That may well be," she replied calmly, "but I am only a sojourner in this country, a pilgrim, and their names mean nothing to me. Now tell me, who are you?"

With the sullen conviction that he was somehow

losing all the advantage that the Sword ought to have given him, Arnfinn grumbled: "What image do you see when you look at me?"

The lady looked him up and down. "My eyes tell me that you are the magician who is called the Ancient One, who is now lord of this castle and of much else besides. And I hear your voice as his. But by your words and your behavior I am quite sure that you are someone else, and that you have with you the Sword of Stealth, although I cannot see it. Besides that, when you were out on the balcony a few moments ago I saw your image change before my eyes—that often happens when one is holding that Sword. Sightblinder is powerful, but like the rest of the Twelve it has its limitations."

"I suppose so," said Arnfinn, trying his best to sound like an expert in these matters. He hesitated, then took a plunge. "Lady Yambu, I mean you no harm. Have those guards been set outside your door to keep you in, or to keep others away?"

"To keep me in. The one whose image you now wear has so far treated me with courtesy, but . . ." With a small gesture, as if to appeal to fate, the lady left the sentence unfinished.

"Then I can set you free. But in return you must help me find Kunderu, and free him too. That is all I want."

"I accept your offer," the lady replied with very little hesitation. "With Sightblinder to help us we ought to be able to do that much if we use a little cleverness. I don't suppose you would be willing to let me carry it for a while—? No, I thought not. But still I believe an alliance between us will benefit us both. You see, I am interested in the welfare of another man who is a prisoner here."

"All right." Arnfinn slowly sheathed the heavy Sword. "You and I have an alliance, then. I would be willing to bet that you know more about castles than I do. What do we do first?"

"I think, Your Ancient Lordship, that we must begin by exploring and finding things out. If everyone here in the castle sees in you the same image that I do, which I suppose is quite likely, then that part should be easy enough. If not, we improvise. Out into the corridor, then I suggest turning right. I believe that will lead us into more interesting territory. You go first, I'll walk half a step behind, as would be appropriate if you were really the one you look like. You turn to me if we meet someone and you wish advice on any point. Or I'll whisper in your ear if and when I think it necessary."

Arnfinn was willing to accept this plan, and said as much. Opening the door, he led the way.

The two guards had returned to their posts beside the door, but again they backed away making obeisances as soon as he appeared.

Ignoring them, Arnfinn turned to the right and strode on. As soon as they had rounded the first corner, the lady whispered in his ear: "Above all, we must do our best to avoid the real master of this stronghold. And if we—but wait."

She laid her fingers on Arnfinn's arm. Just beyond the next turn of the short hallway, someone was approaching.

It was a young man, walking alone, who came into sight. Arnfinn, with some surprise, recognized him as the one he had struck down to regain the Sword. Now the youth was wearing a disreputable servant's smock, and he recoiled instantly as soon as he saw Arnfinn.

At once the lady, looking over Arnfinn's shoulder, said to the other: "Zoltan, you need not be afraid. This is not who you think."

The youth in the smock let himself sag against the wall. "Ben?" he inquired softly.

Arnfinn shook his head. "I am not Ben."

"Who are you, then?"

But again Arnfinn would answer that question only with stubborn silence.

The lady interceded. "Zoltan, we can discuss that matter later. Right now we are on our way to release a couple of prisoners—including the one in whom you and I are interested. And as soon as we've accomplished that, we can all start on our way back to the mainland. Our anonymous ally here should have no trouble in arranging passage for us all aboard a boat."

Zoltan brightened quickly at this news. "And just where are these prisoners to be found?"

"I know where to start, at least," the lady answered, somewhat to Arnfinn's surprise. "At ground level, just off a certain courtyard. Come along, both of you, I'll show you."

Under Lady Yambu's unobtrusive guidance, and with Zoltan following two steps behind in his role of humble servant, they proceeded down some stairs and out into the open night. Small gatherings of people, almost entirely male and military, were in the various courtyards, and parted silently to give the three room to pass. Arnfinn rejoiced; apparently there were times, as Lady Yambu had suggested, when all onlookers saw the one who carried the Sword as the same person. There were salutes and deep bows directed at Arnfinn, and a few heads turned to look after him and his two companions, as if in wonder as to where the Ancient Master was going with the lady and the wretched-looking servant; but no one asked a question. He acknowledged the salutes with a vague gesture, and did his best to look as if he knew where he was going.

As the three were crossing one of the wider open spaces, there came a faint sound from high above. Looking up in the direction of the tallest tower, Zoltan saw the griffin, small with height, and with the figure of a man astride its back. It went leaping out of the aerie into the night sky. The creature's wings worked powerfully, and in a moment it and its rider were out of sight among the stars.

Some of the onlookers in the courtyard dropped

their gaze from the starry sky to Arnfinn, then looked back up into the night again, as if they could not believe their eyes. But if their suspicions were aroused, they were not expressed, at least not within hearing of their great lord who apparently stood before them.

Lady Yambu was again holding Arnfinn by the arm, as any lady might hold that of her escort. This allowed her to exert a slight pressure by which she guided him in the direction she wished to go. In this way they crossed the central courtyard with its grim high altar, charred and empty now, and reached a small closed gate. Here, too, guards stepped aside. Arnfinn himself pushed the gate open.

When some of the guards would have followed the three into the dark, grottolike space behind the gate, Lady Yambu whispered in the ear of her lordly escort. And at his gesture the intruding men fell back, one of them first handing him a torch.

And now at the last moment before they passed into the darkness beyond the gate there was another delay. An officer came hurrying across the wide courtyard, approached Arnfinn, and whispered to him so quietly that not even Lady Yambu could hear. The message was that one who claimed to be Lady Ninazu had reached the island in a small boat and insisted on seeing the lord of the castle.

Arnfinn's heart leaped in his chest. He was ready to order that he be taken to Ninazu at once, or she be brought to him. But her presence would add another complication to the rescue of Kunderu, and besides he was still ashamed to face her. His duty lay here, trying to free her brother as rapidly as possible.

"Have her wait," he replied to the officer, who murmured his acknowledgment of the order and faded away.

But still the delays were not over. There was a fresh outcry on the far side of the court.

\* \* \*

Lady Ninazu, on finding herself locked into the dank waiting room, had wasted no time in futile shouts and protests. Instead, she gave up rattling at the door after only a couple of ineffective shakes, turned to Ben, pointed dramatically at the lock, and ordered: "Break it open!"

Ben liked the locked door much less than she did, but he had a tactical suggestion. "Your pardon, my lady, but there's likely to be someone in the corridor outside who would take notice if we did that. It might be wiser to take a look at the windows first." Their place of detention was on the ground floor, and a quick glance through the windows showed a darkened areaway outside that offered some prospect of escape.

The lady thought for a moment, then nodded her agreement. Ben found that the inward shutters opened easily. Then to his disappointment, but hardly to his surprise, he discovered an iron grillwork on the outside of the windows that effectively prevented any passage. The bars looked no more than ornamental, not really the kind of barriers you would find in a dungeon, but they were discouragingly thick and his first trial of bare-handed strength against them achieved nothing.

There were voices in the corridor outside the door; that way still did not look attractive. Ben concentrated his attention on one of the windows while the lady looked on with approval. She would have liked, Ben was sure, to urge him to greater efforts, but she evidently realized that nagging at him now was only likely to slow things down, and with a major effort was managing to restrain herself.

As Ben cast about for something to serve him as a wrecking bar, his eyes fell on a wooden bench that made up a large part of the plain furnishings of the room. A brace that ran along the bench's back was long and stout enough to serve as an effective lever, he thought. Ben picked up the bench and with a few swift movements knocked off its ends and legs against the stone wall. A moment after that he had violently separated the back and seat from the component that he wanted. The whole process had made only a moderate amount of noise.

Now Ben had his sizable chunk of timber, long as a man's body and thick as his arm. With this inserted between the bars, Ben was able to pry at them and start them moving. But he was able to bend the ironwork only a small distance before his timber lever was balked by coming against the heavy masonry at the side of the window.

But now the tenure of the metalwork in its sockets had been much weakened. Ben dropped the lever. Taking his time, he tried out several grips, getting his hands into the most effective positions that he could find. Then he exerted all the strength that he could summon up.

He could feel the veins in his forehead standing out, and what might have been the tearing of muscle fibers in his quivering arms.

Gasping, he let go and slumped against the stonework. The bars were not going to yield. Not yet, anyway. He had to rest for a few moments.

While he was resting, panting and leaning against the wall, the lady came closer, bright-eyed, to watch him. But still, thankfully, she had no advice to offer or orders to declare.

He looked at her, and nodded his appreciation for her noninterference. Then he bent to his task again.

It just came down to this. That he was going to have to bend these bars. He could not afford to remain locked up here, helpless, until someone came along who recognized him.

With a small explosion, one end of one bar came free of its mortared socket in the wall. The break sent small fragments of stone and brick spraying almost silently out into the night.

Once more Ben rested, gasping. A gap had been created now, but it was probably not wide enough for even a slender lady to slide through. Probably, he thought, two more bars were going to have to go.

Still, he could use only his bare hands. But now he could shift his grip and obtain a great advantage in leverage. In only a moment the next bar had assumed a U-shape, looking as if it might now fit the hoof of some giant riding-beast.

Again he paused, just long enough for a few gasping breaths. His hands were callused from a lifetime of hard use, and when he looked at them he saw that the skin was still intact. Good. He was going to need all his blood and energy.

The lady, her patience wearing out, began to nag at Ben in a whisper, sounding like the angry child she was. If only, she was saying, she could get to speak to the Ancient One himself, all would be well. She would have these incompetent officers who had delayed her boiled in oil. And then, when at last she reached her brother and made sure of his release, she would have Ben rewarded—

Ben ceased to pay attention. He forbore to ask her just why this Ancient One, if he was truly her great friend as she claimed, still insisted on keeping her brother locked up. Instead he gently hoisted the lady through the window, then forced his own great shoulders out. He had to bend the second bar yet a little more before he was quite able to fit through. Then he and Lady Ninazu were standing side by side on the dark pavement, with nothing between them and the stars.

Ben whispered: "Now, where are the prisoners kept? Have you any idea, ma'am?"

She raised her eyes. "My brother will be found high in that central tower. If we were on the other side of it I could point out to you the very windows of his room. But—before we go to him, I think I ought to talk to the Ancient Master." She paused, looking around her uncertainly.

"Are you sure that would be a good idea, my lady?"

"Of course it would. Who are you to question my

decisions on such a matter?"

"I am no one, my lady." He wondered if the time would come when it would be good policy to strangle her.

"Of course you are not." She looked round her and appeared to get her bearings. There were several exits from the areaway in which they stood. Ben prepared to follow, at the most cautious distance she would tolerate. At the earliest opportunity he meant to separate himself from her and start in earnest to look for Mark—or try to make contact with Lady Yambu, if the opportunity offered. He felt reasonably confident that she was here somewhere.

Boldly the young lady started walking straight toward the central tower, the one she had indicated earlier. Ben followed, out of the areaway and into a relatively well-lighted court. But before he had moved more than a score of paces, there was an outcry behind him.

What seemed like a whole company of soldiers were running after them; the uniforms seemed to come pouring out of every passageway and crevice in the stones. There was no way to avoid them. Before Ben could quite decide that the time had come to fight to the death, the odds were hopeless, and he and the lady were both closely surrounded.

"My lady," an officer shouted, "you were told to wait!" There was no great courtesy in his tone.

Lady Ninazu flared back with angry words, which seemed to make little impression on the officer. Ben had just resigned himself to the probable necessity of making a hopeless fight after all when a shout from somewhere in the middle distance made him wait again. "What— ho? What have you there?" The voice, unfamiliar to Ben, was harsh and masculine.

Ben, turning slowly and carefully, beheld a tall, ghastly, half-reptilian figure. From the fervent descriptions often given him by Zoltan, he had no difficulty in recognizing one who had to be the Ancient One himself.

The call had interrupted Lady Ninazu's heartfelt and outraged protests; she too had fallen silent for the moment. Like Ben she had turned to look across the courtyard to where the tall, malignant figure stood waving at their captors.

A moment later Ben, experiencing a sensation of dislocation, realized that the small, pale face looking toward him over one of the figure's shoulders was that of Lady Yambu. And that the face of Zoltan, looking not at all like that of a defeated victim, was peering at him past the other. Even at the distance Ben thought that Zoltan looked as if he would have liked to wink but did not quite dare.

Ben let out his breath, making a sound somewhere between a chuckle and a sob.

The guards who had surrounded Lady Ninazu and himself were saluting the monster across the courtyard, and they were not slow or slovenly about it. In response to gestures and shouted orders from that commanding figure, they put up their weapons and withdrew.

Ben, moving on shaky legs, led the way across the courtyard. Lady Ninazu, for all the demands that she had made to be taken to the new master of this castle, was not so eager now, and hung back slightly. A moment later Ben and the two ladies, along with Zoltan and whoever had the Sword, were shut inside the little grottolike enclosure surrounding the deep, black pool.

When at last Arnfinn, Zoltan, and Lady Yambu were inside the grotto, Zoltan pulled the gate closed after them again. Then he and Arnfinn looked around them uncertainly. It was a narrow place, open to the sky but closely confined between high walls into which fantastic niches and decorations had been carved and built out of the dark stone. The grotto was only a small place, but still the single torch, in the hand of the Sword-bearer, seemed inadequate to light it.

Almost all of the ground space was taken up by the surface of the black, deep-looking pool, with only a rim of pavement around its edge. Ben looked in puzzlement at the surrounding walls, and the two ropes that went down into the still water. On the far side of the pool, a dim mouth blocked by heavy metal bars was open in the stone, the beginning of a watery tunnel that led out of the pool to some unknown destination.

But Lady Yambu paid no attention to this setting. She went directly to the edge of the well, where the two secured ropes went down into cold, dark, quiet water. She knelt down there, close by the great iron ring to which the ropes were fastened, and rested her fingers on the ropes, one hand to each.

Closing her eyes, she said: "The two of them are still alive down there—I have just enough of the art myself to be able to feel that. Still alive now, but I fear that hauling them back up into the air is likely to kill them."

"The Prince is down there? Under water?" Zoltan was outraged.

*"Down there?"* echoed Ben.

The lady ignored the mild outburst. "Before we haul them up, we should have a counterspell prepared, and someone with skill enough to make it work."

As if involuntarily, she and Zoltan both raised their eyes to the impressive image of the great wizard that stood beside them.

During the last few minutes Arnfinn had been making a firm resolution to strive for suavity and dignity befitting a master magician in all he said. But he forgot his resolution now. "I haven't got," he protested, "magic enough to chase a flea."

Meanwhile Lady Ninazu had been very quiet, almost ignoring the others. She had backed up slowly, moving from the others, and away from the pool as far as the confined space would allow, until her back was leaning against one of the enclosing walls. She had been staring down at the black water and its secrets as if she could guess what those secrets were, and found them frightening.

Now, suddenly, in a tight voice she announced: "Kunderu is not down there. I don't see how he can be."

"If you are the daughter of Honan-Fu," the older lady told her, "then your father is down there. Along with someone you do not know."

The girl appeared to find that relatively acceptable, but still it frightened her. "My father," she repeated thoughtfully.

"So I have been told. Quickly, are you enchantress enough to save these men's lives if we pull them up at once?"

Ninazu nodded abstractedly. "I am a very good enchantress. I could do more than that."

"That will be sufficient for the moment," said Yambu in her queen's voice, and gave a signal. Swiftly Ben and Zoltan stooped over the ropes. Seizing one at random, they began to haul.

As they were working, Lady Yambu straightened up and whispered to the one who had the Sword. He nodded, and in a moment had opened the gate again and was calling out to the soldiers in the court, telling them to bring plenty of food and hot drink, blankets and dry clothing for two men.

Within moments Ben and Zoltan had pulled a human figure out of the water. Lying on the stone pavement with steam forming in the air around it, it appeared to be little more than a whitish blob of ice. The clothing and all the details of its shape were so rimed in pale needles and granules as to render the figure quite unrecognizable beyond the fact of its humanity. It was quite large enough to be the Prince. Only an occasional twitching of the limbs, and a slight, fitful turning back and forth of that ice-encrusted head showed that any life at all remained.

Lady Ninazu, meanwhile, remained drawn back as far as possible from the rescue operation. She had fallen silent again, and the fear she had displayed before was now intensified, and focused on the frozen man.

Suddenly she raised her head, with a motion so sharp and sudden that others turned to look in the same direction. There was only the square darkness of the central tower rising against the stars, punctuated at a few points with the narrow sparks of lighted windows.

"He's not down here," she announced positively. "He's up there." And she raised an arm and pointed with assurance.

"Are you going to help these men?" Yambu demanded in a threatening voice. "You must do it now."

The younger lady might not have heard. She continued staring at the tower.

Yambu went to her and shook her. When that rough treatment had no apparent effect, she slapped Ninazu in the face. The swing was more like a man's blow than a woman's, and it brought forth a little shriek of sheer astonishment.

The slap took Arnfinn by surprise. He shouted at Lady Yambu and took a step toward her. But she ignored him and did not shift her attention from Ninazu.

The older woman pointed with a bony finger to the form stretched on the pavement. "Help this man!" she barked.

And Ninazu, yielding to the other's will, moved closer to the icy figure. Murmuring softly, she began to work a spell.

With a sudden gasp the man on the pavement began to breathe again. The sound of his breathing, hoarse and deep, came as a new presence within these dark stone walls.

Meanwhile the hands of others had been gently picking and brushing the frost away from the Prince's gray-blue face. Already much of the frost was falling and melting away from his body.

After that first deep breath, Mark's body was racked with convulsive shivering. But his breathing continued, gradually steadying into an almost normal rhythm.

And now Zoltan and Ben were drawing the second body up out of the dark water.

And again Ninazu was retreating, shrinking back against the stones of the confining wall. She murmured: "That can't be him, I tell you. He's up in the tower."

Once more Yambu had to bully her. "As I have told you, this man is your father. And you will help him, now, if you want us to help you any further."

The younger woman's eyes turned to Arnfinn. She raised her hand in a gesture of appeal, with wondering eyes, as if she was amazed that he would allow her to be so insulted.

He was silent for a few moments, looking from her to Yambu, and back. Then he said to Ninazu: "My lady, help him. If you please."

Ninazu nodded, with acknowledgment of his command if not belief. Her look was one of dazed incomprehension.

But she turned back toward the pool and repeated the spell that she had used before.

Both victims were now undoubtedly alive and breathing, but neither of them was fully conscious, and it was obvious that both were going to need further help.

There was a rapping on the gate, and Ben opened it to admit soldiers who had come delivering food, hot drinks, the clothing and the blankets that had been ordered, a whole mound of them. Arnfinn went to help Ben take delivery.

Zoltan, attending to the two semiconscious men, muttered: "If we could only get them out to Draffut now—we need a boat for that."

"There is—" Ninazu began, and then stopped as if

she thought she had better say no more.

"There is what?" Arnfinn asked. "What, my beautiful one?" he coaxed.

"There is a small boat here," Ninazu went on reluctantly. "The workers who maintain the pool use it to get back into the channel that leads from the lake into the well."

By bending over and peering back into the tunnel's mouth, it was just possible to see the boat where it was tied up. Reaching it would require opening a metal grillwork that blocked the tunnel entrance.

The grillwork could be opened only from inside the grotto, and Ninazu demonstrated how. In a moment Zoltan was splashing through the water, pulling in the little boat.

Meanwhile Ben and Yambu were frantically busy getting the two victims into dry clothes and trying to feed them broth and brandy. Then they put them into the boat.

"We must get them to Draffut," Ben decided. This was a tactical decision, and Ben was in command.

Zoltan, at Ben's orders, got in and started paddling. The boat was a tiny thing, unseaworthy, really meant for only one occupant. To take it out on the lake with three people was chancy, and to put any more in it would be suicidal.

Now Lady Ninazu approached Arnfinn. "I insist," she dared to say, "that you take me to my brother at once."

# CHAPTER 17

AT about an hour past midnight, the man who called himself the Ancient One had jumped astride his griffin and launched himself confidently into the night air from atop the highest tower of his captured castle.

His main objective was to find out what was happening on the mainland, in particular what had happened to his garrison at Triplicane. The last winged messenger to reach the castle from there had croaked out an almost indecipherable tale of calamity, a disturbing though incoherent report of what sounded like mass slaughter confused with entertainment, the performance of some show. To the Ancient Master it at first sounded like diabolically clever treachery by some member of that garrison.

As soon as the creature had delivered this message, it had simply flown off again into the night, in direct disobedience to orders. That had been more than an hour ago, and the flyer had not returned. Nor had any of the others.

It was also the powerful magician's intention to discover what had suddenly gone wrong with his winged scouts. When he had climbed to the high aerie where his griffin rested, he had found the place empty except for the griffin, the cages and roosts used by the lesser beasts deserted. The two humans who were supposed to be in attendance on the beasts had looked on helplessly, fearful of their master's wrath; the Ancient Master had only glowered at them, a look that promised much, before he hurried on.

Ordinarily he would allow no one but himself to ride the griffin, and unless he gave the griffin special instructions it would refuse to carry anyone but him.

Besides the difficulties on the mainland and the trouble with the scouts, there was another problem also requiring the wizard's attention tonight. Something bizarre was reportedly moving around out in the lake, tipping boats and terrifying troops. All in all, the Ancient Lord had already become sufficiently concerned to take the first preliminary steps toward calling up a certain squadron of demons he had been keeping in reserve, a group that could be mobilized with relative ease. And the calling of demons was not a step that this wizard took lightly; he knew from bitter personal experience how great could be the dangers in trying to use such creatures as servants or allies.

Once he was well airborne, soaring high over the lake, he was able to see that a great many more lights were burning in and around Triplicane than was usual at this hour of the night.

From this altitude he could also see that the lakeside manor occupied by young Lady Ninazu was illuminated even more prodigally than the rest of the town. He decided that he would probably look in at the manor before returning to the castle, whether or not the garbled report of disaster proved to be a false alarm. There was no doubt that Ninazu could be an entertaining wench. There were several things about her that the wizard found especially intriguing, and if he had not been so busy trying to consolidate the gains he had won from Honan-Fu, he would have spent more time with her, or perhaps brought her to the castle—

The griffin was rapidly bearing the magician closer to the town and manor. Now he observed that the open field close before the manor was also encircled by torches, some of which had burned out, though a number were still guttering. They shed enough light upon that field to let him see that it was littered with what appeared to be the bodies of many soldiers, in uniforms of gray and red. The sight banished all thoughts of pleasure for the time being. The wizard who rode the midnight air commanded his griffin to descend. He needed no magical subtleties now to be sure that the report of disaster had not been false.

He was unable to count the bodies quickly enough to have the total before he landed, but certainly there were more than a hundred of them. More than half, at least, of the entire garrison.

What had caused the officers to gather their men here? And what had struck the troops down, once they were assembled?

The wizard landed and at once leaped from his steed's back, drawing Shieldbreaker as he did so. The griffin, as accustomed as any beast could be to even stranger sights than this grim field, sat down as a dog or a lion might, with its forequarters high and its avian forelegs straight. In this position it waited quietly.

The Ancient One, Sword ready in his right hand, looked about him. Shieldbreaker was quiet, indicating that no enemies were lurking in the immediate area now. All across the field the bodies lay in a kind of random distribution; here a pile of several together, there a scattered few, there again an open space. And everywhere the ground could be seen it was lightly trampled, as if by hundreds of human feet.

There was something odd here, something beyond the fact of the slaughter in itself. It took the wizard another moment to realize what it was: many of the signs of a conventional battle were missing, including the inevitable broken weapons, the bits and pieces of equipment cast aside. He could hear no moaning wounded. And in fact, he realized after another moment, there was no blood at all to be seen. The men of his army had fallen in scores, perhaps in hundreds, but not one of them appeared to have drawn his weapon or tried to defend himself.

The light of the moon, now close to setting, combined with the orange glow shed by the guttering flames of the remaining torches, showed him a great, silent mystery.

The magician was not really surprised that no one had yet appeared from the manor or elsewhere to mourn the dead or begin the rituals of burial. The only real surprise, he thought, was that no robbers had yet appeared either. None of the bodies looked as if they had been rifled. Pouches that would hold personal belongings were still intact, here and there rings still showed on fingers.

It was only now that the Ancient Master noticed what appeared to be wagon tracks, running here and there across the short grass and the barren earth. He paced the field eagerly, muttering a short spell that served to enhance his eyesight temporarily. Yes, perhaps half a dozen four-wheeled vehicles, pulled by loadbeasts, had been here briefly, had circled, had unloaded at least part of their cargo and then had loaded up once more and moved out. It appeared that the wagons had departed in the general direction of the southern end of Lake Alkmaar, where it was drained by the outflow of the Tungri. The magician knew from scouting reports that the last road running in that direction ended at a dock, a few kilometers out of town. And at that dock was the beginning of the downriver water-route leading to the lands of the south and west.

There must be some connection, the magician thought, between the wagons and the massacre. But what that connection might be was not immediately apparent.

He intended to find out.

For a time now the Ancient One, raging silently at his bad fortune in being thus victimized, walked back and forth among his dead.

And only after he had walked upon this field of corpses for a time, his thoughts busy with other matters than the physical reality around him, did he realize that not all of the fallen men around him were as yet completely dead.

It was a sound that told him, a soft and intermittent little noise that came and went like breath, and yet did not much resemble any other sound that he had ever heard from human lips. He located the source of the sound, and approached it, and saw one of the fallen bodies moving slightly, shaking lightly on the ground.

Only then did it occur to the wizard that the sound he was hearing might possibly have some relationship to human laughter.

He bent down, and with his strong hands seized this man who unlike his fellows was still breathing, and hoisted him to his feet in an effort to compel him to tell what had happened. But despite his magic the only reply that the magician could elicit was a continuation of the ghastly rhythmic croaking, forced out between swollen lips. The victim's eyes were puffed shut as if with weeping, his whole face was swollen and discolored, and he appeared to be in the last stages of exhaustion.

The wizard now called upon deeper powers, making a renewed effort at enchantment. But still the man died, standing on his feet and trying to laugh, before he could be forced to speak more coherently.

The wizard withdrew his magic, letting the body fall.

Well, if one man had survived, so might another. The magician prowled, striding swiftly, until he found another of the fallen figures stirring, this one a little more vigorously than the first.

In response to a spell directed at him by the magician, this man even managed to get to his feet.

And now he came shambling toward the wizard, a quivering, blank-faced survivor, his uniform begrimed, his weapons still unused at his belt. He stumbled to a halt within a long stride of the Ancient Master.

Commanded to speak, the man rasped out: "The wagons . . . Show of Ensor . . ." The words trailed off.

"Go on! Speak! Speak, I command you!"

". . . dancing girls came out. Men in the front row grabbed 'em. I was thinking, why couldn't I have been standing there, get a chance at a good feel at least. . . . Then . . ." The man's voice died again.

"Then what?"

"Then . . . we all . . . the laughing started."

"The laughing? Speak up clearly!"

"Yessir. Laughing. Like—hee, hee—first there was this big man, in a strongman's costume. He stood behind the girls. And then—*ho, ho*—there was this little clown—"

The soldier swayed on his feet. Sounds, almost recognizable as a kind of laughter, bubbled from his lips again, the last laugh turning into a bright red bubble of blood.

The second man fell dead. The Ancient One bent over him, gesturing. But all the powers of magic that the wizard could bring to bear were ineffective now.

The magician stood back and sent forth a calling spell above the fallen. But there was no spark of life left in their ranks to respond to the power he emanated.

The Ancient Master turned abruptly until he was facing toward the manor's torchlit gate, which was standing closed. That gate had been deserted by those who were supposed to guard Lady Ninazu, and by every other human presence as well.

The wizard had already heard enough about the mysterious figure called the Emperor to think that he could recognize him in this strange new "little clown."

"And now the damned villain has taken flight—got away somewhere—before I could come to grips with him. But no matter. I'll get my hands on him eventually."

He who called himself the Ancient Master remained standing in the middle of the field, his mind and soul engaged now with the next step in the process of summoning up his demons. His eyes, more reptilian than human now, stared at nothing. As he stood there, all but oblivious to his physical surroundings, the stars turned indifferently in their high smooth paths above him. An hour of the night slid by, and then another.

Then suddenly the Ancient Master moved again. Signaling his griffin to follow him, and with the Sword of Force gripped firmly in his right hand, he strode on toward the manor's front gate. Surely someone in there would be able to give him a better report than either of those he'd heard so far.

There were still no attendants in sight as the Ancient One approached the closed grillwork of the gate, but a single shout was enough to bring them out of hiding. Figures in servants' garb scrambled about, and the gate was quickly opened for him from inside.

"What has happened here?" He swept an arm behind him, indicating the field of fallen men. "Why was I not informed of this?"

The steward, summoned by lesser servants, had already appeared and was struggling to find answers. "The flying messengers have all disappeared, dread lord."

"I know that. Someone could have brought word in a boat of what had happened here. Did you see what happened?"

"Not I, sire. But there was nothing that we could do to help your men—"

"Yes, yes. I'll hear about your problems later. Where is Lady Ninazu? She, if no one else, ought to have been aware of what was happening out here. Don't tell me she slept through it all."

"Sire—" The steward was more devastated than ever. "Sire, the lady has disappeared."

"What?"

The servants, though none of them would admit being eyewitness to anything important, took turns in trying to tell the story of the night's events—or rather in trying to avoid personal responsibility for its telling. But eventually it came out in a fashion. After the destruction of the garrison, they had discovered first the lady's absence, and then that a boat was missing. Then a drowned sentry had been found in the water near the docks. And then—

It was at approximately this point that the magician observed one of the stablehands staring at the griffin, as if he had never seen anything like such a beast before, which his Lord knew was not the case.

"What ails you?" the Ancient One demanded sharply.

The man stumbled and stuttered. "Sire, it is only that I had thought that there was only one of them. I mean the one that's still in the stables. The loadbeast one."

"What in all the lands of the demons are you raving about?"

The man stuttered and staggered his way through an explanation of sorts. A trip to the stables to view what he said was really a griffin revealed a very ordinary loadbeast, with no detectable tinge of magic about it at all.

"And you say that *I* came riding on this peasant's animal, and left it here?"

"It must be that I am wrong, sire. Very wrong."

"Either that or you are very mad. Or else someone has been playing jokes." The magician issued terse orders for the man to be locked up until he could return to question him some more, or have him brought to the island for that purpose. But there was no time to investigate this matter now. Indeed, the whole trip to the mainland had taken the Ancient One longer than he had expected. By the time he remounted his griffin and urged it into the air again, the sky in the east was beginning to turn pale with the first faint hints of dawn.

The affair of the slaughtered garrison represented a setback, of course, and he had not made much progress toward solving it. Still, the wizard remained basically confident of his position. With Shieldbreaker at his side, and his demonic reinforcements on their way, he could not see that he had anything seriously to fear.

By now the water of the lake, stretching in a flat plain far to left and right beneath his griffin's wings, was no longer black with night. Now it was glowing very faintly with the reflection of the first beginnings of daylight in the sky.

Something, some moving presence in the lake, drew a slow dark line across that faint metallic glow. Some object tall as a tree, in its majestic passage through the water, was leaving a long triangular wake. The object was a towering, almost man-shaped figure that waded on two legs between two of Lake Alkmaar's little islands—

The Ancient Master uttered a soft exclamation, followed by several magical incantations. Then he murmured a command in his griffin's ear, and the creature turned aside from its direct course to the castle. Down they went.

The wizard had been worried when his subordinates told him of what was happening out on the lake at night, that some strange presence there was wreaking havoc on his boats. And he had become all the more worried, as paradoxical as that seemed to his subordinates, when it became clear that this strange new enemy was not actually killing any of his men. He feared that he could recognize a certain signature in that reluctance —and now in the first tentative light of day that recognition had been confirmed.

The Ancient One commanded his steed to circle Draffut at low altitude, and at a respectful distance. The wader stopped, and his great head turned, following the flight of griffin and wizard without apparent surprise.

At last the shadowy giant, half-enveloped in a rising billow of morning mist, called out: "I am here, little man. Bring here your Sword and try to kill me, if you will."

But the man who rode the griffin knew better than to attack any unarmed opponent, let alone this one, with the Sword of Force. Instead he turned his mount without replying, and sped on to his castle, landing at the high aerie. Soon he would have demons on hand to do his fighting for him.

# CHAPTER 18

THE faint splash of Zoltan's paddle could still be heard receding down the tunnel when Lady Ninazu moved away from the others and came around the edge of the grotto pool to Arnfinn, who had already drawn a little apart. He saw her eyes gleaming with the reflection of distant starlight as she drew near him, and he heard her say: "I am ready now, my Ancient Lord, for you to lead me to my brother."

Arnfinn dreaded the thought of having to lie to her any longer. "And if I were to tell you, my lady, that I do not know where he is?"

Her gaze flickered away and back to him. Her chin lifted in conviction. "Then I would think that you were pleased to jest with me, great lord. You are the master of this castle, and must know what is within it. And, even if you did not, I know where Kunderu is."

"Where?"

In solemn silence Ninazu turned slightly away from him, and raised one slender arm to point. Her small, pale hand extended one finger toward the top of the castle's central tower.

Arnfinn said: "If you can lead me to your brother, Lady Ninazu, then I will set him free."

Her marvelous eyes searched him. "You promise that?"

"I swear it."

181

The solemnity of her regard lasted for only a moment longer. Then it melted in the ghost of a smile. She said: "We can start from here, in the grotto, and go along a secret way. Kunderu and I used it often when we were children."

She turned away from Arnfinn, and to his surprise began to climb along the wall, stepping on an irregular series of carved and built-in decorations that made a kind of fanciful stairway. Arnfinn raised the torch he was still holding and looked at the wall. The narrow, uneven steps that Ninazu was climbing gave the impression of not being a real stair chiefly because they went nowhere at all, ending in the middle of the wall where there were three shallow decorative niches. Beyond that point the inner wall of the grotto stretched up flat and unclimbable. Lady Yambu and Ben were watching her with curiosity as she went up.

When she was very nearly at the topmost step, Ninazu turned, and beckoned to Arnfinn with one finger.

He followed her. It was only when his climbing feet had attained a man's height above the surface of the pool that he was able to see that the stair went somewhere after all. What had looked from below like a blind decorative niche, set between two more shallow niches just like it, turned out when seen from this angle to be the genuine entrance to a passageway.

Ninazu's smile became more impish, or perhaps simply more childlike, when she saw Arnfinn's surprise —or rather the surprise of the person whose image he was wearing in her eyes. She said to him: "My father delighted in building such tricks as this. And when Kunderu and I were children, we found new uses for them." She giggled.

The passage into which she now led Arnfinn was narrow, barely wide enough for one person, and windowless. Chill air blew through it gently from somewhere up ahead. And as they went it soon became so dark that Arnfinn, following the lady, had to put one hand in front of him and touch her back to make sure she was there. He had the Sword sheathed now, and his left hand rested on its pommel.

The passage climbed, on little steps. He knew that they must now be threading their way upward through the enormous thickness of the outer wall of the keep itself. After some minutes of silent ascent they emerged, to Arnfinn's surprise, in the prosaic environment of a lofty storeroom. Obviously the place, with dust and cobwebs everywhere, had not been much used of late.

Now he could see Ninazu again, by the faint moonlight coming in through a tall, narrow window. Still smiling, she led him through the cavernous storeroom and opened a creaking door. Together they peered into the corridor outside, which was lighted only by remote torches, and locally deserted. Motioning for Arnfinn to follow, the lady moved out into the hall and turned to the right, where the corridor soon ended in a peculiar little balcony, open to the night.

The balcony, when they had gone out onto it, seemed to come to a dead end. But when they walked around a decorative column, they came to another narrow, unsuspected opening in the wall.

Before he followed Ninazu into this dark doorway, Arnfinn looked around to get his bearings. They were already at a considerable height above the dark lake, and about to enter the base of the castle's central tower.

The wall through which this second hidden passage ascended was not as massive as that of the lower keep, but still it was a good three meters or more in thickness, allowing plenty of room inside it for the narrow, hollow way.

They had barely started up through this second passage when Ninazu turned her head to gibe at Arnfinn like a little girl. "Admit it! You, the high lord of the castle, didn't even know that these tunnels were here!"

"I have already admitted it."

They moved on, with impervious darkness closing in on them again.

Into the darkness Arnfinn said: "These secret passages must not extend all the way to your brother's prison room, or else Kunderu would have used them to get out."

The lady ahead of him stopped suddenly, and he could hear her suddenly indrawn breath.

Then she moved on, climbing more stairs, but only for a short distance. Before Arnfinn was expecting the climb to end they came to a window that looked out over the darkened lake, under the starry sky. A few lights, small fires, speckled the distant shore. Here Lady Ninazu stopped. Arnfinn could faintly distinguish her profile against the stars as she stood looking out.

After some time had passed in which she said nothing and gave no sign of moving on, he prodded: "Well? Aren't we going on?"

"I don't know," she said after a time. And it seemed to Arnfinn that her voice was strangely altered.

"You don't know?"

She didn't answer.

Arnfinn persisted. "I thought you were so anxious to see that your brother was set free."

Still Ninazu had nothing to say to him.

He squeezed past her where she was standing at the window, and then sat down just above her on the narrow stairs. He did not know why, but he was rapidly developing a sense that doom was closing in on him.

Presuming on his supposed authority, he spoke to Ninazu more sternly: "Answer me! Are you afraid of what we're going to see when we find him? Are you afraid that he's no longer alive?"

"I know that he's alive," she answered instantly, as if disgusted that such a question could even be raised.

"What, then?"

In answer she sank down on the narrow stair, sitting just below him and leaning on his knees. "Great lord," she murmured. "Hold me. Help me."

"I will! I will!"

"Have you any magic that can heal the heart and mind?"

"Ah, gods, Ninazu! Whatever magic I have to offer you is yours!"

And after that she would say no more, but clung to Arnfinn's legs and wept. She would not move, nor respond to his questions, nor answer his entreaties. They sat there through the long hours of the night.

Ben, wearied with a day and a night of struggle and flight, had fallen asleep more or less wedged into a stony niche at the base of the grotto wall, near the steps that did not look like steps. Roused now by faint sounds, he awoke to find the head of another old campaigner, Lady Yambu, pillowed on his ample stomach. Ben shook her lightly, and in a moment she was wide awake, head up and listening in the earliest light of dawn.

The sound that had awakened Ben came again, softly. It was the faint splashing made by a paddle in the tunnel.

"Zoltan's back," Ben whispered, and moved to crouch beside the pool, straining his eyes into the darkness of the tunnel's mouth across the narrow reach of water. The grillwork gate, unlocked last night, was still swung back.

Ben and Yambu were both on their feet and watching when the boat appeared. There was only one occupant—a tall man in his early thirties, now looking very much like his old self. When Mark stood up and stepped ashore, Ben seized him in a fierce, silent embrace, then held him at arm's length. "You're well?"

"Well enough." Mark sounded like himself. "Zoltan got us out to Draffut; and he, all the gods be thanked, was able to restore us. Then Zoltan stayed there with Honan-Fu, to explain to the constabulary about Draffut, and the Swords."

"The constabulary? I talked with Haakon, and some officer, Cheng Ho. They're planning to move against the castle?"

Mark nodded. "With Draffut's help. Lady Yambu, a thousand thanks for your efforts on my behalf. Zoltan has told me of them."

The lady smiled remotely. "They were efforts well invested, I should say."

Ben sighed, feeling the relief of being able to hand over responsibility as well as that of seeing the Prince alive and well. "What do we do now?" he asked his leader.

Mark looked around at the confining walls, and up toward the cleverly constructed niche where Ninazu and the Sword-bearer had disappeared. He said: "We can't take the boat out into the lake now. It's too light, and they'd kill us from the walls when we came out. So we find a place, somewhat less inconspicuous than this one, in which to spend the day. Honan-Fu was able to give me a hint or two."

As the first light of morning began to creep into the narrow passage where Ninazu and Arnfinn had spent much of the night, the lady stirred, then jumped to her feet to look out of the window. Arnfinn, straightening his stiffened limbs to stand beside her, was in time to see the Ancient Master returning from the mainland on his griffin. The winged creature landed a hundred meters away, atop the one tower of the castle that was even taller than the one from which they watched.

Ninazu stared at this aerial apparition in amazement. When it had vanished into the aerie she turned to look at Arnfinn, and some of her sudden tension left her again.

"I understand," she said. "That was a deception, of course. A magical counterfeit of yourself, a phantom launched so that others would believe that you had left the castle, while all the time you really were with me."

And she took him trustingly by the arm.

Arnfinn drew in a deep breath. "Of course," he said. Then something made him turn his head. There was no danger to be seen in the half-light of earliest dawn. There was nothing alarming to be heard. But something was certainly wrong.

"What is it?" he muttered. "I feel sick."

The lady looked pale, and her eyes were closed. "It is only demons," she murmured. "As my lord knows very well."

"Demons." Arnfinn swallowed. "Where?"

Ninazu did not answer. She was leaning on the stone sill of the narrow window again, gazing out. The sky was now as clear and innocent as it could be at dawn.

Fiercely Arnfinn determined that, no matter what, he was not going to be incapacitated by these queasy sensations that seemed to come from nowhere. Nor was he going to waste any more time if he could help it. Looking about him, he took note that the passage going on above them was no longer a well of total darkness. Light, very faint and indirect daylight, was coming into it from somewhere higher up. Now Arnfinn could see that after a few more steps the passage turned inward in a sharp bend. These walls were not thick enough to accommodate much turning. A room of some kind, with windows, must be just ahead.

Arnfinn drew a deep breath. "Of course," he repeated. "I am the lord of this castle. Now I am going on, into that room above us. Are you going to follow me?"

Before the morning's sun had risen entirely above the cliffs that served as distant guardians of Lake Alkmaar's eastern shores, the demonic presences summoned by the Ancient One had begun to manifest themselves more strongly in his vicinity.

As yet the demons had not become physically visible, but they were making their presences known in their own way. A vague, inward sickness was spreading throughout the local human population, a malaise, a foreboding that descended on people with the power of physical illness. Only a few magicians, already inured to such evil, were immune to the effect.

The demons here, like all their brethren scattered about the world, were very old, within a few years of the age of Draffut himself, as old as the changing of the world itself from Old to New. Not since that great changing of the world—or so said the magicians who claimed to know about such things—had any new demons been created. But despite the demons' antiquity, some of them still had very little experience in the world of human affairs.

On this morning the first physical manifestation of their presence took the form of a clouding of the atmosphere before the eyes of the Ancient One, who was standing atop the highest tower to watch their arrival. Soon, other human watchers in and near the castle were able to see something of them too.

Then the leader of this demon-pack, whose name was Akbal, appeared more distinctly to the human who had summoned him, in the form of a smoky column that hung in the air close in front of the high tower.

"Hail, Master Wood," said a voice that issued from the faint, dark column. "I am surprised to see you in this time and place." It was not a human voice, nor was it loud. The only man who could hear it was reminded, as he usually was on these occasions, of dead leaves being blown through loosely piled bones.

"All times and places are mine now, Akbal," the man replied. "How many others have come with you?"

"There are five others, Master Wood."

The man sighed. If any other human beings had been with him atop the tower, close enough to hear that sound, they might have found it surprising that such evidence of commonplace humanity could issue from those lips, which had now resumed their reptilian form again. "It is a long time," he said, "since any have called me by that name. A very long time indeed."

"Then by what title shall I know you, master? I know that Wood is not your true and secret name—"

"It is quite good enough. Yes, it will do. Now, Akbal, to business. Are you strong?"

"Indeed, Master Wood. I do not mean to boast, but I have grown considerably in strength since either you, or that accursed one I now see wading in the lake, has seen me last. I take it that he, the Accursed One, is the reason for this summoning."

"You gauge my purpose correctly, demon. Now attend me carefully, Akbal, and you others, also."

While the shadowy forms of five other demons hovered in the air nearby, their leader, Akbal, was given his instructions by their human master.

The briefing did not occupy much time. When it was over, the demon professed to be pleased that he had been chosen to lead an attack on Draffut.

Then Akbal and his cohort, drifting lower over the lake, moved out to several hundred meters' distance from the castle, and the same distance from Draffut, whom they began to engage in a dialogue.

The humans who were able to observe this confrontation from the islands, or from the mainland, could not hear most of what was said. Only the magician who had called up the demons was able to hear most of their talk, by means of magic.

But all of the humans who watched could see how one of the lesser demons, perhaps stung by some taunt from Draffut, suddenly took on physical form—that of a giant, sharklike fish—and in this shape went plunging from the air into the water.

Before the water of the tremendous splash had fallen back, the great fish had darted to attack Draffut.

Grabbing one of its jaws in each hand, Draffut lifted the hideous creature thrashing from the lake. The demon emitted a terrible and most unfishlike scream as its jaws, white shark-teeth showing, were stretched to the point of dislocation and beyond.

The body of the fish steamed and seemed to dissolve in air as the demon shed as rapidly as possible the physical form that it had so recently assumed.

Honan-Fu and Zoltan, cowering together on the sandy shore of an islet near where Draffut was standing in the water, were doing what they could to shelter themselves from demonic observation. In Zoltan's case this consisted of little more than keeping his eyes shut and attempting now and then to heap sand over his own body. Honan-Fu presumably had rather greater powers at his disposal, but judging from the urgency of his muttering he was little more sanguine about the results.

The two, before the demons' arrival, had already held brief conversation with some members of Honan-Fu's old constabulary. The officer Cheng Ho, after talking briefly and privately with the Emperor, had dared to row himself out here during the night to talk to Draffut, and had been delighted to welcome his old lord Honan-Fu back to the land of the living. But Cheng Ho had been prudent enough to row away again before these demonic fireworks had started.

Draffut now turned his head to the two men remaining with him, and observed their concern. The giant said calmly: "I should perhaps explain that my compulsion against hurting people does not extend to demons—indeed I would like nothing better than to destroy them completely. But the death of any demon is practically impossible to accomplish, unless one has access to its hidden life."

"Which, in this case," gritted Zoltan between clenched teeth, "you do not have."

"Alas, that is true. Still, I am not helpless, and can defend myself effectively, as well as any companions who are careful to stay close to me." Draffut turned away to survey the situation once again.

By now the demon whose jaw had been nearly torn

from its joints had melted back into insubstantiality. And it was still fleeing, deep now in aerial distance, and still howling with persistent pain.

At the moment there appeared to be no other challengers ready to take its place.

"Most of them," Draffut confided quietly to his two human companions, "respect my powers too much. If they were willing to make a concerted effort they might destroy me, but they would be hurt in the process. Probably they would all be badly hurt. Courage is a virtue, as you know, my friends, and therefore demons have it not."

Meanwhile the wizard Wood, high on his battlement, was thinking that the six demons as a group ought to be powerful enough to destroy the Lord of Beasts utterly—and yet they hung back, cowardly as usual, and would not accept the pain that would be necessary for them to accomplish his will.

He vowed their punishment if they did not obey his orders; and they understood that it was no idle vow.

So now Akbal, leader of the pack, drifted toward Draffut once more. Akbal alone of this group of demons had skirmished with Draffut in the past—in the far past, those old days when the New World was truly new. In those days the powers of Orcus and of Ardneh had moved across the earth. And now Akbal was minded to taunt the Lord of Beasts with his defeat in those days by the demon-lord called Zapranoth. Akbal hoped by this means to encourage his fellows, so that they would be persuaded to rush in a group to the attack whether he went with them or not.

"And remember, dog-god," the boaster concluded, "that we here around you now are stronger than our brother Zapranoth ever was!"

"Around me? You do not stand around me. I see you all clustering together, as if for mutual protection. And I have no doubt that you are stronger liars than

Zapranoth was, and that is saying a great deal. But do not forget, while you are boasting of your strength, that I am still here, while Zapranoth the Liar is long dead."

At that reply the insubstantial forms that danced above the water all hissed and steamed and rumbled in their rage. Akbal screamed: "But you are unable to touch *our* lives, o dog of gods and god of dogs! For we have them all hidden safely. And this time there will be no little human being coming with a spell to save you!"

"Here I am, if you care to attack me. As for human beings, little or great, perhaps you have something to learn of them as well."

This reply so incited the anger of Akbal that, forgetting his caution and his clever plans alike, he too dared to take on solid form alone and try the strength of Draffut. Plunging into the water, the demon strode against him in the shape of an armored man as tall as Draffut was. Chest-deep he waded toward the Lord of Beasts, amid the billows of the morning mist now rising from the lake.

The two grappled. But still the ancient power that had made Draffut what he was endured in him, the power of that other lake, the Lake of Life, older by far even than Wood and his magic, as old perhaps as the Great Worm Yilgarn. And the demon Akbal, rage and struggle as he might, was unable to withstand him.

With a last desperate effort the demon managed to twist away. He lunged into a retreat, half-drowning himself before he could completely shed the material body he had adopted for the trial.

The Beastlord roared with laughter at the sight. "And you call yourself stronger than Zapranoth? Only in lies and malice, it may be."

And now the entire squadron of angry demons gathered in conference, each trying to convince the others that they ought to hurl themselves in a group against Draffut and overwhelm him. But each demon's fear of him was too strong; and it was with relief that they heard the voice of their human master, summoning them back to the castle. Rather would they face Wood's punishment than Draffut now.

Prince Mark, who with Ben and Lady Yambu had been peering over the top of the low wall that separated the grotto from the adjoining courtyard, watching the demons, suddenly sprang to the top of the wall as the demons again clouded the air almost directly overhead. "In the Emperor's name," Mark shouted to the demons, "I send you far!"

Ben, who knew the Prince and his powers, had been more than half anticipating some such action. But Yambu cried out in surprise. Her cry was echoed by a whistle from above, deafeningly shrill, which stirred the clouded air above the castle. And then another whistle sounded, like the first but slightly different in its pitch; and then another and another. Louder and louder rose the chorus, at last becoming a mad shriek that seemed to split the sky before it was transformed into a lower, polyphonic howling. This last sound was as filled with fear and rage as any human outcry might have been.

And then in turn the howling faded. And with its fading there diminished also the cloudiness of the morning air, and the sense of sickness that had afflicted almost everyone. The sound of the demonic voices faded rapidly at first, and then more slowly, and more slowly still, so that no human being who heard it was ever quite sure that it had really come to an end.

But whether or not the sound of their departure had ever ended finally, the whole collection of demonic presences that had befouled the air above the castle were now indubitably gone.

Wood, who was still standing with Shieldbreaker in hand upon his highest battlement, had never expected anything like this. He did not see Mark jump up to give the order—the courtyard and grotto were out of his direct line of sight—but he heard the man's voice raised in the shouted command that sent the demons scattering.

He had heard almost nothing of the Prince's voice before, and he did not recognize it now. But again there leaped into his mind the stories his advisers, Amintor in particular, had told him about Mark. Never had Wood really believed that Prince Mark possessed such power over demons, but he would certainly have raised the subject in his planned interrogations of the prisoner.

Wood for the moment could only wonder whether Mark was in fact his prisoner still.

And if conceivably Mark was free, what then of Honan-Fu?

The Ancient One determined to investigate, and quickly. But now, with the morning mist beginning to blow away, and the sun coming into its full powers, Wood saw that Draffut was deliberately approaching the castle. Coming closer in full sunlight, the shaggy head and shoulders of the wading giant loomed above the last tendrils of the fading mist. An impressive figure, certainly, but small seen from this height. In fact it seemed to Wood that the God of Beasts was somewhat diminished from the creature he had been thousands of years ago.

Using a touch of magic to amplify his voice, Wood shouted out a taunt to that effect.

Draffut heard him, and paused to look up toward him. The Lord of Beasts needed no magic to amplify his voice when he chose to use it at something like full power.

"Whatever the centuries may have done to me, small man, I think they have done worse to you. For you are sadly changed."

"Changed? Yes, you animal, changed indeed! But stronger now, I assure you, than ever I was then!"

# CHAPTER 19

STARTING the long climb down from the griffin's aerie where he had been standing as he watched his demons routed, the Ancient Master took note again of the absence of small flyers, and reminded himself grimly that for the time being at least he was going to have to rely upon human eyes and ears, stationed in these high towers and elsewhere, to gather intelligence about what was happening on the lake and along its shores. He would of course use magical methods of observation when they seemed appropriate. And if a desperate need arose he could always mount his griffin again and ride out to see for himself.

But for the time being the problems of gathering intelligence outside the castle could wait. There was another question for which he had to find the answer as soon as possible: What had happened to his demons? Who, what power, had been able to sweep them out of the sky like so many drifting cobwebs?

Having descended the ladder that led immediately down from the tower's top, he started down the stairs, meanwhile casting about him with his own magical powers for an answer. But Wood was unable to confirm anything about the event he had just witnessed except that the demons were definitely gone. Whatever force had banished them had left no trace of itself behind.

As soon as he reached a level of the tower where

there were soldiers within easy call, Wood summoned several, then hurriedly sent them scurrying on ahead of him, bearing his orders in different directions.

First of all he wanted to make sure that his important prisoners were secure. Particularly the one named Mark—Prince of Tasavalta, said to be the adopted son of a blacksmith named Jord. And the natural son—if the stories Wood had heard were true—of the enigmatic magician now called the Emperor.

Could it really be true that this child of the Emperor, or anyone else, innately possessed such powers? Wood doubted that, but so far he had been unable to discover any other clue to an explanation for his demons' disappearance.

Mark had shown no sign of magical ability during his first brief confrontation with the Ancient Master. But if Mark was now shouting demons out of the sky, it could be assumed with a fair degree of certainty that he was no longer bound under the water by Wood's enchantment.

Reaching the lower levels of the castle, Wood now passed from the base of the aerie tower into the central keep. In a moment he had reached the room that he ordinarily used as his headquarters. On entering this chamber, his first act was to call for General Amintor.

Before the general had arrived, a messenger came running to the wizard with information on the prisoners. The two men who last night had been sunken in the well were missing this morning. Not only that, but Lady Yambu was gone from what had seemed a secure cell in a tower.

There was additional unlikely news. Lady Ninazu, who had arrived in a small boat last night and had been put into a waiting room to await her lord's pleasure, had also disappeared along with her strange attendant. The bars on a window had been forced—

"She came out here, to the castle, last night?" It was on the tip of the wizard's tongue to demand to know why he had not been told last night of her arrival; but he, of course, had spent much of the night over on the mainland.

A subordinate said nervously: "Your Lordship, if you will allow me to remind you, I informed you of the lady's presence shortly after she arrived."

"You informed me? When was this? Where?"

The officer quailed. "In the central courtyard, last night, sire. It was about an hour after midnight."

The man who made this statement now to Wood had not, in the past, impressed the magician as being more than ordinarily stupid. And he appeared to be currently in full possession of his faculties.

Wood looked at him steadily. "Are you completely sure of this?" he asked.

"It was last night, Your Lordship. Just as Your Lordship was entering the grotto with Lady Yambu. When I—"

"Wait. Wait. Start over. Tell me all the circumstances of this supposed encounter between us."

The soldier he was questioning grew increasingly nervous, but Wood was patient. As the story came out it forced all of his other problems temporarily out of his mind. Someone, as recently as last night, had been successfully impersonating him within the castle. So successfully, indeed, that the idea of an impostor had never entered the minds of even his close associates.

General Amintor had entered the room during the course of this questioning, had quickly grasped the situation, and now had a suggestion to make.

"Sire, this strongly suggests one thing to me—that the Sword of Stealth has been introduced into your castle by one of your enemies. In fact I know of no other way such an impersonation could be accomplished."

Wood could think of at least two other possibilities in the realm of advanced magic for achieving such an effect. Using one of these himself, he was accustomed to being able to alter his own appearance between two modes, more or less at will. But he had to admit that Amintor was very likely right about the Sword.

The Ancient One's next step was to order a full alert of all his troops, and then a thorough search of the castle, and the fringe of island surrounding it, for the escapees.

Then Wood informed his chief subordinates of where he himself intended to be during the next few hours while the search was in progress. If they believed that they saw him anywhere else during that time, they would be looking at an impostor. In that event they were to keep the masquerader under surveillance and bring word to their real master at once.

Having issued these and a few other orders, Wood turned his attention to the castle's garrison and the other components of its defenses. In what other way might they have been undermined without his knowledge?

But here, at least, the reports he got were reassuring. Just under four hundred troops were present, well armed and ready for duty, within the castle walls. The morale of the men had reportedly been somewhat shaken by the events of the past few hours, and the Ancient One decided that his next step ought to be to address that problem.

He commanded a general muster of all the troops except a few sentries who were to continue manning the walls. He intended to speak to his soldiers and reassure them.

Certainly, he thought, the garrison ought to be more than adequate to defend these formidable walls against the strongest attack that the ragged followers of Honan-Fu could mount—assuming the old wizard had any followers left, and assuming he had indeed managed to make good his escape to the mainland. Now that a search for the prisoners had started, reports were coming in to Wood of the chance discovery of secret passages within the castle, and that kind of an escape no longer appeared such a remote possibility.

Particularly with Draffut roaming the surrounding lake . . .

Mustering almost all his men in a formation to hear their commander speak meant necessarily delaying the search for the escapees, but Wood determined to take that risk.

From what the officers and the sergeants could tell him, it was not the doubtful capabilities of Honan-Fu that worried his troops. It was the mysterious fate of their mainland garrison, and, even more than that, it was Draffut.

Wood could understand that last apprehension, because in a way he shared it. But he was not going to allow any kind of fear to demoralize his men.

He strode out onto a high balcony, overlooking the assembled troops, hundreds of faces squinting up into the noon sun.

"Hear me!" he roared in his amplified voice. "I know what bothers you, and in a way I cannot blame you, because in your ignorance you cannot help yourselves. Let me instead enlighten you.

"To begin with, you have all heard rumors about what happened to the garrison at Triplicane. The truth is that they relaxed their vigilance when I was not there to protect them, and a powerful magician struck them down. He fled the field afterward, not daring to face me directly. I am here, and as long as I am your leader he is not going to come back. Enough on that subject.

"The next most popular subject of rumors is yonder monster out in the lake. He's fierce enough against boats, and, I grant you, against demons too, as some of you have been able to see for yourselves this morning.

"But, as those of you who had to swim last night can testify, he is too tenderhearted to so much as scratch the skin of any human being. Did we lose a single man to him last night, for all his pranks and bellowing?"

There had indeed been, as Wood well knew, at least one man reported drowned among the occupants of the capsized boats. But one man, among the dozens who had been tipped into the lake, might well have been sheer accident. At least no one was brave enough to raise the subject of that one man now.

"No, we did not!" Into the uncertain silence Wood shouted his own answer to his own question. "And we'll lose none to the great dog, today or ever!"

For some time he continued in this vein, and when at last he paused to consider the temper of his audience, he thought that they had been considerably encouraged.

In a somewhat lower voice their master went on: "No, we can hold these walls against him. One sword or one pike or one arrow may not be able to do him much damage—but let him stand within our reach, and we can hew the flesh from his bones eventually, so he'll have to back away or die. The walls here are at least twice as tall as he is, and he cannot climb them as long as we are alert and ready to discourage him in the attempt. And, let me say it again, he cannot, I repeat he cannot, ever do any one of us the least harm!"

It was as rousing a climax for his speech as any Wood was able to conceive at the moment, and he let it end there. The troops, at a signal from their officers, managed to produce a cheer that had some energy and some flavor of spontaneity about it. Marching rank by rank out of the courtyard, they seemed to their Ancient Master to be moving with new determination.

When he came in from the balcony, officers were waiting for him with more good news for the defense. There was plenty of stored food on hand, provisions prudently stockpiled by the castle's previous owner, against the possibility of a siege that had never come. And there would of course be no difficulty about fresh water, even supposing that Honan-Fu and his allies could really manage to mount and maintain a siege.

All in all, Wood foresaw no real problems in his defense of this castle, unless an attack should be made with sudden, overwhelming force. And there was no reason to anticipate anything of the kind.

He had business outside these walls that he was anxious to get on with. But that business would require that he travel a considerable distance, and he did not want to leave the castle while there was a possibility of a successful impostor still lurking within.

Once more Wood summoned General Amintor, and when the limping old soldier had arrived, discussed with him the friendly reinforcements that were supposedly on their way. Some of Amintor's lieutenants ought now to be leading those troops—perhaps five thousand men in all—here from the west. This force was to form the nucleus of a large army that in time would move into the north, challenging Tasavalta and the other powers of that region for supremacy.

Wood announced his intention of sending Amintor out now, riding the griffin. The general was to meet this army of reinforcements, which was still probably a two week march away, and survey its size, condition, and rate of advance. Then Amintor was to report back to Wood, within twenty-four hours.

Amintor, experienced warrior that he was, could not entirely conceal his dismay when he heard about the means of transportation that he was to use. Wood had noticed in the past that the general preferred not to get too close to the griffin.

"The griffin," Wood assured him, "is very fast and reliable. It should be able to manage the distance in that time without any trouble. Well, what do you say?"

The general thought briefly, then asked: "Will the creature obey my orders, sire?"

"It will obey all the orders that you may need to give it. However, it will come back to me here tomorrow, whatever you may say to it in the meantime. See that you are on it when it begins its return flight."

Amintor bowed. If the thought of flying on a griffin terrified him, he was at least not trying to shirk the duty, and that was all that Wood could ask of him.

The two men climbed to the aerie—Amintor getting up stairs and ladders slowly on his bad leg—and Wood gave the necessary magical commands. A moment later, squinting into the afternoon sun, he had seen the griffin and its somewhat reluctant rider off.

Naturally Wood had remembered to inform the officers conducting the search of the fact that he was leaving his headquarters room, and of his destination. One of these officers met him on his way down from the high tower, with word that the impostor had been spotted. Someone looking exactly like Wood himself —in which of the two modes of his appearance the informant did not say—had been glimpsed by several people, looking out of one of the higher windows in the little-used central tower of the castle. As yet no attempt had been made to close in on the offender.

"That is good. I myself will lead the way." Resting his hand on the hilt of Shieldbreaker, Wood smiled grimly and set out to deal with the impostor.

# CHAPTER 20

ZOLTAN too had managed to get some rest and nourishment. After rowing Mark and Honan-Fu out to Draffut, he had waited in the small boat until the Lord of Healing had healed the damage done by the Ancient Master's magic, had restored the two men by holding them in his hands, and set them on an island. By that time some people from shore, members of the constabulary, were beginning to come out to Draffut, emboldened by whatever conversation the Emperor had held with them. Eventually Zoltan had gone back with some of these people to the docks at Triplicane.

Meanwhile Mark, as soon as he was healed and had rested enough to feel nearly recovered, insisted on returning to the castle, where Ben and Yambu were still in peril. But Honan-Fu declined to go with him, deciding instead to stay for the time being on the small island where he had been placed by Draffut. This afforded the old wizard an advanced position from which he would be able to command the amphibious assault he was already planning in order to retake the castle.

The town of Triplicane, like the rest of the territory surrounding Lake Alkmaar, was now free land once more. The only effective troops in the area still loyal to the Ancient One were now confined within the castle walls. The people who welcomed Zoltan ashore were rejoicing over this state of affairs, but by this time he was

203

almost too tired to care. He talked briefly with some of the leaders of the constabulary in town, enjoyed a good meal, and then stretched out on a borrowed bedroll inside a shed.

Zoltan did not awake until midafternoon. When he came out of the shed, he discovered that preparations for an amphibious counterattack against the castle were farther advanced than he supposed, and the attack was to be launched during the coming night.

Already a surprising number of boats had been gathered from around the lake. Some of these were craft that had been successfully concealed from the invaders; and some were the very boats that the soldiers of the Ancient One had used in their invasion. These craft had been seized at the town docks after the destruction of the garrison, and were now to be turned against the enemy. Also included in the invasion fleet were two large rowboats that Draffut had overturned during the night, then righted and emptied so they could be easily rowed ashore.

Transport for several hundred men was thus available. Nor had there been any difficulty in gathering sufficient arms. Besides the weapons that had been successfully hidden away during the brief occupation, enough more had been picked up from the field in front of the manor to arm at least a hundred men.

Zoltan had heard that there were a few military survivors of that massacre, and he had even talked to one of them, a young private soldier in a dirty uniform of red and gray, who was now confined under guard in a shed next to the one in which Zoltan had been sleeping.

The youth appeared somewhat fearful of what was going to happen to him next, but the main impression that he conveyed was of sheer gladness in being still alive.

"Why are you still alive, do you suppose?" Zoltan asked him curiously after the prisoner had told him a brief version of the disaster.

The other young man shook his head, as if at some wonder he could not understand no matter how he tried. "I don't know. I just don't know. When that show started, everyone around me, almost, started laughing. . . . Were you there?"

"No. But I've talked to someone else who was."

The former enemy shook his head again. "I just don't know why I'm still here. Everyone was laughing, but I just didn't see nothing to laugh at. Them girls having their clothes ripped off, that wasn't funny. Nobody had ought to do that. And the little fella in the clown suit, he acted like he was trying to protect 'em, even if he got himself killed. I wouldn't have had the guts to do that, but I didn't think it was funny either."

"No," said Zoltan. "No, I wouldn't have laughed at that."

"And all the rest of my company are dead, they tell me, and here I am still alive. It's strange. I'm just lucky, I guess."

Zoltan left him in the shed. The young man was still marveling at his own survival, and ready to tell the story again, if someone else would listen.

It was well after dark when the assault force finally pushed off, some two hundred men and a few women in more than twenty boats. Zoltan, having eaten heartily again, and armed from the common stock of weapons, was aboard one of them.

At sunrise, as soon as the brief sickness brought on by demons had suddenly abated, Arnfinn had gone on alone into the hidden rooms of the central tower. By that time he had temporarily given up trying to persuade Lady Ninazu to come with him. He didn't know what was wrong with her—as near as he could tell, she was afraid that her brother would not be here after all. Or else she was afraid he would.

As Arnfinn soon discovered, there were four rooms

in this hidden suite, two on the level entered from the tunnel and two more just above, on the highest interior level of the tower. He spent an hour alone in these rooms, searching them carefully, making sure in his own mind that Ninazu's brother was not here. No one was, except himself. Nor was there any sign that anyone had lived here very recently, nor was there anything about the rooms to make Arnfinn think they might have been used as a prison.

The four rooms, two on one level and two on the next, connected by a single narrow interior stairway, occupied the top two stories of the central tower. The tower narrowed slightly here, toward its top, and none of the rooms were very large. All of them were furnished, and they did contain plenty of potential hiding places: there were beds with spaces beneath, disused cabinets and wardrobes, and closets stuffed with junk, much of it children's toys. Arnfinn had done as thorough a job as he possibly could of searching through all these nooks and crannies, making sure that neither Kunderu nor anyone else was lying in concealment.

Each room was lighted and aired by two narrow windows, built out in a slight bulge of wall and equipped with interior shutters, most of which were standing open. Arnfinn supposed a slender person might have been able to squeeze his way in or out through one of these windows, or at least could do so if there were anything but the sheer face of the wall outside. There were no other visible entrances or exits to the apartment, except the tunnel through which Arnfinn and Ninazu had come up.

As Arnfinn went through these rooms he received a strong impression that no one could have occupied them for a long time, perhaps for years. A thin film of dust covered all horizontal surfaces, and there was unmistakable evidence that some of the waterfowl so plentiful around the lake had taken advantage of the open windows to come in from time to time.

Several times during the hour that he spent alone in these rooms Arnfinn had interrupted his examination of the place to look out into the dim passageway again and speak softly to Ninazu, trying to persuade her to join him. He had almost given up on being able to do this, when he looked up from the examination of a cabinet and saw her standing in the doorway of the passage, looking in at him.

For a moment neither of them spoke. Then Arnfinn said gently: "Your brother isn't here after all."

She looked back at him helplessly, saying nothing. Her elaborate long dress, not made for boat rides and climbing through dark passages, was smudged and slightly torn in a couple of places, and her hair hung round her face in disarray. She was absolutely the most beautiful thing that Arnfinn had ever seen.

Arnfinn, now feeling as helpless as the lady looked, cast his gaze around the room in which they were standing. It was on the lower level of the apartment, and roughly semicircular in shape. There were chairs and dusty tables in the middle of this room, as if for some kind of bookish work, and shelves of books around the curving walls. Arnfinn had learned to read, better at least than most of the people in his village. But he had never seen as many books as this, and many of the titles were in languages he did not know. Even those in his own language were hard to understand. At least some of them, he was sure, must have something to do with magic.

He said: "I suppose you and Kunderu must have lived in these rooms. There are beds in the two rooms upstairs."

"Yes, my brother and I lived here much of the time." Ninazu came closer to him, walking slowly into the center of the room. It was as if she had forgotten again that there was something here of which she was afraid. "We were always together when we were children. We made up our own games, Kunderu and I. Even when we were very young we knew we were both going to be magicians."

"Like your father."

"Oh, father, yes. Father pretty much let us do whatever we wanted." The lady shrugged. "He was usually busy with his own work."

Arnfinn felt a tremendous relief that she was at least talking to him rationally again. "What about your mother?" he asked. "You've never told me anything about her."

Ninazu drew symbols with one finger in the faint dust on a workbench. She said: "I don't know much about her. She died when Kunderu and I were very young."

"That must have been very sad for you."

"I don't remember." Ninazu's voice was remote. She turned away from Arnfinn and went to a set of cabinets, tall and ornately carved, that stood against the flat interior wall beside the doorway to the adjoining room, and below more shelves of books. She pulled open the doors of one of the tall cabinets, and then stood looking at the diverse objects arrayed on the shelves inside as if she had expected to see something rather different. Many of the things on the shelves were hard for Arnfinn to recognize. There were bones and a stuffed bird, and little piles of what looked to him like rather ordinary rocks.

The lady was pointing at one of the small piles of rocks now. She said thoughtfully: "Kunderu was trying to evoke a demon once, when he was only twelve. He was using these. Father found out before he got very far and made him stop."

Arnfinn was aghast. "Fortunately!" was the only comment he could find to make.

Lady Ninazu looked at him with almost open rebellion in her eyes. "My brother could have controlled a demon, with my help."

"But—Ninazu, a *demon*! You felt the ones outside

just now. How could you have wanted—that? How could your brother want it?"

Ninazu's gaze had become almost demure. "*You* have never dealt with demons, lord?"

"That—that's beside the point."

She shrugged boldly. "We didn't know quite what it was going to be like. But we could have managed, we could have stayed in control, Kunderu and I together." Then the growing, visible anger of his wizard-image crushed her opposition, and she shrank back timidly. "Oh, great lord, we were very young."

"Yes. You were. You must have been. Demons are tremendously dangerous, and I am glad that you did not succeed." Arnfinn spoke with great conviction, as if he really were a wizard and knew what he was talking about. Maybe, after this morning's brief whiff of demons in the tunnel, he knew enough.

Ninazu looked at Arnfinn strangely now. "I have told you, my lord, my lover, that you were our first success."

"I?"

"Yes, lord. I see that you are pleased to have another jest at my expense."

"How, in what way, was I a success for you? When? I want you to tell me."

Ninazu stood with downcast eyes, almost in the attitude of a child fearing punishment. Still her tone dared to be reproachful. "It was two years ago, lord. A little more than two years now . . . but you know all this as well as I do, lord. You know it better."

"Tell me, I say. I want you to tell me what you are talking about, what happened, just as you remember it."

"Yes, lord. I am talking about the help we gave you, Kunderu's help and mine, that enabled you to find your way here across the ages."

"Across the what?"

Ninazu ignored the question. "We were looking for something that would—irritate our father, show him what we could do, that we could be magicians too."

"The help you gave *me*?" Arnfinn was struggling to understand, but at the same time not at all sure that he wanted to understand.

"You and I have talked about all this before, my lord and lover." Ninazu sighed. "Many times we have laughed about it in our bed."

Arnfinn was very tired. He sat down on a stool before one of the tables. "Never mind that. I would hear it all again."

The lady leaned against the other table, her arms folded. She recited: "Kunderu and I were very angry at our father for being so oppressive all the time. We had been experimenting with ways to get back at him. We worked and worked, until finally our efforts—brought us in touch with Your Lordship, across the gulf of years."

Arnfinn couldn't understand what she meant by the gulf of years. "You were trying to evoke a demon, I suppose. And you got me instead."

"Have I displeased you, great lord, with my poor telling? Did it really happen in some other way?"

"I don't suppose so, Ninazu. No, you must know what happened. I am sure it must have happened as you say." Arnfinn rested his chin on his fist and tried to think.

Ninazu was musing aloud, as if she too were grappling with some kind of puzzle. "You could have found someone else in this time to help you, I suppose. But Kunderu and I were the ones you chose." Suddenly grief and fear overwhelmed her again. Raising her head, she cried out: "Kunderu, where are you?"

A gull-winged lake bird had been just about to land on the sill of one of the open windows behind her, and her sudden outcry frightened it off. The bird veered away from the tower, letting out a loud, harsh cry.

Ninazu screamed, and spun around in terror.

Arnfinn experienced a sudden insight. "It was only

a bird, Ninazu. Are you really so afraid of your brother as all that?"

"You are wicked to say that!" Then, aghast at her own boldness, she brought her hands up to her mouth.

"You were afraid to come into these rooms when you thought he might still be here."

"I love my brother, and I will save him!"

"Are you sure that he is really a prisoner? How are you so sure? These rooms are not a prison," Arnfinn pointed out. "We got into them easily enough, without passing any locked doors or guards. Kunderu, if he was here, ought to have been able to get out the same way. Besides, it doesn't look to me like anyone has lived here for a long time."

"He was here!" Ninazu whispered the words with tremendous conviction.

"He's not here now. Maybe he's somewhere else in the castle. Or maybe somewhere else altogether."

Lady Ninazu's eyes had closed, as if she were in agony. "Kunderu is here somewhere," she breathed, softly but with great intensity. "My brother is here, and I am going to save him."

"All right, if you say so. But I don't see or hear anyone in these rooms but us. He's not here now."

"Great lord," she breathed more softly and hopelessly still, "I had thought that you were going to help me."

And with that Ninazu slumped down into one of the dusty chairs and abandoned herself to the saddest, most hopeless weeping that Arnfinn had ever heard.

In a moment Arnfinn was at her side, all his efforts to be firm and practical crumbling into dust. "I will help you. I will help you, whatever you say. Whatever I must do." And he held her fiercely, in bewildered helplessness.

Mark, with Ben and Lady Yambu nearby, had been standing atop one of the lower parts of the grotto wall when he shouted at the demons to disperse.

"The same shout that sent them off," Ben commented, "will draw some people here. People of a kind I fear we'll like no better than the demons." He gestured at the wall with the hidden exit. "Let's move on up."

"Yes, it would seem to be time for that."

With Mark in the lead, the three of them climbed to the niche where Ninazu and the latest Sword-bearer, whoever he was, had disappeared. They entered the dark tunnel that they found there, and advanced cautiously. As they climbed farther they began to speculate in low voices on the possible identity of the person who was now carrying the Sword of Stealth.

Yambu, ascending between the two men, said that she now felt reasonably sure it was the youth Arnfinn they were following.

Ben, who was bringing up the rear, was more than a little skeptical of that suggestion. "That scrawny peasant? I find it difficult to believe he would have had the guts to come after Zoltan and me, and hit Zoltan over the head in that shed. And then, to get aboard a griffin, and ride it out here—"

Here in the dark tunnel where no one could see her, Yambu allowed herself to smile broadly. "What you tell me you went through to get here, my friend, was hardly less fantastic."

Ben grunted something, then swore softly when he stumbled in the darkness. Mark, alertly in the lead, was silent.

The three of them went on up.

Their general plan now was to reach one of the hiding places high in the structure of the castle recommended by Honan-Fu; also Mark and Ben in particular nursed some hopes of being able to get back the Sword of Stealth from Arnfinn, if it was really he who was carrying it again.

Their whispered planning session had not made much headway, nor had they gained much distance upward along their gloomy escape route, when Ben hissed for silence. His two companions halted with him, holding their breath. In a moment they were all able to hear the soldiers arriving in the grotto they had just left. It sounded like one had come over the wall to open the locked gate for the others. In another moment there was a whole squad of them in the grotto, beginning a clamorous search.

Mark, Yambu, and Ben crept on, as silently as possible. Almost at once cries of surprise sounded from below and behind them, indicating that the soldiers had found the two ropes severed and the prisoners gone.

Mark methodically continued upward. The two others followed. Either the soldiers would quickly locate the hidden exit from the grotto, or they would not. After a minute Ben muttered: "I could wish for Wayfinder in a place like this. Or Coinspinner at least."

"Go ahead," Mark whispered over his shoulder. "But you won't have either one of them in hand after you've wished. So let's get on with what we have."

Which was not, Mark added silently to himself, much in the way of weapons. Ben had left his staff behind him long ago, and Lady Yambu was an unarmed pilgrim. Mark himself had brought one dagger back with him from his trip out into the lake, a gift from the officer Cheng Ho passed on to Mark by Draffut.

At least all three of them had eaten heartily last night, and all had been granted an interval for rest. These benefits, along with Draffut's healing treatment of Mark, had restored them all to something approaching normal strength and energy. Before they left the grotto Ben had refilled a couple of last night's drink containers at the well, and slung them on his belt; if they could find a hiding place, they ought not to die of thirst for a day or two at least.

Presently the three came to the end of the first hidden passage, to find themselves in what looked like an ordinary if almost unused storeroom. Mark paused in the entrance to the storeroom, frowning. This was really not what any of them had been expecting. Honan-Fu's directions for finding a hiding place had been hurried and perhaps unclear. The three paused for a brief whispered conference.

There were two doors to the storeroom, besides the one by which they had entered, and the three people had no means of telling which way Ninazu and her Sword-bearer might have taken from this point.

Before the three had chosen a way to go, they could hear movement outside one of the doors.

Quickly and efficiently, making plans with no more than a swift exchange of gestures, they had arranged themselves in ambush, with the men against the wall behind the door.

The door swung in. There was only one soldier, and he had come alone here to look for someone or something, not expecting trouble. He saw Yambu, standing alone in the middle of the dingy storeroom, and he took a step toward her and started to ask a puzzled question.

He never got the question out. A moment later, Ben was able to unbuckle the swordbelt from the soldier's body; he needed to pick up the soldier's dagger, too, and use the fine point to bore another hole in the belt before he could buckle that belt around his own waist over the strongman costume. While he was thus engaged, Mark dragged the lifeless body out of sight.

Yambu signed for silence, then made another gesture, pointing back over her shoulder. There were faint sounds, as of cautious footsteps, in the tunnel through which they had come up. Evidently the enemy had found the hidden entrance to the tunnel and were already following them up from the grotto.

The three went warily out into the corridor from which the lone soldier had entered. Mark shrugged over the choice of directions, and turned left. Moving in that direction, they quickly reached an ascending stairway, which took them steeply up again. Going higher within the architecture of any castle was very likely to bring you to a more defensible position. The structures were, after all, designed with defense in mind.

This stair went up a little way without a break, or any other exit, and then emerged onto the cylindrical outer surface of the tower. At this point it became almost uncomfortably narrow, with only a sheer drop on the left side, and continued up around the outside of the tower in a spiral.

The stair did not quite reach the top, but came to an abrupt end some three or four meters below a gap in the parapet encircling the roof. From the top of the stair a removable wooden ladder extended the rest of the way to the top. The three went up this ladder and found themselves on the tower's flat, circular stone-paved roof, some ten paces in diameter.

There was a small roof cistern here, which had some water in it; Ben's jugs were probably not going to be necessary after all. Most of the tower's rooftop was open to the sky, but at the side of the roof opposite the cistern a small, half-open shed had been constructed, to serve as shelter for a lookout and perhaps for a small signal fire. Some wood was stacked for this contingency. In another place a pile of head-sized stones had been neatly pyra-mided, a routine provision of armament for any last-ditch defenders who wished to discourage their enemies from following them up the stairs.

The wooden ladder was obviously another means to that end, and Ben had already taken advantage of it, pulling the ladder up briskly after them. None too soon, perhaps. The ladder had only just been removed when Yambu took a quick glance back and down upon the exterior stair and saw red and gray uniforms coming up.

"Hush!" she warned her companions softly.

Listening, all three of them were able to hear a

dogged, soft, dull thudding noise.

"Shieldbreaker," Mark breathed unhappily.

The other two nodded. They had all heard before the sound made by that Sword as it was carried into combat range of its bearer's enemies, whoever they might be.

Whoever now had the Sword of Force in hand was coming along their trail, up the exterior stairway. But whoever he was, he could not get at them, at least for the moment.

"But listen again," Ben whispered, frowning. "I could swear that there are two of them. Two Swords."

Straining his ears, Mark found that he could indeed make out an extra, doubled thudding.

"There cannot be two," Yambu objected softly but angrily, as if she were quietly outraged that the rules of the Sword-game might have been changed without her being told.

"Wait," whispered Mark. "I wonder. Yes, that must be it. Sightblinder."

The others frowned at him, then Ben's face brightened suddenly with understanding. "Yes, we've been following Sightblinder, or trying to. If that peasant, or whoever he is, is in some room of this tower just below us . . . and his Sword is doing an imitation of Shieldbreaker—yes, that would do it."

"Ho, on the roof!" The voice was powerful, and so loud that some manner of magic, or Old-World technology perhaps, must be in use to augment it.

"Do you suppose we ought to answer?" Yambu whispered very softly.

Mark and Ben exchanged frowns, giving the question silent consideration.

"Ho, there! This is the master of the castle speaking! Let your ladder down for us at once! You are trapped, and I will show you mercy if you come down now!"

\* \* \*

After exchanging looks with her companions, Yambu made answer with a rock, which she handled over to the edge of the roof with wiry strength, and dropped just over the head of the stair below. Prudently she refrained from looking over the edge to observe the exact result. There was an explosive crash, and small rock-fragments sang through the air in all directions.

There were no more shouted demands after that. Listening carefully, the three on the roof could hear the people on the stairs quietly retreating.

Things settled down for the time being into a waiting mode.

The only place from which anyone could see the top of this tower was the top of the only higher tower, where the aerie was, at least a hundred meters distant. And if the three retreated under the lookout's shelter they would be invisible even from there, and probably immune from any speculative stones or arrows launched from that high place.

The afternoon was wearing on. As was perhaps inevitable, the talk among the three people on the roof turned to the Swords and their various powers. Long before the day was over, Mark had time to reminisce about the occasion upon which he had carried Sightblinder into the camp of the Dark King himself.

"And the Sword of Stealth has another power that is more subtle than the one of which we are always aware. The verse tells it: 'his eyes are keen . . .' I scarcely understood it at the time, but when I looked at the Dark King and his magicians, I could *see* their evil."

# CHAPTER 21

W OOD, ascending the exterior stair that curved around the tower, with the great Sword Shield-breaker thudding softly in his right hand and a squad of picked troops at his back, knew that he had reached the top of the stair no more than a few minutes behind his quarry. Quite possibly it had been a nearer miss than that. He did not actually see the wooden ladder being pulled up out of his reach, but he saw the supports where it had rested, and he surmised its very recent removal. And Shieldbreaker was now signaling the near presence of his enemies. Wood could not see or hear them on the roof above, but he knew that they were there.

He smiled lightly to himself. He could hear a duplicated thudding, keeping time like a faint echo with the sound of his own Sword, and in the first moment after the Ancient Master heard that echo he realized where it must be coming from. It was coming from the Sword of Stealth, in the impostor's possession; and that Sword now had to be somewhere very near at hand.

Before calling on his prey to surrender, Wood took a moment in which to survey the general situation. Whoever was on the roof might well be trapped there, though for the moment in a snugly defensible position. Plainly there was no way but this stair to reach the tower's roof from the outside, short of using chains and grappling irons slung over the parapets—matters might eventually

218

come to that—or by flying. The wizard took a moment in which to curse the decision that had made him send his griffin away with Amintor. But there was no help now for mistakes already made.

The outside stair on which he stood was undefended by any roof or even a railing. It curved three quarters of the way around the central tower, and at several points well above its curve, too high to be reached, were windows, indicating the presence of interior rooms. But there were no windows below the stair, or otherwise readily accessible from it. And not only were the windows high, but they were narrow, not much more than archers' slits; perhaps a child or a very thin adult might have been able to squeeze through one of them. And not only were the windows high and narrow, but they were slightly overhanging the stair, each pair of them built out in a small projecting bartizan.

It was quite possible, of course, that some kind of trapdoor gave access to the roof from inside the tower. The impostor, who had been seen looking out of one of these tower windows, could have gone up to the roof from the inside and then pulled the outside ladder up. Wood could wish now that he had personally taken a more thorough inventory of the castle and its architecture during his brief peaceful tenure.

Only minutes ago, before starting up this outside stairway, he had detailed men to search the interior of the tower for a way to reach the roof, or at least the upper floors, whose existence was indicated by the windows. Those men were to report to Wood before they closed in on their quarry, but so far they had not reported any success in finding an interior way up.

He was being foiled for the moment, it seemed, by some more of the architectural whimsy of Honan-Fu.

Now the Ancient Master, with his Sword ready —truth to tell, he had never been much of a swordsman —and speaking in his most terrible amplified voice, called upon those who were above him to surrender.

"Ho, on the roof! Ho, there! This is the master of the castle speaking! Let the ladder down for us at once! You are trapped, and I will show you mercy if you come down now!"

There was only silence up above. His answer came in the form of a heavy, head-sized rock, dropped over the edge of the parapet by anonymous hands, hands that worked blindly but still managed to choose their aiming point with what would have been deadly accuracy had it not been for the Sword of Force. Shieldbreaker altered the rhythm of its monotonous thudding voice just slightly, putting mild emphasis upon a single syllable. The blade moved as if with its own volition, pulling Wood's hand after it in a single economical movement. Shieldbreaker flashed in the sun, arcing above the wizard's head. The rock, precisely intercepted in midair, shattered into a hundred screaming fragments, none of which touched Wood. The soldier who was just behind him on the stair muttered a low oath; one of those stone fragments had left a bloody track across his face.

The Sword of Force, the keenness of its edges undented by that blow, again was almost quiet, chanting its low rhythmic song of rage and barely suppressed violence as if it were singing to itself alone. And still the gentle echo of its counterfeit persisted, coming from somewhere nearby.

With a silent, emphatic gesture Wood ordered his squad back down the stair; even though his Sword would protect him personally against rocks or any other weapons, his escort was vulnerable here, and there was no point in wasting useful men.

The sound made by Shieldbreaker subsided as the Ancient Master carried it back down the stairs, and the echo of its imitation faded from his hearing also.

Once he had reentered the tower again, the wizard detailed a few of his men to make another ladder, or else bring one of the proper size over from another tower if that would be quicker. Of course, even if another ladder

could be set in place atop that exposed stair and somehow kept there, the top of the central tower would still
be very easy to defend. Undoubtedly there were more
rocks up on the roof, and even when rocks were exhausted, still only one man would be able to come up a
ladder at a time. And anyone standing on that last stone
step, where it would be necessary to stand to set the
ladder into place, would be an extremely vulnerable
target to more stones dropped from above. A man
carrying Shieldbreaker might win through, of course
—depending on how much the defenders knew about
the Sword. Wood did not intend to take unnecessary
personal risks to get at them, nor did he mean to hand
over the Sword of Force to any of his subordinates.

Remaining inside the tower himself, he led a quick
exploration of the accessible levels, and confirmed what
his people were telling him, that these ended one or two
floors below the top. So it was possible, he supposed,
that the only way to get into those upper levels without
tearing part of the tower down might be from the roof.
But yet Wood could not be absolutely sure of that—and
suppose the impostor was able to get out some other
way, and do more damage?

Still, every course of action had its risks. The
Ancient Master decided to temporarily abandon his
search for another way into the upper rooms, and
started toward the highest tower of the castle, from
whose top it ought to be possible to see the top of the
central tower, and who was on it. Before he had even
reached the base of that tower, a report was brought to
him. A small flyer, carrying some object, had been seen
to land on the roof of the central tower. One witness said
that the thing the flyer carried had been a water bottle.

Wood swore oaths of great intensity. He yearned for
his griffin, to be able to go and pluck the renegade
water-carrying beast out of the sky. Draffut had somehow perverted Wood's corps of winged scouts, or some
of them at least, to the cause of his enemies.

But in a way the news about the water bottle was reassuring—if water was being sent by that means to the people on the rooftop, that suggested they were pretty effectively prevented from getting it any other way.

On the roof of the central tower, Mark, Ben, and Yambu rejoiced to receive the written note that the flyer had brought out to them from Triplicane, along with the unnecessary leather bottle of water.

The handwriting of the note was recognizably Zoltan's. In it he assured them that Honan-Fu's counterattack was going to be launched tonight.

From her small pouch of personal belongings, Lady Yambu got out a little metal mirror, and began an effort at heliographic signaling to some of the boats in the lake, and then to the people in green and gold uniforms who were now gathering on several of the small islands. There were a number of boats near those islands now, and enough constabulary troops in gold and green on boats and islands to make it unlikely that Wood would want to send out his own amphibious force, risking his own remaining fleet of lake-going craft, to challenge their possession. But her signaling drew no response.

When the three on the roof strained their eyes in the direction of distant Triplicane they thought they could discern another gathering of boats along the dockside there.

Their talk came back to their enemy, and the Sword he carried. The sound of Shieldbreaker had faded away very quickly after Yambu dropped that discouraging rock. And with Shieldbreaker withdrawn, its voice muted, the echo-sound presumably made by Sightblinder had faded too.

"Where is Sightblinder then?" Ben asked, scowling.

Yambu had a logical answer ready. "Well, if it was not on the stairs when we heard it, then it must have been in one of the rooms just below us."

When the people on the rooftop at last peered

cautiously over the parapet, they were just able to catch a glimpse of someone passing inside one of the projecting windows below them.

"Should we call out to them?" Mark asked his companions.

Before they could decide that question, a deadly distraction came from the direction of the castle's highest tower, in the form of a desultory bombardment with rocks and arrows. Their tower was too far away from the other, more than a hundred meters distant, for this attack to be effective, and it was not pursued. But the three on the roof tended now to stay within the shelter of the lookout's roofed shed.

Continuing to take a cautious inventory, they discovered a trapdoor in the approximate center of the roof. On the upper side of the trap there was no sign of any lock.

Mark asked: "What do we want to do about this? Open it and see what's under us, or block it up?"

Ben offered: "We've more or less come to the conclusion that the Sword-bearer is probably down there. What do you say, do we go after his Sword again?"

They debated it a little, and Ben's tentative effort to lift the trap discovered it to be locked somehow from below. Mark eventually decided it would be better to block the trap, for the time being.

It was not hard to find the proper materials for the job of blocking the trapdoor. The pyramidal pile of defensive rocks, in the busy hands of Mark and Ben, was soon being transferred right on top of it.

"There," Mark grunted some time later, setting the last rock in place atop the reconstructed pile, and pausing to wipe sweat from his face. "*You* might be able to push that trap open from below now, but I doubt there's another man anywhere who could manage it."

Ben squinted at the pyramid of stones and shook his head. "I wouldn't care to try."

The three on the roof got through the day, taking

turns napping in the shade of the lookout's shelter. As old soldiers, they were all accustomed to not thinking about food for long intervals, and otherwise they were comfortable enough for the time being.

The patience of experience saw them through the day.

The night began with the three people on the roof taking turns at watchful listening and rest. It was about two hours before dawn when the enemy made an almost silent attempt to put a new ladder into place upon the upper end of the external stair. Lady Yambu happened to be on watch at the time. Listening attentively and timing her moves carefully, she put another rock neatly over the edge. This time the Sword of Force was evidently not on hand to fend it off. The missile fell for almost the full height of two men before it struck something. There was a muffled impact, followed by a fading, wailing cry, as of a man departing under the full acceleration of gravity. There followed the faint but rapid sounds of scurrying feet going back down the stairs. Then silence reigned again.

Early in the night there had been a discussion among the leaders of Honan-Fu's assault force as to whether they should try to recruit Draffut to pull some of their boats into position for the final attack. In the end it was decided that they should all row themselves into position, leaving Draffut to do whatever he thought best to help them in his own way. The Lord of Beasts had indicated that he would do something, but perhaps because he did not trust their human councils he had kept his exact intentions to himself until the flotilla of constabulary boats were ready to put out into the lake.

Zoltan watched from a distance as the Lord of Beasts left the lake and moved up into the hills, his head overtopping half the trees he passed. Draffut passed out of Zoltan's sight for a while, and when he returned he was carrying the stripped trunk of a pine tree that had been twice taller than himself. When he came down among the people again they could smell the aromatic sap oozing from the torn bark.

Draffut announced to Zoltan and those near him that this was going to be his scaling ladder.

The boats did not begin to move into their final positions for the assault until about midnight. Honan-Fu's planning allowed several hours for them all to get into position. The idea was to put men ashore simultaneously on all sides of the island, getting ready to assail every part of the castle's perimeter at once.

Knowing just where Draffut planned to land, Zoltan could see the Beastlord wade ashore, for the moment undiscovered by the castle's lookouts. The towering figure emerged from the water on the spit of sand that extended from the island's northern end, and before the enemy had spotted him, he was running toward the castle. When he was within reach of the wall that towered over him, the Lord of Beasts wedged the base of his treetrunk into the sand, and leaned the upper end against the castle wall, which it slightly overtopped.

At this point shouts of warning, cries that trembled on the verge of being screams of terror, went up from Wood's human lookouts. Draffut responded to them at once, with the most bloodcurdling bellow he could produce. In the next moment he was swarming up his improvised ladder, and a moment after that he was crouched apelike atop the thickness of the wall.

The sentries who had been manning that portion of the wall were there no longer, having delayed not a second in getting out of Draffut's way. There were a few more, now standing paralyzed with terror at a little distance, and Draffut waved his arms at them and bellowed again, effectively frightening them away.

Now he could get down to work. Wrapped around

his body under his thick fur Draffut was wearing a couple of rope ladders, fabricated by the women of Triplicane in twenty-four hours of intensive work. In a moment the Beastlord had looped an end of one of these ladders over a merlon on the nearest parapet, then tossed the rest of the ladder out over the wall, so that the other end, if its length had been correctly calculated, would now be trailing on the ground.

He trusted that the people in the boats were already responding to his noise, and that by now the first troops of the landing were no more than moments from the beach.

Moving rapidly along the top of the wall, edging past a slender watchtower already abandoned by its defenders, Draffut disposed of his second rope ladder in the same manner as the first, and at a distance of some thirty meters from it.

As he was engaged in this operation, an arrow flew at him from somewhere, and stuck in a fringe of his heavy fur, almost between his eyes. It would be too much to expect that he could frighten all of the enemy away, and now some of them were waking up, regaining at least a minimum of courage. It was time for him to see what he might be able to accomplish at ground level, before his advantage of surprise and shock was entirely dissipated.

He let himself over the inner surface of the castle's thick outer wall, hung briefly by his hands, and then dropped into a courtyard. The shock of his huge weight dropping on the bones of his legs and feet was tremendous, but he was almost immune to internal injury of any kind. The powers that enabled him to heal others worked almost automatically within his own body.

From the courtyard where he had landed, a small postern gate opened through the outer wall. It was defended by some guards, and Draffut, three times as tall as a man, moved boldly toward them. He was able to frighten away this gate's defenders with another bellow and a blow of his fist against the wall near them, making the stones quiver. Then he sprawled on his belly to get a good look at the gate. There was an inner gate, a simple affair of wood reinforced with iron bars, and easy enough to pull open. When this was done he lay there groping with one hand beyond the inner gate, into the deep penetration of the wall, until he reached an outer gate and could punch it open too. Now he had provided yet another means of entrance for the attackers.

Meanwhile more arrows were sinking into his fur. And a javelin, hurled by some unseen hand, flew near Draffut as he rolled over and got to his feet again. He looked about him. There were no more gates here to be broken open, but there, at about the second floor level, a stony bartizan pierced with archers' slits looked out over what would otherwise have been a blind expanse of exterior wall. If those openings were enlarged sufficiently, they would provide another means of ingress once the people outside could get a ladder of modest length into position.

Thrusting a finger into one after another of the archer's slits, Draffut willed power into his hand. The stones softened, and one by one the openings dilated until he could pass his whole hand through each of them. The ancient power of the Lake of Life was working in the Beastlord still, and it was capable of temporarily animating even the very stones of a castle wall.

A small swarm of arrows stung his back. Turning round, he was unable to spot his assailants, who were keeping under cover as much as possible, but he did behold a much more welcome sight. The troops of Honan-Fu, in green and gold, were already in small numbers atop the wall where Draffut had just strung up the ladders. More were coming up the ladders all the time, but the attackers were not maintaining their foothold unopposed; already the defenders in red and gray were coming out in comparable numbers to meet them, and the fight was beginning briskly.

Draffut could take no direct part in the fighting, much as he might sympathize with those who were fighting to regain possession of the castle. And now another movement caught his eye—leaning over the parapet that guarded the flat top of the central tower of the castle, two or three human figures were gesturing to him. These were mere signals of encouragement, it seemed. One of the figures he thought was Prince Mark, but he had no time to make sure now, and in any case their identity was not of the first importance.

More wounds, from both javelins and arrows, were accumulating on the tough hide of the Lord of Beasts. The overall effect was increasing pain, though each hurt in itself was scarcely more than a pinprick to him. He paused now to brush from his body some of the hanging weapons whose points had snagged under his skin. At the same moment he saw by torchlight another javelin coming at him, and he blew his breath upon the weapon in midflight. In midair the spear was turned into a giant dragonfly. The creature veered away from Draffut and went darting innocently over the castle wall, going out above the lake. Before it had got so far as the shore, he thought, it would probably revert to inert matter and plunge into the water.

"I must get on with the job," the Beastlord muttered to himself, tearing a moderate accumulation of barbs out of his hide, and wincing with the pain. Yet even as he removed the weapons, more darts assailed him.

Now he went scrambling over one of the comparatively low interior walls of the castle, reaching another courtyard. At the base of a wall there was another gate leading to the outside, this one the main entrance by the docks.

With one wave of his fist Draffut frightened away the knot of soldiers who were gathered just inside this gate. In another moment he had knelt in front of it and knocked it open.

He stopped, staring helplessly at what lay before him, just at the edge of the docks, beneath the fragments of the shattered gate. And suddenly it was as if the world had ended for him, the world in which he had been doing what he could, for many thousands of years, to serve humanity.

*What is that I see? What is it?* And yet the Lord of Beasts knew only too well what it was. It was just that for a moment he could retain the comfort of being able to refuse belief.

But only for a moment. The God of Healing stood up unsteadily, like a man dead on his feet, so horrified that for the moment he was unaware of what he was doing. More darts, unnoticed, pierced his skin.

There had been a human being, a soldier, standing just on the other side of the last gate when it went down, and the momentum of the bursting gate had spent itself upon him.

Draffut could do nothing but stand motionless, his eyes riveted upon that crumpled, mangled body in its uniform of red and gray. He had just killed a human being. That he had not suspected the presence of the man, had not intended to commit the slaughter, meant nothing to him now.

Then his paralysis broke and he lunged forward, reaching through the gate to seize the lifeless thing and bring it to him with urgent tenderness. Meanwhile a terrible whining howl escaped his lips.

He held the body up with both hands. With all his energy he willed his healing power into it. Meanwhile more arrows, unnoticed, struck him on his flanks and back.

Draffut willed to achieve healing, but this time his

powers could not heal. The damage to the small body was too great, death was a finality.

He, Draffut, had killed a human being.

He let the limp and bloody body fall. Then, shrieking out one horrible doglike gowl after another, Draffut dragged himself somehow over the castle wall, and fled into the darkness of the lake.

# CHAPTER 22

ARNFINN was the first to hear the thudding sound. About two hours had passed since he had entered the hidden rooms at the top of the tower, and an hour since Ninazu had joined him there. Full daylight had long since come outside. Their conversation had taken an increasingly tender turn, and they were in one of the upper rooms, making their way with many sweet pauses toward the bed, when the Sword Arnfinn was wearing began to make a muffled pounding noise. Listening carefully, he needed only a moment to determine that this sound was proceeding in sympathy with a similar pounding that seemed to be coming in through the high windows from outside.

Putting Ninazu gently aside, Arnfinn drew his weapon and stood looking at it in puzzlement. Ninazu's surprise as she gazed at the Sword was even greater. It was as if she had not known until now that her companion was carrying anything like it, but now she was ready to accept the weapon's presence as one more indication of his superlative wizardry.

Then suddenly a man's voice, unnaturally loud, came blasting in through the high windows. "Ho, on the roof!"

"On the roof?" Arnfinn whispered, looking up.

"Ho, there!" The voice blasted in at them again. "This is the master of the castle speaking! Let your

231

ladder down for us at once! You are trapped, and I will show you mercy if you come down now!"

Arnfinn felt himself able to make at least a fair guess as to who those people on the roof were.

"But who is that shouting?" he whispered to Nina-zu, perturbed. "Where is he?"

"There is a stair outside, going up the outside of the tower to the roof. But no one out there can see in here." Ninazu frowned. "It sounds like your voice, shouting."

What further comment she might have had on that point Arnfinn never learned. There was a violent explosion somewhere very close outside the windows, followed by a muted outcry. Hardly had Arnfinn's ears ceased ringing from that blast when he could hear whoever was on the stairs quietly retreating.

He went on listening, in fear and total bewilderment, without any idea of what was happening now. He could only hope that his fear was not evident to this lady he wanted to help and protect.

This time it was Lady Ninazu who asked the question. "What was *that*?"

"An event of magic," said Arnfinn, swallowing. "Don't worry, I will protect you. Are you all right now?"

"Yes, great lord." She sounded confident in his protection.

"I have decided," he said, and had to pause to swallow again, "decided that it would be well for us to make contact with those people on the roof, whoever they may be."

"Do you think, lord, they will be ready to surrender to you now?"

"Actually it is not surrendering that I had in mind particularly. But I would like to talk to them at least."

Standing on the foot of one of the beds, Arnfinn located the trapdoor in the roof—there was a false panel concealing it, as Ninazu showed him. Arnfinn unlocked the trap, and tried to raise it.

He strained, pushing upward with all his force, but

nothing happened. Some weight above was holding the door immobile.

At last, determined to make contact now, he called out. "This is Arnfinn here! I have the Sword of Stealth!" And he hammered on the trapdoor with the pommel of his Sword.

"Arnfinn?" Lady Ninazu questioned gently. "If that is one of your names of power, lord, it will be safe with me."

Arnfinn gave her a sickly smile, knowing that she doubtless saw the cowardly grimace as something else entirely.

Presently there were sounds from overhead as of heavy weights being moved.

At last, when he pushed on the trap again, it swung up.

Gray daylight flooded down into the bedroom. Arnfinn, looking up at three people who were standing on the roof, found himself, with some relief, confronting huge Ben and gray Lady Yambu. Zoltan, who had been with them in the grotto, was gone; Arnfinn remembered he had seen him getting ready to row the boat away. But Arnfinn could not recognize the tall, brown-haired man who was now with the familiar pair. Certainly he did not see in this tall man one of the victims who had been pulled nearly dead out of the well some hours ago.

It was plain, from the way the lady and the huge man deferred to this newcomer, that they recognized him as their leader.

Arnfinn glanced back at Ninazu, who was scowling to see Lady Yambu again.

"We heard someone shouting on the stair," Arnfinn opened the conversation lamely.

"Your twin," Mark informed him. The Prince, even familiar as he was with Sightblinder's capabilities, was studying the shape that Arnfinn presented with fascination. "So, you are Arnfinn."

"I am. What of it?"

"Nothing. Never mind. I thank you for whatever contribution you made to helping Honan-Fu and me out of the well."

"That was you?"

Mark nodded. "Yes. I am glad you opened the trap . . . your twin upon the stair just now had Shield-breaker with him. I suppose you heard what it did to the one weapon we tried against it."

"I heard the sound it made, whatever happened. And this Sword—"

"Performed an imitation, yes. We heard it. A word of advice, though, my friend. Don't use the Sword you have there against Shieldbreaker. Can I trust you not to do so?"

"It would be better," said the big man, "if one of us three had the Sword of Stealth instead."

"I agree," said Mark, his eyes not leaving Arnfinn. "But we should not be fighting this young man—we all have our real enemy to fight."

Mark was thinking back to his own boyhood, when he had run away from a small village, to find himself alone and far from home, with only the terror and beauty of a Sword to keep him company.

"Hard to get rid of, isn't it?" he went on, speaking to Arnfinn gently, indicating the Sword the other carried. "And hard to keep. I know something of how that goes."

"You?" The youth was obviously suspicious of him. "How would you know?"

"I'll tell you about it someday. So, if you refuse to give it up, then keep it. Perhaps you can do as much good with it as we three could. But mind what I have said about the Sword of Force. It'll mow you down like a blade of grass if you go armed against it, whatever weapon you may have in hand."

Ben grumbled privately, and would have tackled the youth again to reclaim Sightblinder, but Mark held his big friend back. The Prince was not going to have their two small groups fighting with deadly effect against each other; and it would be hard to fight against anyone who was using Sightblinder as a physical weapon because you would not be able to tell which way they were swinging or thrusting it.

"Lady Ninazu and I intend to remain in the apartment," Arnfinn called up to them.

"All right. Just as well. We three will keep to the roof for a time; they already know we're here and it lets us see what's going on." Mark hesitated, then called down. "What're you going to do if the real Ancient One finds that tunnel and comes up after you?"

Arnfinn had no ready answer for that. At last he said: "Even if he is proof against the magic of this Sword, the men with him will not be. Am I right?"

"Right."

"Then I will be able to confuse them at least."

Mark added: "Let me say it again. One thing you'd better do if he comes against you with Shieldbreaker, and that's disarm yourself. Your Sword won't help you against that one—he'll see you as you are anyway. But he won't dare attack you if you're disarmed."

Arnfinn nodded, though in his heart he still half suspected this advice might be a trick.

The trapdoor to the roof was closed again, but left unblocked and unlocked. Before this closing, Mark and Ben came down to look the apartment over, and to their satisfaction they found a warclub, hung up as a decoration, that would become an eminently practical weapon in Ben's hands. And before retiring to the roof again, they blockaded the tunnel entrance with a wardrobe. The barrier thus formed would hardly be proof against a determined assault, but would at least serve to give warning that the entrance to the apartment had been discovered.

Left to themselves again, Arnfinn and Ninazu got through the remainder of the day in the hidden rooms of the uppermost interior level of the tower. There was some dried food still in a cabinet, preserved with a touch of magic that left it reasonably flavorful; indeed, it was better than most of the food Arnfinn had eaten during his lifetime. And there was wine, of which he had but little experience, so that it went to his head and left him feeling giddy.

Now that she had come back to this apartment, Ninazu did not want to leave. And Arnfinn was in a way as subject to her enchantment as she was subject to the power of the Sword he carried. Whenever he looked at her, with Sightblinder held tightly in his own hand, he saw a mystery that seemed to him divine. This is, he thought, the mystery of courtly love that minstrels sing about. And I, though only a peasant . . .

When night fell, they quietly locked the trapdoor again, and then spent the night together in one of the beds in one of the highest rooms. Whether it had originally been Ninazu's bed, or Kunderu's, Arnfinn had no idea.

The two of them were roused roughly in the hours before dawn, when the racket of Draffut's invasion awakened the entire castle. Jumping out of bed, the lady and Arnfinn moved from window to window, trying to see what was going on outside, where the sounds of battle were unmistakable.

Then there was a pounding on the locked trapdoor above.

On the morning the battle had started, on a lower level of the castle, Wood rejoiced to see the at-first-mysterious rout of Draffut. This eucatastrophe was closely followed by another stroke of good fortune for the Ancient Master—his griffin had returned, and could now be seen circling in the clear morning sky above the aerie tower.

Wood's first elation at this sight was somewhat dampened by the fact that the beast was riderless.

Running out of his tower, across a first floor roof in the gray light of a clouded morning sky, Wood waved his arms in practiced gestures. The eagle-eyed creature saw him at once, and came gliding swiftly down to land on the low roof near him.

In a moment Wood had reached the griffin's side, and was rifling its saddlebags, in search of a written message from Amintor, or at least some clue as to what might have happened to the general. But there was nothing in the containers, not even the small amounts of food and other supplies that Amintor had had with him on his departure. The general might, of course, have fallen to some kind of enemy action. Or deserted. Or he might have consumed his supplies, Wood supposed, and then fallen from the beast's saddle at high altitude. If so, that was that. Such an accident would not have been impossible, though decidedly unlikely; the griffin knew that it was supposed to return with the man who had ridden it away.

The griffin now turned its fierce impassive gaze upon its master, who glared back at it in frustration. The beast was possessed of many valuable powers, but those of speech or any other intelligent communication were not among them. The poorest of the small flyers could do better in that regard. For Wood to try to question this mount now would be about as profitable as grilling a riding-beast on what had happened to its human rider.

But the discovery of Amintor's fate, and even that of the expected army of reinforcements, would have to wait. Wood's main consideration at the moment was that he now had the griffin back for his own use. Smiling grimly, he vaulted into the saddle.

By the time Wood got back his griffin, Mark, Ben, and Yambu had changed places with Arnfinn and Ninazu. Mark and his people had gone down from the roof through the trapdoor, meaning to take a more active part in the fighting for the castle, at least to divert part of the defenders' strength.

Arnfinn, with Ninazu at his side, had gone out on the roof to see what was happening, with a vague plan of using the Sword to create a distraction of his own. He was ready to destroy Ninazu's real lover if he could.

There seemed to be fighting everywhere on the walls and in the courtyards below, and as near as Arnfinn could tell, the invaders in green and gold were winning. Before Arnfinn could decide on what false orders he ought to shout, to do his rival the most harm, there was a rushing in the air above him, as of giant wings, and he looked up. He was just in time to see Wood on his griffin come swooping down with intent to destroy the impostor and, if at all possible, capture another extremely useful Sword for himself in the process.

In a moment the griffin had landed on the rooftop. But no sooner had its master leaped from its back, than it flew away again, to circle the tower at a little distance, ignoring his commands to attack the man who stood armed across the diameter of the roof from him. The creature was as confused as any of the humans by the powers of the Sword of Stealth—the beast did not know which of the two images of Wood it saw on the rooftop was the one it ought to obey. And as one of the two Woods it saw was ordering it to attack the other, it held back in confusion.

Meanwhile, the troops of Honan-Fu were adding to the griffin's difficulties by firing arrows and slinging rocks at it from below.

When Wood leaped off his griffin to the roof, Arnfinn saw facing him the hideous image of a reptilian warrior. The youth recognized the Sword of Force in the hand of this enemy, and heard the deadly thudding he had heard before through the high windows of Ninazu's bedchamber.

Ninazu, who had never seen Wood in his reptilian guise before, looked on this terrible arrival with profound loathing, and a fear that made her shrink closer to Arnfinn.

The half-human warrior ignored her. He looked Arnfinn over as if he could see him perfectly well, with growing, amazed contempt. Then the enemy strode toward him with easy confidence, raising Shieldbreaker casually, as if to strike against some unresisting target.

Arnfinn, with Sightblinder in hand, looked into the inward nature of this enemy, as he had scanned the two thieves on the road so many days ago, and had scrutinized the Prince, and Ninazu herself, a short time past. What he saw now revolted him.

Arnfinn dropped his own weapon as the Prince had told him. Now Sightblinder lay inert upon the stone paving of the roof, and its imitation of the other Sword immediately ceased.

Lady Ninazu had drawn her breath in sharply when Arnfinn cast Sightblinder down. But when Arnfinn turned to her in an agony of concern, he saw to his amazement that she was gazing at him as lovingly as ever, and nodding her approval. In a flash he understood. It was as if she were saying yet again: "A clever trick, my lord. This time you have made this hideous enemy see you as only a gawking peasant. I am sure it is all part of your invincible plan."

But now Wood, finding that he faced an unarmed opponent, retreated a step or two and cast down Shieldbreaker. He dropped the weapon close behind him on the rooftop, safe for the moment from any hands but his. He had heard too many warnings, and he knew better than to try to fight any unarmed man, even this woeful-looking peasant, with the Sword of Force in hand. The Sword would never harm an empty-handed foe, and, by drawing virtually all of Wood's physical strength into itself, would leave him helpless.

As soon as Wood threw down Shieldbreaker, Arnfinn grabbed up the Sword of Stealth again.

Now it was Wood, caught Swordless and unprotected, who for the first time experienced the full effects of Sightblinder's power. He saw the other man, who moved toward him, first as a roiling cloud of thicker demon-smoke than any Akbar or his surviving cohort were likely to produce. From this sight the wizard recoiled, sure for the moment that he once again confronted his ancient foe, the ultimate arch-demon Orcus. Wood stumbled back, and farther back, around the sharp curve made by the encircling parapet. Even as he shrank involuntarily from that image, it altered, the cloud turning pale and becoming laced with inner lightning. And now it seemed to Wood that he was confronted by an avatar of Ardneh himself.

And yet again the advancing image altered. It was that of a mere man now, deceptively ordinary in appearance, who walked on two legs and smiled at Wood and seemed about to give him orders, as he had commanded him of old, orders that the great wizard would be incapable of refusing. It was the image of John Ominor, an emperor of evil memory even to such as Wood.

"I tell you," the image of John Ominor commanded him, "to leave us alone."

Almost, Wood obeyed. Almost. But the sheer ferocity of his inner purpose saved him, kept him from yielding to that command through mindless terror. He stumbled backward.

Then he turned aside to regain Shieldbreaker, which was still lying where he had cast it down. The peasant, seeing this, disarmed himself by hurling Sightblinder at him from behind; the bright steel missed Wood, bounced on the hard roof before him, and skittered away to lie available for the taking. With a lunge Wood darted forward and grabbed up the Sword of Stealth. Magic aside, this one would be a tool with which even awkward hands could kill an unarmed man.

Ninazu, in the background, was calling out encouragement of some kind to her hero—but neither man was really aware of what the lady was now saying.

Then suddenly she had their attention. Now that Wood had Sightblinder in hand, she saw him as her brother Kunderu, and screamed, a scream that distracted both men for a moment.

Arnfinn now saw two Ninazus. One of them was standing in place and screaming, while the other smiled at him encouragingly as she approached, holding out her arms as if she wanted to give him comfort. Her small white hands were empty. Both Ninazus had the same smudges on face and gown, and the dress of each was torn in precisely the same way. The Sword of Stealth, meanwhile, had completely disappeared, as had Arnfinn's opponent.

The youth realized barely in time what this combination of appearances implied. Ninazu with her soft arms outstretched had almost reached him. He threw himself aside barely in time to dodge the invisible blow of Sightblinder, a blow that lodged the blade firmly in one of the wooden supports of the lookout's shelter.

And then Arnfinn's eye alighted on a Sword, another Sword, that was lying naked on the paving just across the roof's diameter. Running across the roof to grab up Shieldbreaker, Arnfinn looked back over his shoulder and saw his own father standing with his back to Arnfinn, wrenching at something connected with the shelter post, some object that was concealed behind him as he strove with all his might to tear it free—

Arnfinn grabbed up Shieldbreaker, and felt the gently thudding, remorseless power of it flow into his right hand. Now he could see with perfect clarity that it was his reptilian enemy who was struggling to pull loose a Sword, and who now turned to face Arnfinn with Sightblinder in hand.

Wood saw what Arnfinn had picked up, and hastily threw Sightblinder down, disarming himself again almost as soon as he had managed to get the weapon free.

And Arnfinn promptly cast down Shieldbreaker. He felt sure now that was the proper move to make, because he had seen his crafty enemy do it when their positions were reversed.

"I will help you, my love!" cried out Lady Ninazu suddenly, in a strong voice. And, before anyone could move to reach Shieldbreaker again, she had darted near the enemy and grabbed up Sightblinder.

There was an outburst of sound from somewhere below the tower, men's voices cheering, followed by calls for the Ancient One himself to surrender.

But no one on the roof heard that. For the moment it seemed that none of the three people there were capable of moving. Arnfinn was frozen, looking at an image of his own father, who stared back at him in utter horror. Then he saw Ninazu as Wood in duplicate. And then Arnfinn saw her briefly as herself, and he could not understand why that should be, while she still held the Sword.

Her gaze swung round to Wood, who was now hesitating as to whether he dared try to make a rush for Shieldbreaker or not. The griffin, crying fiercely, was circling the tower swiftly, coming closer now in rapid orbit.

"You," the multiple, flickering image that was Ninazu said to the wizard. "Gods and demons, I see you clearly now. Clearly at last. How could I ever have—you make me want to puke!"

And then her gaze turned back to Arnfinn. Aided by Sightblinder's second and more subtle power, she was seeing him now, for the first time, for what he really was.

The changing image that was Ninazu shook its head. "Ahhh," was the sound that came from her throat, in a voice that was made up of many voices, and even if there were no words the tones of that sound spoke with great eloquence of utter denial and refusal.

She backed up farther, away from Arnfinn even as he took a step toward her, and farther still, even if it meant climbing up on the parapet behind her.

The Sword slipped from her grasp, and for a moment he saw her clearly. Her long dress tangled her feet and she started to go over.

Arnfinn was halfway across the roof toward the spot where she had disappeared when the claws of the griffin struck him down.

# CHAPTER 23

THE sun had moved well past noon before the last mopping-up operations had been concluded in the castle. But organized resistance had effectively collapsed much earlier when Wood was seen making good his own escape aboard his griffin, with Shieldbreaker in his hand. Besides the Ancient One himself, probably none of the intruders in red and gray had been able to get away.

Dead and wounded lay everywhere, indoors and outdoors, but none of the other fallen were near Arnfinn where he lay dead on the tower roof. Or near Ninazu, who now, still breathing, lay on a setback only a few stories down.

The victorious Honan-Fu had reached his daughter's side as soon as he was able to do so. Those who had been first to reach her had noted the twisted position in which her body lay, and no attempt had been made to move her.

Honan-Fu was squatting beside her broken body. Sadly, tenderly, fearfully, his hand was stroking his daughter's hair. He had already sent orders to his best physician to come at once and attend Ninazu. But that man was undoubtedly very busy elsewhere, and even if he heard the order and obeyed, it seemed unlikely that human medical care of any kind could make a difference.

The wizard had already helped her as best he could

244

with his own magic. It appeared that in this, as in so much, his magic was not going to be enough.

As time passed, a few other people gathered around the father and daughter, to watch and listen. Ninazu's breathing was harsh and irregular, and her eyes were closed.

"If only," someone inevitably said, "we had Woundhealer here . . ." But of course the Sword of Mercy was nowhere near.

"If only the lord Draffut—" said someone else. And that line of wishing had to be allowed to die also. Draffut had not been seen or heard of since he had fled out into the lake at the height of the battle.

Ninazu's eyes remained closed, even when her father spoke to her. Her body had been covered with a blanket now, up to the chin, but the ominous lines and angles of her broken limbs and body showed through the covering.

Suddenly her father, in an awkward movement, sat back on the roof. He looked a totally exhausted old man, as if his physical energy and his magic had given out at the same time.

"Now my daughter is dying," he announced in a harsh voice. "And I am childless."

No one responded at first. Then Lady Yambu asked quietly: "What about Kunderu?"

Honan-Fu looked over at her as if he did not understand what she was talking about. Then comprehension seemed to dawn on him. He said: "Of course, you were with Ninazu, and listening to her. I suppose she talked about her brother Kunderu; she always did. But Kunderu died two years ago. It was at the same time that she—became ill."

Yambu appeared to understand now. But Zoltan did not. "Became ill?" the young man repeated.

"For the past two years," said the old man sitting on the roof, "her mind has been deranged."

Prince Mark was nearby, resting on one knee. He

had carefully moved Sightblinder to a place just in front of him, where he could keep an eye on it. Now the Prince asked Honan-Fu: "She knew that her brother was dead?"

"She knew it, but she could never accept the fact. And at the same time she blamed me. It was more than I could bear, to hear her speak of him as if he were still alive—worse, as if I were holding Kunderu prisoner and punishing him. My son and I had our disagreements, even quarrels, but I never did that. I never could have done that. . . .

"And so, I had the manor on the mainland refurbished as her house. At first she seemed content to live there, or so it was reported to me, though she was always expecting Kunderu to come back to her.

"But it was someone else who came to her instead. The man who had been the real cause of her brother's death—though Ninazu would never believe that. The man who became—no, I cannot call him her lover. He was never that. He used her, that was all. Trying to get at me, to overthrow me. And I was too busy with the academy, and other matters, to discover what was going on. Always, even after Kunderu was dead, I was too busy . . ."

And now at last the eyes of the young woman opened. She did not try to speak, and perhaps she could not move. When she saw whose hand it was that stroked her hair, she turned her gaze away, as if she were looking for someone else.

When Ninazu had finally drawn her last breath, and enough time had passed for all of the survivors to rest as well as they were able, Honan-Fu publicly renewed his offer to take on Mark's son Adrian as an apprentice, when the academy was reopened. The student would of course be charged no fee, in gratitude for the help Prince Mark and his people had given Honan-Fu, and the sufferings they had undergone.

Mark had been expecting some such offer, and had had time in which to prepare a diplomatic answer. The truth was that he had already decided, in his own mind, against ever sending his child into the atmosphere of this place.

A few hours later Lady Yambu, thoughtfully walking in her pilgrim's garb upon the docks at Triplicane, was pondering silently upon the fact that she had been unable to catch even a brief glimpse of the Emperor during his short stay in this locality. She wondered that she felt such real disappointment as she did at the implication that her former lover did not want to see her again.

She was beginning to wonder whether the great downriver journey she had been contemplating had ever really been more than a search for him.

Prince Mark sought out Lady Yambu on the docks and expressed his thanks for her help more fully than he had yet done. Then he asked her: "And do you think, my lady, that you have found here any portion of the truth you sought?"

She considered carefully. "Perhaps I have been able to recognize a bit or two of it. But in any case I plan to go on, down the Tungri."

Mark nodded, unsurprised. "I have heard that the Show of Ensor was seen two days ago, loading itself aboard a couple of barges, to go down the river too. The man in the clown's mask was still reportedly in charge."

"Indeed. And have the flying scouts brought any word of Amintor?"

"No word as yet."

Now Zoltan came to join his uncle and the lady on the docks. The young man said that Ben had told him about the mergirl in the Show of Ensor; and he, Zoltan, now asked permission of his Prince to accompany Lady Yambu upon her downstream pilgrimage, in the capacity of bodyguard, or any other way in which she would be pleased to have him. The lady herself, it appeared, had already indicated that he would be welcome.

After thinking the matter over briefly the Prince granted his permission. He said he hoped that Zoltan would return to Tasavalta within a year or two, and would bring with him some useful intelligence about what was going on in the southern regions of the continent. Draffut, before his abrupt departure, had dropped some disquieting hints about developments in that direction. As for Mark himself, though he felt now almost entirely restored to health, he was more than ready to hurry home for a rest in the company of his Princess and his children. He was going to take Sightblinder with him, and he was going to see that suitable compensation for it should be sent to the village of Lunghai.

Ben of Purkinje meanwhile was preparing to return to his own wife and child, in the Tasavaltan capital of Sarykam. But in the course of his preparations Ben paused, more than once, to think over what the Emperor had said to him about Ariane.